I0823864

NETFLIX

STRANGER THINGS

STARCOURT MALL ESCAPE

OTHER TITLES IN THE STRANGER THINGS *UNIVERSE*

Runaway Max

Rebel Robin

Lucas on the Line

The Dustin Experiment

NETFLIX

STRANGER THINGS

STARCOURT MALL ESCAPE

JENNIFER BRODY

Random House New York

Random House Books for Young Readers
An imprint of Random House Children's Books
A division of Penguin Random House LLC
1745 Broadway, New York, NY 10019
penguinrandomhouse.com
GetUnderlined.com
ReadStrangerThings.com

Jacket art by Ian Keltie

ISBN 979-8-217-03273-0 (trade) — ISBN 979-8-217-03274-7 (lib. bdg.) —
ISBN 979-8-217-03275-4 (ebook)

Manufactured in the United States of America
2nd Printing

The authorized representative in the EU for product safety and compliance is Penguin Random House Ireland, Morrison Chambers, 32 Nassau Street, Dublin D02 YH68, Ireland, https://eu-contact.penguin.ie.

To all the strange ones . . .

don't stop being strange.

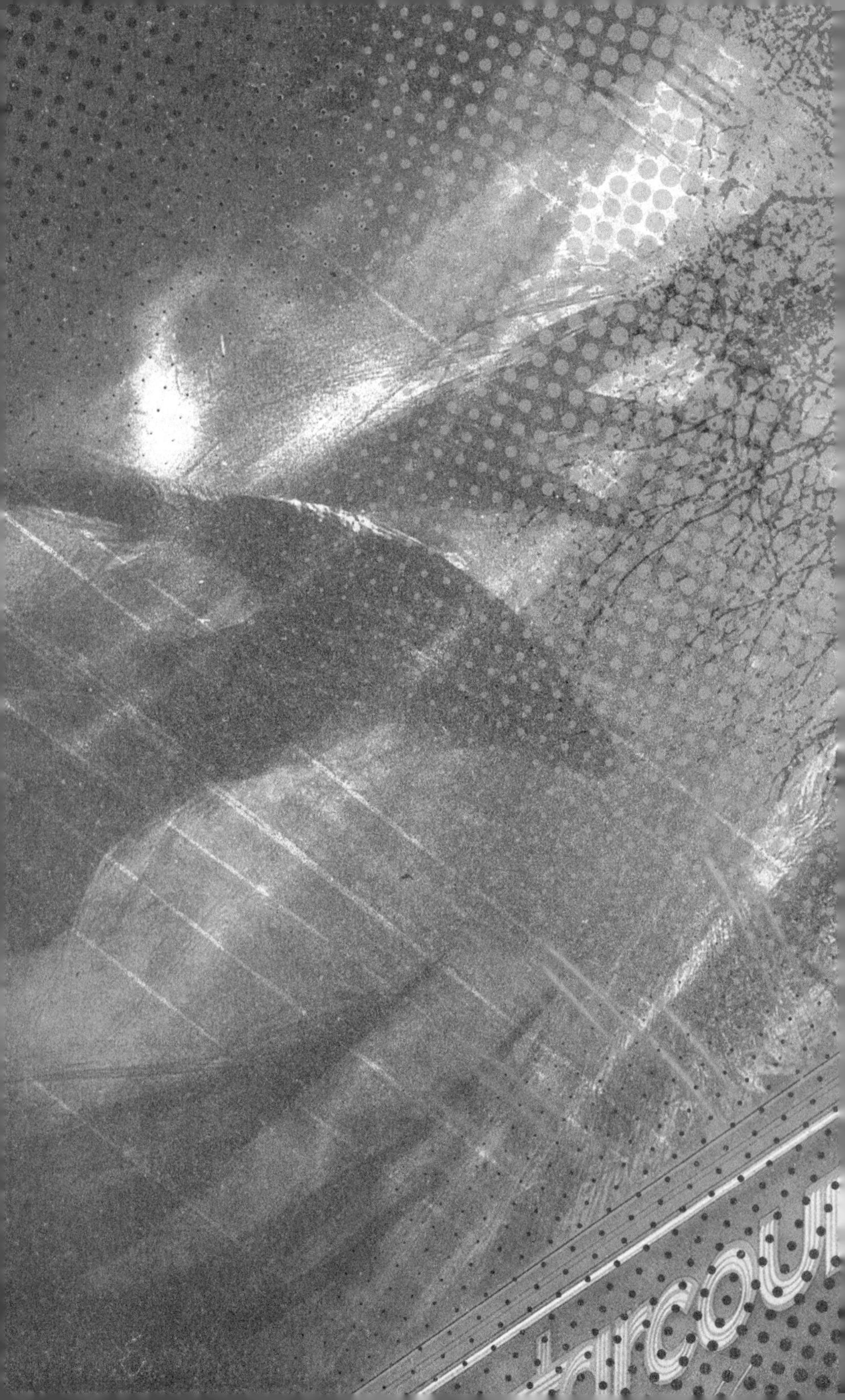

PROLOGUE

"Where am I?" Eleven's voice echoed out, swallowed by the darkness. It pressed against her skin like a living thing, cold and suffocating, wrapping her in a shroud she couldn't escape.

It took her a moment to *sense* where she was.

Her powers unfurled around her, pressing into the walls, feeling the shape of them, the angles and how they slotted together, then pressing into the very molecular structure that bound them. Something resisted, suppressing and muting her powers, trapping her.

Then it hit her.

She was back in that terrible place again—*the lab.* She ran her hand over her head. Her head was shaved down to the flesh, exposing the curves of her skull. She was wearing a hospital gown. The air reeked of bleach and antiseptic, the sharp, acrid sting clawing at her nostrils, mingling with the sour tang of fear that had soaked into her bones.

Her bare feet slapped against the icy tiled floor, the sound of her footfalls bouncing off the sterile walls.

She froze, listening . . . sensing.

Something moved. A rustling in the shadows.

A slight shift in the air pressure that told her one thing.

She wasn't alone.

Fear jolted her. She whipped around, her heart fluttering like a tiny bird.

"Who's there?" she called.

Abruptly, a single bare bulb flickered on overhead, its weak yellow glow buzzing like a trapped insect, casting jagged shadows that twisted and stretched into monstrous shapes. The corridor stretched on forever, a tunnel of torment she couldn't outrun.

"Papa?" Her voice trembled, a fragile whisper swallowed by the void.

The silhouette loomed in the doorway ahead, sharp and menacing, framed by the stuttering light. The white lab coat gleamed, pristine and ghostly, and for a fleeting second, her heart leapt—Papa, her captor, her protector, the only constant in this nightmare.

But as the figure turned, her breath caught. It wasn't his face. It wasn't a face at all. The features melted into a void, a hollow mask of nothingness.

"You did this—you killed me!" the unnatural shrieking voice ripped out.

The *void* creature spidered toward her, superhuman and impossibly fast.

"No, stay away from me!"

Eleven thrust her hand up, hitting the creature full force with her powers.

With a pitiful shriek, it flew back and hit the wall, then exploded. Flesh and blood splashed the walls and splattered across the corridor in a crimson rain.

She relaxed slightly. A trickle of blood dripped down from her nostril due to her efforts. She turned away from the carnage and suddenly—the Demogorgon erupted from a portal that split the floor, her powers having accidentally torn it open.

The creature clawed its way out of the chasm, pulling the crack open. It landed with a thud and turned on her. The monster's petal-like maw cracked open with a wet, guttural snarl, rows of teeth glinting like razors. Claws slashed out, ready to tear her to shreds.

She stumbled back, her scream tearing from her throat, raw and jagged, as power surged through her veins like wildfire. The air crackled, her hands trembling with the force she couldn't yet control, and the monster lunged—

"Nooooooo!"

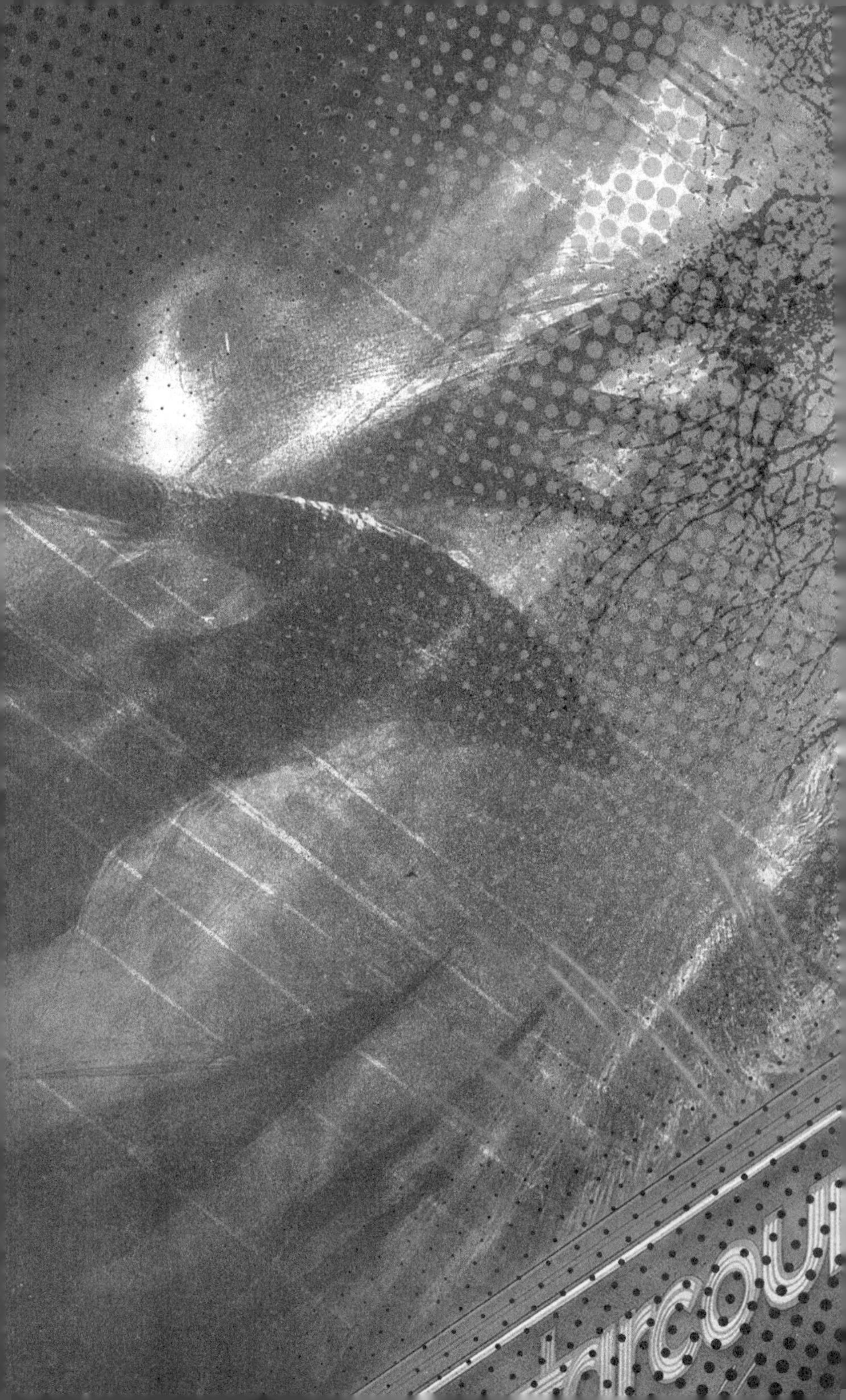

CHAPTER ONE

Eleven jolted awake, gasping, her body slick with sweat that clung to her like a second skin. Her heart hammered against her ribs, a frantic drumbeat threatening to break free. The nightmare still felt fresh in her mind.

She ran her hand over her head, feeling hair curling under her fingertips. It had grown longer, reaching her shoulders. That calmed her slightly.

It took her a moment to realize where she was—Hopper's cabin. She must have fallen back asleep after he left for work early that morning. Her tiny room was a chaos of her own making. Her quilt lay in a crumpled heap on the floor, dragged down in her thrashing.

As she looked around, she felt more ashamed. The nightstand teetered precariously, the lamp swaying as if caught in a ghost wind, its bulb flickering from the jolt of her powers.

A glass of water had shattered beside it, the shards glinting like tiny mirrors, its contents pooling on the warped wood in a glistening mess. She stared at the wreckage, her chest tightening. This happened too often—her dreams bringing her back to the lab, back to the terror of fighting the creatures from the Upside Down.

She glanced out the window. At least Hopper wasn't home to witness it. She picked up a picture that had fallen, its glass shattered—Hopper with a goofy grin, holding up a large fish.

"Gross." El frowned and shook her head. *People are strange*, she thought. *They get happy about dead fish.* She tossed it aside with a clatter. Despite the chaos, the familiar wood-paneled walls and homey decor broke through the remnants of her nightmare, grounding her in the present. She wasn't in the lab. She was safe. *Safe.* The word echoed hollowly in her mind as she pressed her palms to her face, trying to scrub away the phantom blood, the terror that lingered like a shadow.

Her breaths came in shallow bursts, each one a battle to reclaim herself.

"It's okay . . . I'm *home.*" She whispered the unfamiliar word. For so long, that lab had been her only home. But no, that wasn't a real home. Her home was here in this cabin with her father.

Not Papa.

Her true father. This was home.

"Papa's gone," she whispered to remind herself, still surprised by all the events that had shredded her past and destroyed the lab. The portal to the Upside Down was closed—she'd made sure when she went back there. It was a dark but reassuring reminder of something important.

She was finally free.

Well, sort of.

While this was a superior situation to her imprisonment as a test subject, sometimes it still felt like she had traded one prison for another. It was summer and all her friends were on break, but much to her dismay and staunch protests, Hopper had her on a strict lockdown.

"Don't leave the cabin—stay put!" he had ordered her before he left for work, like she was a criminal being detained, not his daughter. "And no Mike when I'm at work. Got it?"

That had drawn her groans and objections, all of which he'd silenced.

She glared at him. It was a father-daughter standoff. Nobody was backing down.

"After you're home? Mike?" she pleaded.

Now it was his turn to groan and object and tear his hands through his hair dramatically, but they'd settled on that compromise, which left them both dissatisfied and surly.

Terrific . . .

She glanced at the clock on the wall. It was barely noon.

El let out a deep sigh. That meant six more hours at least until Hopper was home from work and she could see if Mike could come over.

She wished Hopper would relax and let his paranoia subside, not that she could blame him. They'd been through a lot in their short time together, and Hopper feared dark forces still hunted her. And he was probably right. But now the lab had been exposed and shut down.

And more importantly, she wasn't alone anymore. She had friends—real friends—and she had Mike, who she loved *kissing* more than anything, much to her father's distress.

With a smile, she remembered the Snow Ball dance and their tentative first kiss. More recently, their kisses had blossomed into full-on make-out sessions on her bed, which left her lips sore and aching for more and drove her father crazy. He had this ridiculous *three-inch* rule to keep her door open, which was totally unfair if you asked her, and gave her zero privacy.

She often broke it, using her powers to slam the door in his face, further angering him. But she was determined not to let her father's overprotectiveness come between them.

"Mike . . ." she whispered, missing him with a sharp stab. She started digging for the brick-sized walkie-talkie that Dustin had rigged up for them with RadioShack parts.

She found it lodged under the crumpled quilt. A smile emerged on her face. She jammed the button and spoke into the receiver.

"Mike, do you read me? Come in?"

Static, then nothing.

"This is Gold Leader. Do you copy?" she tried, repeating something she'd heard Dustin say more than once, though the reference went over her head, like so many inside jokes her friends shared, which left her feeling like an outsider. Or more like the alien in that movie they always talked about.

She remembered another catchphrase they often deployed for laughs. The phrase popped in her head, overheard in one of their old basement hangs.

"E.T. phone home," she tried into the walkie-talkie, her final attempt.

Static, then nothing.

She sighed and tossed it on her bed in defeat. Mike was probably doing what all teens did in the summer—or so the TV and teen mags told her. He was probably out with friends having carefree fun. And El was stuck inside.

She glanced at the stack of teen rags Hopper had picked up from Melvald's General Store in town in a desperate attempt to keep her occupied. It wasn't working.

He'd plopped them in her arms before he sped off for work. She already knew there was no way Hopper had picked them out himself. Joyce must have helped since at least they were "age appropriate." She studied the glossy cover of *Seventeen* that showed a gaggle of bronzed teen girls with perms and neon shades and suits all in a row, as if the bands in a juvenile rainbow, sunbathing by a sparkling blue pool—"Make Your Teen Dreams Come True This Summer."

It was summer break in Hawkins. Outside, the world buzzed with life she could only imagine. She pictured kids tearing down the streets on their bikes, the clatter of chains and the whoosh of tires blending with their laughter. Others might be sprawled on lawns, slurping melting Popsicles that stained their fingers red and blue, or cannonballing into the community pool with shouts that echoed through the humid air.

Freedom was out there, tangible and taunting, but not for her. Eleven was a prisoner in this creaky cabin, hidden deep in the woods under Hopper's ironclad rules, its ugly wood-paneled walls pressing in like the bars of a cage.

She tugged on a bright pink shirt with bold triangles and navy pleated shorts, hoping to emulate the effortless beauty of the girls on the magazine cover, fluffing her hair in the mirror on the closet door, grateful yet again that it had grown into bouncy curls that framed her face and high cheekbones. She smiled at her reflection, but the glass was warped, making her look elongated and monstrous. She huffed and shut the door with her powers.

Slam.

Bored, she shuffled to the window, her bare feet sticking slightly to the worn floorboards, and peered through the smudged glass, hoping for some distraction, anything really. Or better yet, for Hopper to come home early so she could summon Mike to come over.

No such luck, she thought, deflating. No brown Chevy Blazer rumbled up the driveway. Nor did Mike materialize on his bicycle, pedaling up the gravel driveway to sneak in and kiss her.

Kissing again, fluttering her insides, making her feel jittery and alive.

She waited another minute, studying the area around her purgatory. Sunlight filtered through the dense pines, casting golden streaks that danced on the leaves, warm and inviting. A squirrel darted across the yard, its tail flicking as it scampered up a trunk, free in a way she envied. But that world might as well have been on the moon.

Suddenly, something broke the silence, jolting her from her reverie.

"Come to Starcourt Mall—where summer dreams come true!"

The TV blared to life with a jarring jingle. She jerked her eyes to the living room, feeling uneasy. She hadn't touched the remote, its plastic bulk still resting on the arm of the sagging couch.

She must have accidentally turned it on, bored and looking for some entertainment.

The screen filled with a commercial for Starcourt Mall, a neon wonderland of '80s excess. Teens with big hair and brighter smiles slurped milkshakes at Scoops Ahoy, their laughter tinny through the speakers. Others darted through the arcade, fingers flying over joysticks, or browsed racks of clothes in stores with names she didn't know.

The ad taunted her—it was a mirage, shimmering just out of reach.

She turned away, the TV's glow fading into the

background as she spotted the note taped to the fridge. Hopper's messy scrawl glared back at her: *STAY PUT—OR ELSE! I MEAN IT!*

"Ugh," she groaned, hearing his stern voice lecturing her though he wasn't even home.

Boredom gnawed at her, a hunger she couldn't satisfy. She flopped onto the sagging couch, its springs creaking under her weight, and the remote levitated into her hand with a flicker of thought. She focused, her brow furrowing, and it hovered there, a small victory against the monotony. *Click. Click. Click.* The channels flipped—soap operas with dramatic gasps, game shows with flashing lights and forced smiles, infomercials hawking gadgets she'd never use. Nothing held her. She turned off the television.

The silence of the cabin pressed in, broken only by the hum of the fridge and the occasional chirp of a bird outside. She sighed, a sound heavy with frustration. She grabbed the pile of teen magazines on the coffee table.

Teen Beat, Seventeen, Bop Magazine—their glossy covers promised a world she didn't inhabit. She reached for *Teen Beat,* the paper crumpling under her fingers, and flipped it open. The pages were a kaleidoscope of color—bright photos of girls with permed hair and boys with cocky grins, articles with titles that leapt out like accusations.

"Summer Bucket List: Teen Summer Guide!" *Flip.* "Summerize Your Style!" *Flip.* "Boys of Summer: Heat Up Your Relationship!"

Each headline twisted the knife deeper, a reminder of

what she lacked. Every exclamation pointing out what she was missing. She didn't have a summer bucket list. She didn't even know what "summerize" meant—did it involve sun or clothes or something else entirely? And Mike . . .

Her stomach flipped at the thought of him, his shy smile, the way his hand had felt in hers at the Snow Ball. But that was weeks ago, a memory fading like an old Polaroid. Why wasn't he answering her on the walkie-talkie? He had sworn that he would keep her company today. What was he doing? Worse, what if he'd forgotten her?

What if their spark, that fragile thing she'd felt growing, was fizzling out like a dying firework? The uncertainty gnawed at her, a quiet panic she couldn't voice. She kept expecting the walkie-talkie to crackle to life, but it remained stubbornly silent.

Too silent.

Frustrated, she flipped to a quiz, the bold text catching her eye: "Relationship Quiz: Hot or Fizzling Out?"

The questions stared up at her, each one a judgment. *Does he call you every day?* No. The phone in the cabin sat silent, its cord coiled like a snake. *Do you go on fun dates?* No. She hadn't left the cabin, let alone held hands under the stars. They hadn't gone out since the Snow Ball. *Are you spending the summer together?* No. He was out there, living, while she was stuck here.

Her frown deepened with each question, her fingers tightening on the magazine until the pages crinkled. Hopper had meant well, she knew that, but this only made her feel worse—more alone, more *different,* a freak among the pages of normalcy.

A sudden gust of frustration surged through her, hot and uncontrollable. The magazines exploded off the table, pages fluttering like wounded birds caught in a storm. They scattered across the floor, some tearing at the edges, others landing face down in the puddle from the broken water glass.

She stared at the mess, her breath hitching. The cabin felt smaller now, the walls closing in, the weight of her isolation pressing down like a physical force.

RAP!

A sharp knock at the window shattered the silence, jolting her upright.

Her pulse spiked, a drumbeat of fear pounding in her ears. A dark shadow loomed outside, distorted by the glass, its edges sharp and threatening. Did the scientists from the lab find her? She tensed, ready to deploy her powers in self-defense. She crept toward it.

Her tremulous voice echoed out.

"Who's there?"

CHAPTER TWO

Eleven watched the dark shadow hovering outside the cabin window. Fear spiked, the fresh nightmare flooding back. Her body tensed, every muscle coiling as dark memories flashed through her mind—the lab, Papa, the Demogorgon. Did they find her?

Her trauma flared, adrenaline sparking in her veins like a live wire. She raised a trembling hand, power humming in her fingertips, ready to strike. The air vibrated, the lamp flickering as her energy built, a deadly weapon.

For a moment, she saw it again—the dark shadow emerging from the gate in the lab, a rift to the Upside Down, the maw with razor-sharp teeth cracking open to kill her.

Her breath caught, her vision tunneling. She wouldn't go back. She wouldn't let them take her. The window rattled, the glass vibrating with the force of her will, and she braced herself to unleash everything on the intruder—

Then the shadow shifted, and a familiar flash of red hair broke through her panic. Eleven's hand faltered, the power dissipating like smoke. She blinked, her heart still racing, and the tension drained from her shoulders.

It wasn't a monster.

It was Max.

El lowered her hand, the lights steadying as the cabin returned to normal. Relief washed over her, tinged with embarrassment and a little fear. If she'd attacked, then she could've accidentally ended her friend's life.

A trickle of blood dripped from her nose, which she quickly wiped away. Her heart sank. Maybe Hopper was right—maybe she deserved to be on summer lockdown after all. She backed away, ducking down into the shadows.

Rap! Max tapped the window again, more impatiently this time. Still, El held back and didn't answer. For a second, it looked like Max left, disappearing with her skateboard tucked under her arm. But then—*Bang!* She rattled the front door insistently, making El jump. She banged again.

"El, open up already—and let me in!" Max called out. "I know you're in there. I saw you lurking in the shadows."

Max's face pressed against the glass, her grin wide and mischievous.

"Fine," El said, giving up. "But enter at your own risk.

Hopper thinks I'm still in danger."

Max rolled her eyes. "Please, I *live* for danger." She tapped her skateboard against the window frame. "Now, quit stalling—and open up already. It's scorching hot out here."

El focused, her mind reaching out, and the front door creaked open with a soft push of her powers. The hot morning air rushed in, carrying the scent of pine and damp earth, a stark contrast to the cabin's stale air.

Max clambered into the cabin, her white sneakers scuffing against the creaky floors, and propped her board against the wall. She untied her ponytail and shook out her wavy copper hair, brushing dirt from her jeans, her energy a burst of light in the dim cabin. She was dressed in a colorful striped shirt paired with jean cutoffs.

"Kind of shabby," Max said, her tone teasing as she surveyed the cluttered living room—the worn, mismatched furniture, the stack of Eggo boxes in the overflowing trash, the faded curtains. "This is where you live?"

Max kept walking through the cabin, not waiting for an answer. "Not that I can talk—my trailer's a total dump. Leaky roof, busted couch, you name it." She made a beeline for the pink boom box sitting on the dresser in El's room and flicked it on.

"Footloose" blared from the tinny speakers, the upbeat rhythm filling the cabin with life.

Eleven stood rooted in the living room, still catching her breath. "What are you doing here?" Her question was direct, lacking the usual social nuance. But Max wasn't fazed. She plopped down on the bed and started flipping through a stray magazine that El had left open.

"Skating at that makeshift park those punks built in the woods," Max answered, casually flipping through the pages. "It was sick! I caught a few good runs. Until the cops broke it up. They said we were . . . *disturbing the peace* and *it was an accident waiting to happen.*" She looked up with a smirk. "I guess they had a point there. It was kind of janky."

"Hopper?" El asked, her eyes widening. She joined Max on the bed.

Max nodded. "Yeah, but don't worry. He's busy hauling those punks down to the station. Probably gonna make them squeal and call their parents. They act tough until—" *Wham!*

She brought her hand down on the bed.

El smirked. "Until . . . Hopper."

"Exactly! Anyway, I made a quick escape and stumbled on your little hideout here. Spotted you through the window. Figured you might need someone to break you out of"—she gestured vaguely at the cabin—"Hopper's Soviet prison."

"Soviet prison?"

"Yeah, like something out of a spy movie." She formed a gun with her hands. El couldn't help it. She snorted a laugh. But then she remembered Hopper's note taped to the fridge.

STAY PUT—OR ELSE!

Max noticed, her expression softening. "Everything okay?"

El nodded, but the lie felt heavy.

Max set the magazine down. "Come on. I told you all about my bogus skate adventure turned *Escape from Alcatraz*."

"Alcatraz?" El said.

Max shook her head. "It's this movie . . . Never mind. *Escape from Hopper* is more like it. So, what is it? You can tell me, El."

El's eyes darted to the magazine in Max's hand with its vibrant summer spread. The story of her recent hijinks at the illegal skate park only solidified how left out Eleven felt.

She glanced away, her voice barely a whisper. "I've never had a . . . real summer. Not like that . . ."

The admission stung, a confession of her outsider status. She longed for the experiences glamorized in full color. She'd come a long way since escaping from the lab, but she still felt different, like a puzzle piece that didn't fit.

"Bummer," Max agreed. "But totally fixable. 'Summer Bucket List,' that's a good starting place . . ." She tapped the listicle with suggestions to "Max Your Summer Fun." But then she narrowed her eyes. "Wait, is there something else?"

El shook her head, looking down.

"Let me guess," Max said, setting the magazine down and giving El her full attention. "I may not have your Spidey sense, but I can sniff out boy trouble from a mile away . . ."

Those words hung in the air.

El nodded, a confession. One word.

"Mike . . ."

"Wait, what did that jerko do?" Max said, ready to take El's side.

"He's not answering." El nodded toward the humongous walkie-talkie on her bed. "And he promised . . ."

Max frowned. "Is this the first time? Or has he done this before?"

El shook her head. "Before."

"What a jerk. They don't have jack to do. It's summer! I bet he's goofing off at the arcade with Lucas, shoving quarters into *Dig Dug* . . . "

The way she said *Lucas* caught El's attention.

"Did something happen?"

Max rolled her eyes. "I dumped his ass. *Again*. He was driving me crazy."

"Crazy, how?"

"Right, we were supposed to be hanging out last night, but then Mike, Dustin, and Will crashed our date. Like totally rude! Then Lucas was cracking dumb jokes, trying to impress them, and not taking my feelings seriously."

"That's why you . . . *dumped his ass?*" El said in a stilted voice, repeating the phrasing that felt alien on her tongue.

Max nodded. "Oh, wait . . . that's not all! I didn't even tell you the worst part."

"There's more?"

Max nodded, still pissed off. "Then he dipped with them to play D&D. But not before he . . . farted . . . like on purpose."

"Ew, gross." El scrunched up her nose in disgust.

"Boys, right? They're all putrid. But Mike and Will and Dustin thought it was hilarious. He'd been eating Doritos like all day. His fart was basically nacho cheese–flavored."

"Double gross." El giggled.

"Totally. So tell me, why do we waste our time, only to get hurt? And put up with disgusting behavior? Anyway, consider Lucas officially dumped."

"Wow." El shook her head, trying to keep up with the evolving dynamics. "How many times is that? Three?"

Max groaned. "Ugh, don't remind me. He always finds a way to win me back—like some puppy with those big eyes. But I'm serious this time. No more wasting my summer on stupid boys." She sat up, her grin returning. "Which brings me to my point—summer's way more fun without them. Trust me."

El smirked. She knew it probably wouldn't last. They always got back together. But for now, Max was solo.

As if emphasizing the point, "Girls Just Want to Have Fun" blared from the radio. They both burst into giggles, then cranked up the volume.

"How can you sit still with this song playing?" Max said, coaxing her to dance. At first, El moved awkwardly, unused to dancing to an upbeat pop song. But Max showed her some moves, helping her to find her rhythm.

They shimmied around the cabin with abandon. Max jumped on the sofa, falling back but bouncing up and recovering, much to El's amusement.

Then "Jump" by Van Halen kicked on. El tossed her hair around while Max did a little head-banging, imitating Billy and throwing out some devil horns.

The song faded away and commercials followed. "Welcome to the future of shopping in Hawkins, Indiana! Introducing Starcourt Mall . . ."

El shrugged. "Now what?"

They were both breathing hard, but exhilarated. Max brightened, a mischievous grin lighting up her face.

"Now . . . it's time for more fun!" she said, smacking the power button on the boom box to silence the Starcourt ad.

"What do you mean?" El asked, fidgeting. "What about Mike . . ."

"Trust me—summer's more fun without stupid boys," Max said, rolling her eyes. "Don't let Mike ruin your chance at an unforgettable summer."

"*Unforgettable* . . . summer," El said. Her cadence betrayed her uncertainty.

Max nodded. She grabbed El's hand and dragged her into the living room.

"I'm breaking you out of house arrest. Let's get out of here. What's next, bars on the windows? Your surrogate dad may be the sheriff, but you deserve more freedom." Max gestured around, her tone turning firm. "Live a little, for once! What do you say? Roam free, find some fun—or trouble. Probably both," she added, her grin widening.

But El hesitated, staring again at the note with Hopper's warning. Her fingers twisted the hem of her oversized shirt.

What if Hopper caught her? Or what if danger was lurking beyond these walls, waiting to drag her back to that lab nightmare?

The memory of the Demogorgon's needle-like teeth flashed in her mind, making her flinch.

But Max's words sparked something else—a flicker of rebellion, a hunger for the summer she'd never known.

She frowned, her mind racing with the risks, then nodded slowly.

"Great. And don't worry," Max said. "You won't be alone—I'll be with you. We can look out for each other."

That cemented it. El grinned, the worries dissolving under Max's irresistible charm and enthusiasm.

With a flick of her wrist, El used her powers to unlock the cabin door and thrust it open—*WHAM!*—rattling the walls.

It echoed out like a declaration.

Outside, summer had arrived and the world waited, wild and unknown. And for the first time since Hopper put her under house arrest, El felt the pull of freedom like a thread of hope weaving through the darkness of her past.

Max's eyes lit up. She grabbed her skateboard. "That's right. Girls just wanna have fun, remember? Let's go."

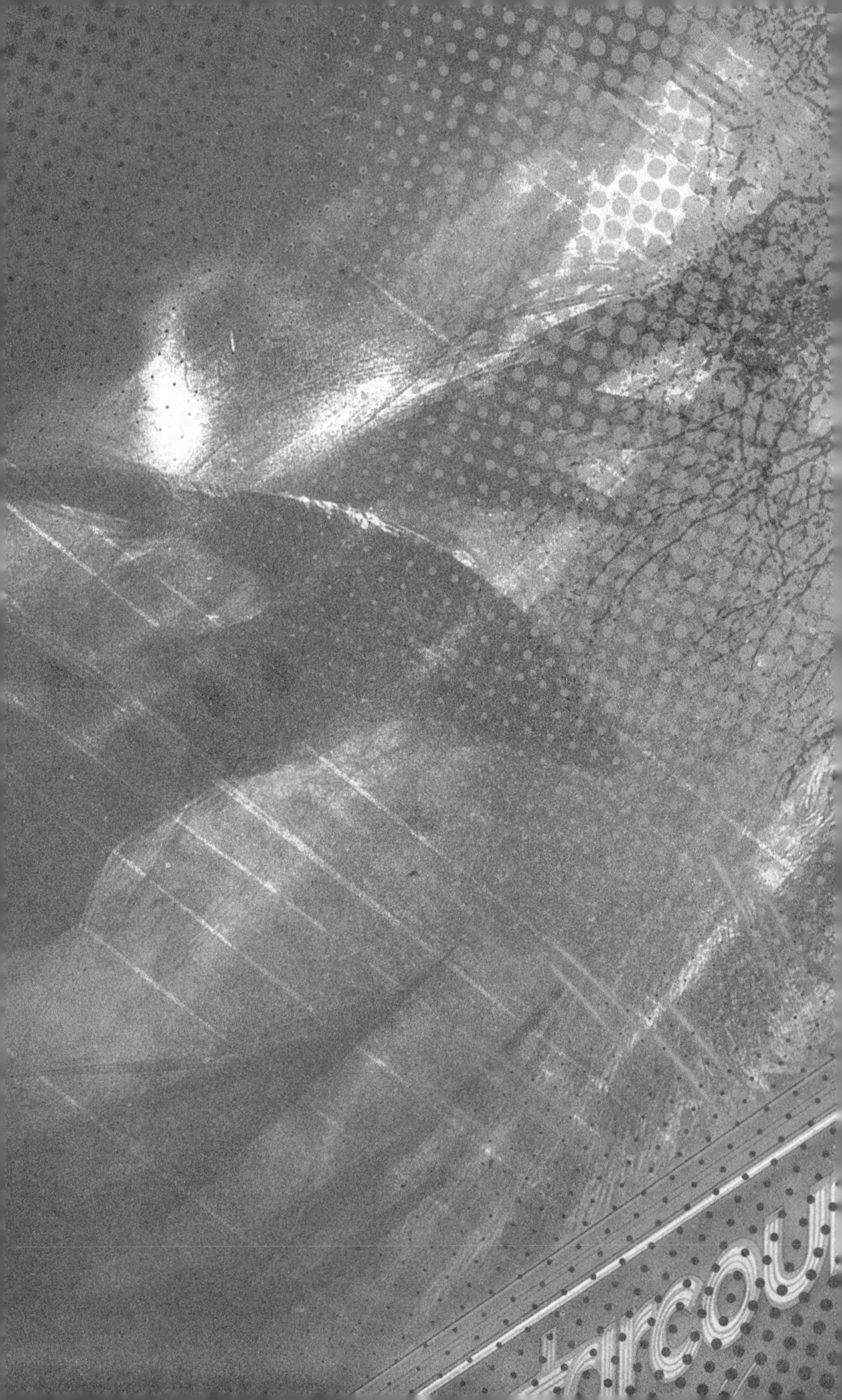

CHAPTER THREE

"Come on," Max said, grabbing Eleven's arm and propelling her from the window seat. "This is our stop."

They hurried toward the front while the bus was still rambling down the asphalt. The bus was nearly empty—*unusually empty*—for the downtown loop. As it slowed, El bumped into Max, the gravity rendering her clumsy.

"Oops, sorry." They both giggled, the thrill of breaking the rules—Hopper's rules—thrumming in their veins.

The bus screeched to a halt on the outskirts of downtown Hawkins, its brakes hissing like a tired beast. The rural fields gave way to a strip of old-fashioned, Midwestern brick buildings housing mom-and-pop storefronts.

Hiss. Pop.

The folding door jerked open, emitting two passengers. El stepped off first, her white sneakers hitting the cracked pavement with a soft thud, the rubber soles sticking slightly to the sun-warmed asphalt. Max followed, carrying her skateboard.

The air slammed into them, thick and humid, carrying the mingled scents of sunbaked tar, freshly cut grass from a distant lawn, and the faint, chemical tang of gasoline from a nearby pump. That perfume was the scent of summer, but it also smelled like something else.

Freedom.

Eleven's heart raced, a giddy thrill pulsing through her veins. She was out of Hopper's cabin, away from his suffocating rules, and the world of summer break stretched before her, wild and brimming with possibility. But as her gaze swept over downtown, that smile faltered, replaced by a sinking disappointment. The vibrant pulse she'd imagined from the magazines—kids weaving through the streets on BMX bikes, their chains rattling; laughter spilling from open shop doors; even the cheerful jingle of an ice cream truck—was nowhere to be found.

Main Street stretched out like a faded photograph, eerily silent under the relentless June sun. The storefronts, once proud, now sagged with neglect. Melvald's General Store anchored the corner, its red-and-white SUMMER SALE! sign flapping limply in the breeze, the edges curling from days of heat. The plate-glass windows reflected the empty streets, their surfaces smudged and streaked, framing a display of dusty canned goods and a mannequin in a faded sundress. It all looked . . . sad.

El shuddered, feeling a sudden chill work its way through her body. A single pickup truck idled at the stoplight, its driver slouched low, staring blankly through a cracked windshield. A crumpled Tab can skittered across the pavement, pushed by a hot gust, its metallic clatter echoing in the stillness, the only sound in this ghost town.

"What happened . . . to Hawkins?" El asked, her voice small, the excitement draining as she turned to Max.

"Starcourt happened, that's what. The new mall—does that ring a bell? You really have been locked up, huh?"

El winced, the accusation ringing true. "Downtown used to be . . ."

"Inhabited?" Max replied with a shrug, kicking her skateboard onto the pavement with a sharp clack, the wheels spinning briefly before settling.

El nodded. "Yeah. That."

"I mean, it's not like Hawkins was ever a hip metropolis." She snorted to emphasize that point. "But it sure was busier than this sorry ghost town."

El trailed behind Max, unsettled by the lack of people and traffic.

Max continued talking while riding ahead slowly. The wheels clacked down the bumpy sidewalk. "Yeah, it's like a zombie apocalypse hit Hawkins. And everyone with a pulse escaped to the mall. Like in *Dawn of the Dead*. My stepbrother Billy loves that super-creepy flick."

"Everyone went to Starcourt?" El asked, recalling the cheerful ads.

Max nodded, weaving on her skateboard so El could keep pace on foot. "Yup, they're probably dropping their allowance at Scoops Ahoy or that new flashy arcade. Downtown's been a dead zone ever since it opened."

"Scoops Ahoy?" El asked. So much about the world still stumped her.

"Uh, right, it's like this boat-themed ice cream shop in the food court. 'Ahoy, matey, would you like to set sail on this ocean of flavor with me?'" Max quoted the cheesy company slogan, but El frowned.

"Boat ice cream?"

"Right, it's confusing. What do sailors have to do with ice cream? Seriously, weird combo. But they do make *killer* ice cream sundaes."

El laughed, filing that away under something to investigate later.

They reached the main drag, but the traffic didn't pick up. Eleven's shoulders slumped, the hollow atmosphere seeping into her bones. She'd pictured a summer like the ones in her *Teen Beat* magazines—kids shrieking with laughter, shops buzzing with chatter, the air alive with the hum of possibility.

Instead, Hawkins felt like a husk, its heart stolen by the flashy allure of the new shopping mall. But Max's words sparked a flicker of curiosity. Starcourt—she'd seen the commercial on Hopper's grainy TV, a dazzling wonderland of escalators, twinkling lights, and teens living the life she craved. Maybe that's where summer hid, just out of reach.

Max started skating slowly down the street, her board's wheels clacking rhythmically against the uneven pavement, dodging cracks and pebbles.

"Come on, El. Don't let it be a drag. We'll make our own fun."

Eleven followed, her sneakers scuffing the ground, her eyes darting to every shadow, every alleyway, her nerves still raw from the morning's nightmare. The air felt heavy, charged with an unease she couldn't shake.

Max weaved away, hopping off the curb and trying out some basic tricks. El skidded to a halt by an alley, waiting.

Suddenly, a hot wind kicked up, scattering trash and raising gooseflesh on her skin. El slowly turned around.

The alley winnowed into darkness, despite the blazing sun. It was blocked by the buildings, casting it into shadow.

"Is somebody there?" El called out, but another gust hit, stealing her words.

The shadows seemed to writhe, an uneasy beat that made her freeze.

She shivered again even in the heat. Her senses unfurled around her.

Something stirred behind a rusted dumpster, a faint rustle that sent her pulse spiking. Her powers hummed beneath her skin, and with a flicker of thought, she nudged the dumpster aside . . . its rusty metal wheels groaning.

Then a rat burst out!

Its oily, sleek body darted across the pavement, beady eyes locking with hers for a split second. El caught a vision of the rat bubbling into a bloody mass, then exploding. Her breath caught in her throat, but before she could do anything, it scampered away and vanished into a storm drain with a wet squeak.

Eleven exhaled, her shoulders sagging, but a chill lingered. That rat and the vision—it felt like a warning.

But . . . of what?

She couldn't answer that.

Suddenly a voice cut through the dark alley. "Hurry up, slowpoke!"

Max's voice sliced through El's thoughts. She was halfway down the block, her board weaving lazy arcs. Eleven grinned, a spark of mischief flaring. She focused, her powers tingling, and Max's skateboard jerked to a halt, the wheels locking mid-spin.

"Hey, no fair!" Max yelped, but her reflexes kicked in—she popped the board up, plucking it from the air with a graceful twist, landing smoothly.

She whipped her head toward the cause of her sudden dismount.

El gave her a slow applause.

"Oh, you're gonna pay for that, El!" Max said in a teasing voice, hands on her hips, her grin wide and wicked.

They both laughed, the sound ringing through the

empty streets. They continued deeper into downtown, searching for something . . . *anything* . . . to spice up their day. A rusted bike rack stood empty, its metal warped from years of sun and rain, a relic of busier days when kids flooded these streets.

Suddenly, a familiar figure emerged from Melvald's, and Eleven's stomach lurched. She froze, grabbing Max's arm.

"Joyce," she whispered, her voice tight. "She tells Hopper everything."

Max's eyes widened, and she yanked Eleven behind a parked station wagon, the paint peeling in long, curling strips.

Joyce Byers, her dark hair pulled into a messy bun, wrestled with a new CLEARANCE SALE! sign, taping it over the old one in the shop's front window. Her blouse was rumpled, her expression harried as she muttered to herself, juggling a roll of tape and a marker. They crouched low, watching as Joyce stepped back to admire her handiwork, oblivious to their presence.

"Think she'd bust us?" Max whispered, her breath hot against Eleven's ear.

El nodded, her heart pounding. "She's . . . close with Hopper."

She made a kissing face, her lips puckering exaggeratedly.

"No way! Will's mom? Really?" Max stifled a laugh, then mimed gagging, her fingers splaying dramatically.

They both dissolved into giggles, clamping their hands over their mouths to stay quiet, their shoulders shaking until Joyce turned and headed back into the store, the bell jingling faintly.

They let the laughter ring out until tears leaked from their eyes.

"So, you really think Hopper's crushing on Joyce?" Max whispered, still grinning. "If they got hitched . . . then would that make Will . . . your stepbrother?"

Eleven looked horrified. "Maybe."

"Will would probably be okay," Max replied with a flick of her wrist. "My stepbrother terrorizes me on a daily basis."

The thought of Will and El becoming siblings sent them both into another fit of laughter, the tension easing as they straightened up, dusting off their knees.

Disaster averted, they continued down Main Street. Max hopped back on her board, her confidence infectious. "Check this out," she called, speeding toward a short set of steps leading to the library's entrance.

El focused, her powers tingling, and gave Max's board a subtle push, boosting her speed.

Max hit the steps, launching into a clean ollie, her board soaring over the concrete with a satisfying clack as she landed. She whooped, pumping her fist, then sped toward a low railing by the post office. Eleven nudged the board again, guiding it perfectly—Max grinded the rail, her wheels screeching, then popped off with a burst of air.

Max handled it gracefully, flipping the board up and plucking it from the air, landing with a flourish.

"Hell yeah!" she said, spinning to high-five Eleven.

"You're my secret weapon, El! You gotta come to the skate park if those punks get it going again."

That's when something caught El's attention, jerking her to a halt.

"What is it?" Max asked.

El pointed to a colorful flyer stapled to a telephone pole. The fresh sign was papered over another flyer, which was dull black and white and sun-bleached, reading:

SAVE DOWNTOWN! NO TO MALL! SAY NO TO STARCOURT! TOWN HALL!

Max skated over, rolling to a halt. She read the flyer's bold print aloud:

"'Starcourt Mall Teen Slumber Fest—*Gremlins* and *Ghostbusters* Movie Doubleheader! Ice Cream Sundaes! Scavenger Hunt! Fifty-Dollar Gift Certificate Prize!'"

Max looked up. "A double feature? Those are two of my favorite movies from last year. And a scavenger hunt? That's a fortune!" Her eyes sparkled with excitement. "We can't miss that! It's the perfect way to kick off summer break."

Now, that sounded more like the teen summer the magazines all promised. A night at the mall with movies and ice cream. Even if they weren't first-run flicks, El had never seen either of them. It seemed like the summer she dreamed of, straight out of *Seventeen*. El grinned at the prospect, but then her face fell. Hopper's voice echoed in her mind: *Stay put—or else!*

Max nudged her, sensing the hesitation. "We'll figure it out, El. You deserve this, whether Hopper likes it or not.

We just need a plan." She tore the flyer off, folding it into her pocket with a determined nod. "This is our ticket to freedom. No way we're missing it."

Eleven nodded, her jaw tightening. Max was right—she couldn't stay locked away forever. Before they could plot further, a commotion drifted from the run-down city park across the street. El tapped Max's arm, her expression turning stormy. "Look over there . . ."

A jeering voice echoed out. "Hey, kid, think you can play on *our* field?"

"Give it back," the kid said in a teary voice. "That's mine—"

Eleven and Max watched as bullies—Kyle Walsh, Becks Carter, and Danny Ortiz—picked on a younger kid by taking his soccer ball and playing keep-away with it. El clocked the crew, summing them up. Kyle was lanky with a greasy mullet and a chipped tooth, his Van Halen tee stained with sweat, while Becks had frizzy blond bangs and a shaggy haircut. The largest kid was Danny, stocky with a buzz cut and scarred fists. He cracked his knuckles, grinning as the kid cowered away from them. But he lunged for his ball, missing badly.

They all cackled at the kid's pitiful effort. Kyle shoved him. Hard. He landed in the dirt and started whimpering. Then the biggest bully, Danny, yanked the red baseball cap off his head and stomped it into the mud.

Max's eyes narrowed, her outrage growing. "Burnouts—

why don't you pick on someone your own size?" she yelled, flipping them off with both hands, her gesture bold and defiant.

That got their attention. Kyle jerked his head up from tormenting the kid.

His smirk twisted into a sneer. "Well, lookee here . . . two dumb girls!"

Becks laughed, sharp and mean, while Danny lumbered forward, his Whitesnake shirt straining at the seams. He bunched his hands into meaty fists.

The bullies gave chase, their sneakers pounding the pavement as they hurtled across the street. Max kicked off on her board, weaving through the empty street, her red ponytail bouncing. El ran beside her, her powers humming.

She glanced back at the park, nudging the soccer ball to roll toward the snotty kid. He picked it up, looking over in surprise, mouthing, *How?*

El smiled and gestured—*Scram, kid!* He didn't hesitate, grabbing his ball and booking it the other way.

"You'll pay for that!" Kyle yelled, jerking El's attention back to him.

He lunged at her, but El flicked her wrist, sending a trash can skidding into his path. He crashed into it, garbage spilling—banana peels, soda cans, and a half-eaten burger splattering the sidewalk. Becks tripped over him, cursing, while Danny followed next, falling flat on his face, red with rage.

"Nice one!" Max said, pulling up and high-fiving El. A

trickle of blood dripped from her nose, but she didn't care. She quickly wiped it away.

But victory was short-lived. The bullies started to recover, irate, their shouts echoing as they scrambled to their feet. But then . . . a low rumble cut through the chaos, the growl of a truck engine. Eleven's heart leapt into her throat as a familiar brown Chevy Blazer rounded the corner—Hopper.

"Crap, it's your dad!" Max hissed, grabbing Eleven's arm. "Move!"

CHAPTER FOUR

Hopper's truck rolled onto Main Street, prowling through downtown slowly. Everyone scattered at the sight of cops—the bullies bolting down an alley, while Max grabbed her board and El's hand. They leapt behind the nearest car, a Pontiac with peeling paint.

"That's bad luck," Max muttered at this unfortunate turn of events. She peered around it as Hopper neared.

"What do we do?" El gasped, feeling her bright summer dreams evaporating.

"We've got to get out of here, that's what. If he catches you out of the cabin, then we're both dead."

El paled. "I think I'm deader."

"Well, that's not going to happen, not on my watch. Hurry, stay low . . ."

Max army-crawled across the sidewalk, gesturing for El to follow.

She shoved open the door of the nearest storefront, and they ducked inside, immediately greeted by stale air and a chorus of electronic music and beeps. The carpet under their feet was ground down with gum and kiddie foot traffic.

This could only be one place—

The Palace Arcade.

That kinetic bastion of games, where kids ran wild until the change in their pockets dried up, and even then, they hung around to watch their friends pump quarters into machines, frantically gunning for top scores on the leaderboard, only to groan at every GAME OVER like it was the end of the world.

The door slammed shut behind Max and El with a *whoosh;* then they crouched down by the front windows, watching as the Blazer slowed, Hopper's silhouette visible through the tinted windows, his sunglasses glinting.

"Think Hopper saw us?" Max asked, breathing hard. "If he did, we're dead."

Eleven's breath caught, fear jolting her as Hopper slowed even more, craning his neck their way. She couldn't afford to get caught or he'd never let her out again. Her powers tingled, ready to create a distraction if he spotted them.

But she didn't have to.

Right then, a blue Camaro roared past, speeding

recklessly down Main Street with tires squealing, nearly clipping a parked car and a pedestrian.

"Watch it!" Joyce yelled, storming out of Melvald's. "If you're not careful, you're gonna drive away what little business we have left!"

Hopper's siren blared, his lights flashing as he peeled off after the speeder—Billy Hargrove, Max's stepbrother, his mullet flapping as he floored it.

Hopper gave chase, and soon both cars vanished from downtown.

Max exhaled, slumping against the window. "Goddamn Billy," she muttered, but a grin tugged at her lips. "I told you stepbrothers can be the worst."

El shrugged. "But he saved us."

"I guess you're right," Max said reluctantly. "He did save our asses. *Technically.* But he didn't do it on purpose. Hell, if he only knew—he'd probably turn us in to Hopper himself."

El smirked. "Stepbrothers. The worst."

"Now you're learning," Max joked back, rolling her eyes.

But then something deeper in grabbed their attention.

"Listen, you hear that?" Max asked, whipping her head toward the sound.

Familiar voices rose from the back of the arcade, drowning out the games' tinny beeps.

"Nice try, but you can't beat my top score," a lisping voice said. "It's not humanly possible. You're just wasting quarters."

Another voice shot back. "Aren't you leaving for camp? I bet I knock you off the leaderboard before you get back."

"A month isn't long enough. You couldn't beat my score in a year. Heck, you couldn't beat me even if I had my hands tied behind my back."

"I'll prove you wrong! Besides, that doesn't make sense. You can't even play with your hands tied behind your back."

"Oh, just watch me!"

Sounds of shoving erupted. A third voice cut in.

"Pay attention, dumbasses! Your game started while you were busy arguing!"

Then a fourth voice. "Why don't we just go back to my house and play D&D like old times? It's way more fun. Not to mention cheaper. I'm almost out of quarters—"

"No, stop asking!" the other three yelled back in unison.

Their shouts grew louder, cutting through the arcade's electronic din.

Eleven focused, zooming in on the culprits. A spark of hope pierced the fear still lingering from Hopper's close call.

She exchanged a glance with Max, her eyes glinting with mischief. "Mike!"

"You've got to be kidding," Max said, rolling her eyes. "Lucas?"

El concentrated, using her powers, then nodded in confirmation.

"Of course, just my luck," Max muttered. "Well, come on. Let's surprise the dweebs making all that noise."

They wove through the Palace Arcade's chaotic maze,

past flickering screens and kids hunched over joysticks, their faces lit by the glow of *Pac-Man* and *Centipede*. The air was thick with the scent of burned popcorn, stale soda, and the faint metallic tang of quarters jingling in pockets. The carpet, sticky with spilled drinks and ground-in gum, squished under their sneakers.

The arcade pulsed with life, a stark contrast to the ghost town outside, and for a moment, El felt like the summer break that she craved lay within reach.

But as El passed by a nearby *Galaga* machine, the screen flickered oddly, stuttering to black before flashing a jagged crimson rift that pulsed like a wound. Suddenly, pixelated rats erupted from the gash, running over the game and trying to break through the glass. Crack! It started to splinter!

"Wait, do you see that?" El said, grabbing Max's arm and pointing.

But the game snapped back to pixelated aliens. No bloody gash. No pixelated rats. She blinked, but the game remained normal, like nothing was amiss. Her skin prickled, her senses still on high alert, but the arcade's hum drowned out the unease.

Max gave her a look. "What is it?" she asked, craning her neck but not seeing anything.

"Uh, nothing," El said, feeling self-conscious about the disturbance. It was probably like her nightmare, her mind haunted by echoes of her past trauma.

They continued deeper into the arcade. Max led the

way, dodging a kid who sprinted past clutching a fistful of prize tickets. The voices grew clearer, a mix of laughter and mock outrage, punctuated by the tinny clank of a game cabinet. El's pulse quickened.

They rounded a corner, and there they were—the usual culprits—Mike, Lucas, Will, and Dustin, huddled around a *Dragon's Lair* machine, its animated knight flashing on the screen. Mike leaned in, his dark hair falling into his eyes, barking instructions as Lucas jammed the joystick, cursing under his breath. Dustin stood back, arms crossed, smirking, while Will hovered at the edge, his expression subdued, almost haunted, his pale skin stark under the arcade's harsh lights.

"Move left, Lucas! Left!" Mike shouted, his voice cracking with urgency. "You're gonna die again!"

"I'm trying!" Lucas snapped, his curls bouncing as he wrestled the controls. "This game's rigged!"

"It's not rigged," Dustin said, rolling his eyes. "You just suck. I told you—you're never knocking me off the leaderboard top spot. It's impossible!"

El froze, her breath catching. *Mike.* Annoyance flickered through her. He wasn't ignoring her calls—but he'd broken his promise to keep her company, instead opting for carefree summer fun with his friends. The annoyance mixed with something else—the way his dark hair dipped into his eyes, the soft curve of his lips.

She wanted to tell him off—but she also wanted something else.

To kiss him.

Which urge was stronger? She wasn't sure, and that was the problem.

Max nudged her, raising an eyebrow. She tipped her head toward Lucas, who was jamming the joystick like a maniac.

"Boys will be boys," she muttered, but her tone was teasing, not bitter. "Listen to me, don't let him off the hook that easily. He'll probably try to sweet-talk you like Lucas. Don't fall for it."

Before El could respond, Mike glanced up, his eyes locking with hers.

She crossed her arms—sending a clear message: *You broke your promise.*

The teen relationship quiz was still fresh in her mind. And how many questions she'd answered *no.* Including, *Does he call you every day?*

"Damn," Mike said, worry drifting over his face.

Lucas saw Max and El standing there, looking hostile, then exchanged a look with Mike—*uh-oh.* Mike moved away from the group, weaving through the arcade, and pulled El behind a *Pac-Man* machine, its blinking ghosts casting yellow light across his freckled face.

"You're here! How'd you get away from Hopper? He'll be pissed—"

"You didn't call me today," El cut him off. She kept her arms crossed tight.

"Uh, about that . . . the day isn't over yet!" Mike stammered. "I didn't say what time, right? I was going to call you . . . *after* . . . I got done. We're heading over to

Will's to play D&D later, and I was going to call you after."

"After?" She started to soften, and Mike seized on the opening.

"Yes, exactly! *After!* How could I forget about you? You're my—"

He didn't finish. Instead, he leaned in, his lips brushing hers in a quick, stolen kiss, soft and warm, sending a jolt through her veins. El's cheeks flushed, her heart racing as she kissed him back, her fingers curling into his striped polo. For a second, the arcade faded—the beeps, the shouts, the weight of Hopper's rules—leaving only Mike, his breath mingling with hers. And in that moment, she forgave him completely.

How could she stay mad? Especially when he was kissing her like this . . .

"Gross!" Dustin's voice cut through, sharp and dramatic. He stood a few feet away, clutching his chest like he'd been shot. "Get a room, you two!"

Lucas mimed puking, sticking out his tongue. "Yeah, save it for next year's Snow Ball, Romeo."

Mike pulled back, his face red but grinning, and flipped them off.

"Jealous much?"

El giggled, her nerves easing, but her eyes darted to Max, who stood with her arms crossed, one eyebrow arched.

Her meaning was clear—*I said don't let him off the hook that easily.* But then, the corner of her mouth curled, betraying a reluctant amusement.

Meanwhile, Will stayed quiet, his hands stuffed deep in

his pockets. El noticed the shadows under his eyes, the way his shoulders hunched, like he was carrying something heavy. The Upside Down, she thought, her stomach twisting. It clung to him, a ghost that wouldn't let go. He caught her staring and offered a small smile, but it didn't reach his eyes.

"Yo, Dustin," Lucas said, slapping Dustin's shoulder. "You're hogging the machine. My turn."

"Nuh-uh," Dustin shot back, feeding another quarter into *Dragon's Lair.* "I'm this close to beating my high score. Besides, I'm leaving for science camp tomorrow—let me have this turn."

"Science camp?" El asked, stepping out from behind the *Pac-Man* machine, her curiosity piqued.

Dustin puffed out his chest, his grin wide enough to show his braces. "Yup! Starts tomorrow. I'm gonna build a robot, maybe even a laser. It's gonna be epic—total mad scientist vibes."

Mike snorted, leaning against the machine. "Just watch, he'll come back like me. Bet you get a camp girlfriend, Dustin. It's pretty much unavoidable."

Dustin's face went pink, but he held up his hands, indignant.

"Never!" Dustin said, his gap-toothed grin flashing. "I told you already. I'm staying a single ladies' man. Can't disappoint all the hotties."

Max rolled her eyes. El smiled shyly.

Dustin continued his rant, oblivious. "My friend Steve gave me advice. Summer is the time to run wild and free—

and sow your wild oats. You can't be locked down. No offense, Mike and El."

Mike laughed. "None taken. Do go on . . . Wild oats, you were saying?"

Dustin nodded. "Lucas, you're on the Dustin summer program, right?"

"Yup, I'm free as a bird," Lucas said, catching a scowl from Max.

"Hey, I dumped his ass—that's why he's single," Max snapped. "Not because he wanted to get in on your *free bird, wild oats sowing* summer."

Lucas and Max glared at each other—but then the moment faded. They both softened, making it clear that the breakup was only temporary, and they'd inevitably get back together. Again.

"Camp girlfriend . . . I still bet he gets one," Will said with a smirk. "Trust me, it always happens when you least expect it. Just look at Mike and El."

"Guilty as charged," Mike said, kissing El again, making her blush.

"No way!" Dustin shot back. "The odds of me getting a camp girlfriend are roughly equivalent to the odds of you beating my top score at *Dragon's Lair.*"

Lucas grabbed the joystick, shoving Dustin off. He dumped a quarter into the machine, firing it up. "By my calculation, the mathematical probability might be low, even minuscule, but it's not zero."

Dustin shook his head in dismay. "We'll see, man. We'll see."

El smiled, the banter washing over her like a warm wave, pulling her into their world. This was what she'd missed while being locked up in Hopper's cabin since she got back from her adventures in Chicago—their dumb jokes, their easy camaraderie, the way they made her feel like she belonged. But Will's silence tugged at her.

He shifted, his sneakers scuffing the carpet, and finally spoke, his voice soft but firm. "We should do a D&D night. You know, like old times."

The group paused, the air shifting. Will's haunted eyes hit them. Mike nodded, his expression softening. "Yeah, Will's right. We haven't played in forever. After we run out of quarters, okay? We can head to the basement."

Lucas opened his mouth to agree, but his eyes focused on the flyer crumpled in Max's back pocket.

"Hold up—what's that?"

Max stiffened, not wanting to invite the boys, especially with her recent breakup, but El, caught up in the moment, focused her powers.

With a flicker of thought, the flyer levitated from Max's back pocket, floating toward the group. Max shot her a look—half annoyed, half impressed—as Mike snatched it from the air, his eyes scanning the bold print.

"'Starcourt Mall Teen Slumber Fest'?" Mike read aloud, his voice rising with excitement. "*Gremlins* and *Ghostbusters*? Ice cream sundaes? A scavenger hunt with a fifty-dollar prize?"

He turned to El, his grin infectious. "Wow, this is perfect! A movie night slumber party with you? And I'll bet you've never seen these films. We can experience them together. I'm in."

Even though he'd seen both films when they came out last year, he couldn't wait for the chance to revisit those two instant classics. Plus, he knew El had never seen them.

El's heart soared, her earlier doubts about Mike dissolving. She glanced at Max, expecting resistance, but Max's expression had shifted, her annoyance falling away.

"Okay, fine. Have it your way," Max said, crossing her arms. "It could be fun. Plus, that prize money? Total score. We could use the extra hands to win."

Lucas pumped his fist, making Max roll her eyes. "Fifty bucks? That's, like, a million quarters! I'm down. That's just what I need to beat Dustin's score. And seriously? They're playing both of those films? *Ghostbusters* is basically my all-time favorite movie!"

Dustin groaned, slumping against the *Dragon's Lair* machine. "Seriously? I'm gonna miss *Gremlins* and *Ghostbusters*? At the mall? This is the worst timing ever." He kicked the cabinet, earning a glare from a nearby kid. "Science camp better be worth it."

Will fidgeted, his fingers twisting the hem of his shirt. "I don't know . . ." he said, his voice barely audible over the arcade's hum. That haunted look flashed over his face again.

Mike clapped a hand on Will's shoulder. "We'll do D&D soon, man. Promise. But this Slumber Fest? It's a once-in-a-summer thing. We gotta go."

Max leaned in, her voice low but firm. "Problem is, how

do we sneak El out? Hopper's got her on, like, maximum-security lockdown."

"You don't have to remind me," Mike said. "He's always watching us. 'Three-inch rule—open the door!'" he said, mimicking Hopper's gruff voice. "'Or else—I'm coming in!'"

"Bummer. Like, no privacy?" Lucas said. "That would drive me crazy."

"Yeah, and he's a cop. And not just any cop—the chief of police. Like, it's basically the worst-case scenario."

"Total mess," Dustin agreed. "He's got like investigative skills. He'll sense if you're lying to him, too."

"He'll never let her go," Mike said, his voice cracking with anxiety. "Especially if he finds out I'm going to be there." He dragged his finger across his throat.

El's stomach twisted. They were right. It was a lost cause. And overnight?

Forget about it.

She pictured his stern face, the way his mustache twitched when he was mad, and the thought of disappointing him stung. But the flyer, now passed around the group, felt like a ticket to the summer she'd dreamed of inspired by the magazines—movies, ice cream, her friends . . . and her boyfriend. Hopper couldn't keep her caged forever.

Mike squeezed her hand. "We'll figure it out, El. No way you're missing this."

Max nodded, her grin returning, all business now. She pointed to El. "Don't worry—I've got a plan. This is my specialty. Evading parental units. We'll outsmart Hopper, hit the mall, and win that scavenger hunt. You're not missing Slumber Fest, El. Not on my watch."

El's resolve hardened, a flicker of rebellion flaring bright. She nodded, her jaw set. "Okay. I'm in."

The group erupted in cheers, Dustin's groan drowned out by Lucas's whoop and Mike's excited chatter about the movies. Max high-fived El, her eyes sparkling with the promise of trouble. Then she pocketed the flyer for later.

For the first time in a long time, El felt like she was part of something bigger, something normal—a summer with her friends, a chance to be a real teen.

But then the moment shattered.

A jeering voice cut through the arcade's hum, sharp and mean.

"What are you losers doing hogging my game?"

CHAPTER FIVE

The bullies cornered El, Max, and their friends in the back of the Palace Arcade. "Step off *Dragon's Lair,*" Kyle said, his shadow falling over them.

"Yeah, nerds . . . scram," Becks added with a cruel sneer, backing him up.

"Or else . . ." Danny added ominously, cracking his knuckles.

El grew annoyed hearing their voices. She jerked around, her powers tingling, and saw them—Kyle, Becks, and Danny, the bullies from the park, their sneers back and uglier than ever.

"Oh crap," Max muttered, turning around. "Those morons found us . . ."

Around them, the Palace Arcade buzzed with the frenetic pulse of 8-bit beeps and electronic flashes, but the air turned heavy with the bullies' arrival.

"*Who* exactly found us?" Lucas asked, turning around in surprise.

The boys stood crowded over *Dragon's Lair,* but they abandoned the game in progress. GAME OVER flashed on the screen with a downbeat jingle.

Max stiffened, her grip tightening on her skateboard. "Those are the bullies I flipped off in the park. Oh, and El threw a trash can at them."

Lucas's eyes widened, his voice cracking with fear. "Well, those aren't just any bullies—that's Troy's cousin. Of all the people to mess with, you had to pick that guy?"

He nodded toward Kyle. El's breath caught, the name dragging up memories of Troy's cruel taunts and the glint of his knife from a year ago. Dustin leaned in as he hissed, "Yeah, Troy's younger, meaner cousin. He's a real dick."

Kyle shoved past Mike, slamming his palm on the *Dragon's Lair* cabinet, making the screen stutter. "Step off, loser! This ain't your personal playground. It's our game now."

Max bristled, stepping forward. "We were here first, jerk. Back off. Don't you only pick on kids younger than you?"

Kyle's eyes snapped to her, his grin twisting. "Oh, it's the skater wannabe." In a flash, he snatched the skateboard from her grip. "Girls suck at skating. Go play with your Barbies."

Max's face flushed with rage. "Give it back!"

Becks sauntered closer to Eleven, studying her neon shirt and bouncy curls with contempt. "What's with this weirdo? Crawl out of a science experiment or something?"

The word *experiment* cut deep, stirring memories of shaved heads and hospital gowns.

El's expression grew dark, a low hum of power sparking beneath her skin. The arcade lights flickered, a sharp stutter that made kids glance up from their games. Her fingers curled, the air crackling faintly, but Mike's hand brushed her arm, his whisper urgent.

"Not worth it, El. Don't."

Her powers could draw attention. The staff might even call the cops. That meant . . . Hopper would bust them. That would be the end of her summer plans.

She locked eyes with him, her chest tight, and forced the power down.

The lights steadied, but a trickle of blood seeped from her nostril. She wiped it away, her heart pounding. The bullies exchanged confused looks, unsure what to make of her.

"Dude, you are a total freak!" Becks taunted. "They should lock you up."

El lunged at her, but Mike held her back.

"Think we need to teach them a lesson," Kyle said with a cruel smile. "About who's really in charge of this arcade." He held out Max's skateboard to tempt her.

Max swiped for it. "Give it back!"

But Kyle jerked it away at the last second, torturing her.

"Consider this payback," he sneered, passing the skateboard to Danny, the muscle in their crew.

Danny raised the deck high over his head. With a grunt, he smashed it against the floor . . . right in front of Max. Then he stomped his foot down right on the middle. Hard.

CRACK!

The wood splintered, wheels spinning uselessly as the board broke right in half. Max cried out in anger and lurched at him, fists clenched, but Kyle shoved her back. She stumbled into a *Pac-Man* machine with a crash, the Slumber Fest flyer falling out of her pocket.

Lucas caught her, helping her back to her feet. Her eyes blazed with fury hot enough to scorch the room. Furious tears pricked her eyes, burning like acid.

"Oops," Danny mocked, tossing the broken halves at her feet. "Guess you're grounded now, princess."

Lucas stepped up, his jaw tight. "You're gonna pay for that."

But Danny pulled him back, putting him in a choke hold. Lucas struggled, futilely. His eyes bugged out, and he was gasping for breath. Danny released him and he fell sputtering to the floor.

Kyle's sneer widened. "Oh, I'm so scared, I'm shaking! Ha, I know you're chickenshit, too. Figures, bunch of crybaby losers. My cousin told me all about you dorks."

Suddenly, his gaze caught the flyer that had fallen out of Max's pocket in the scuffle. "Yo, what's this?"

Becks darted forward, snatching the flyer with a

triumphant cackle. She handed it to Kyle, who scanned it, his grin turning vicious. "Starcourt Mall Teen Slumber Fest? *Gremlins, Ghostbusters,* ice cream, and a fifty-buck prize? Oh, were you dweebs planning to go?"

He held the flyer high, then ripped it to shreds, letting the scraps flutter over Max's head and drift to the floor like ash. She clutched her broken board and glared back at him, her face a storm of rage and humiliation. But she knew they couldn't overpower the bullies. It would cause a scene and possibly damage the arcade. Even worse, it could summon the men from the lab who hunted her. They couldn't risk that.

"Too bad you losers won't make it," Kyle said, tossing the last shred into the air. "Now scram! Get out of my arcade!"

He shouldered past Mike and Will, claiming the *Dragon's Lair* machine. Becks and Danny crowded in, their laughter grating as they fed quarters into the cabinet, the game's tinny medieval tune blaring. The group stood frozen, the arcade's chaos swirling around them.

El's anger surged, a wildfire threatening to erupt. The overhead lights flickered again, sharper now, and the nearby screens stuttered and flashed. She clenched her fists, the air humming, but Mike squeezed her hand.

"We'll find another way, El. They're not worth it."

She nodded, swallowing hard, the power ebbing but leaving her trembling.

Max scrambled to her feet, clutching the shattered halves of her skateboard, her eyes glinting with unshed tears.

"Let's go," she muttered, her voice tight with fury. "It's game over . . ."

The shattered pieces of her board were the price she paid for her earlier defiance. The group retreated through the arcade's maze of flashing screens and sticky floors. Dustin cast a longing glance back at *Dragon's Lair,* where the bullies frenetically jammed the joysticks.

"Those jerks better not mess with my high score," Dustin grumbled, but Lucas nudged him toward the exit.

"There's more to life than the high scores," Lucas said. "At least nobody got hurt in real life."

"Ha, easy for you to say," Dustin muttered. "You've never gotten your initials on the leaderboard."

Outside, the heat slammed into them, the sun glaring off Main Street's cracked pavement. The ghost town stillness felt heavier now, the weight of the confrontation clinging like damp air. Mike led the way, his arm brushing El's.

"How about we regroup at my house? The basement? Make a plan."

Will's face lit up, a rare spark piercing his haunted expression. "Now can we play D&D?" he asked.

The group groaned, but it was playful.

Dustin slung an arm around Will's shoulders, rolling his eyes. "Fine, but only if I'm dungeon master. I've got a campaign ready—goblins, traps, mages, epic loot."

"No way!" Will shot back, a grin tugging at his lips. "Mike is the best dungeon master."

"Don't push it, Will the Wise," Dustin teased, shoving him lightly. "I'm the master of masters. It's a science."

Lucas snorted, dodging a pebble Max kicked. "You're the master of bull, that's what."

El smiled, the banter loosening the knot in her chest. Even Max cracked a reluctant grin, though her grip on her broken board tightened. It was her most precious possession, aside from her Walkman, and now it was destroyed.

"Worst summer kickoff ever," she muttered, still simmering with anger.

Dustin fell in beside her as they cut to the right, heading for Mike's house. He inspected the splintered wood. "Don't worry—I can fix it. Before I leave for science camp tomorrow. Epoxy, duct tape—boom, good as new."

Max raised an eyebrow, skeptical but softening. "Really? You can?"

Dustin nodded. "Yeah, and I can reinforce it too. Improve on it. You know, sprinkle some of my magic dust on it. So those dicks can't break it again."

"No way! You're a genius," Max said, impulsively hugging him, much to Lucas's annoyance.

Dustin blushed . . . hard.

"Hey, hands off—that's my girl." Lucas sniffed, but Max glared at him.

"*Your* girl?" she snapped. "You got dumped, remember? I'm *nobody's* girl."

Everyone laughed at their antics. The group continued

down the cracked sidewalk, joking and bantering, until it abruptly ended as downtown gave way to a neighborhood of modest single-family homes.

"Duh! Duh! Who you gonna call . . . Ghostbusters!" Mike sang. "Remember when we dressed up last year?"

"Admit it, Mike—I was a better Venkman," Lucas said, recalling how they both wore the same costume.

Mike snorted. "In your dreams! I've got more in common with Venkman. I thought we settled this already?"

Lucas thumped his chest. "You wish! I'm smart, witty, and a ladies' man . . . It's a killer combo. You can't compete."

"Dustin's going away," Will cut in. "So, one of you can be Ray this time."

Lucas raised his eyebrows. "Don't look at me . . . Venkman forever!"

As they bantered, weaving down the street, El lagged behind, her attention drifting to a deserted alleyway where shadows seemed to shift unnaturally, a faint rustle prickling her skin.

She shook it off, blaming her nerves, but the uneasy feeling lingered like a chill she couldn't shake despite the summer heat. She'd used her powers to close the gate at Hawkins Lab, cutting off the portal to the Upside Down. The terrible secrets about their experiments had been leaked to the press, shutting the lab down, once and for all.

So, why couldn't she shake the feeling that something dark and terrible was still amiss in Hawkins, like an abscess festering just below the surface?

"You okay?" Max asked, catching the haunted look on Eleven's face.

"Sorry . . . about your board," El said as Max fell into step beside her.

"You're sorry? It's not your fault. Those burnouts think they can get away with this?" Max said, her voice low and fierce. "No way. I swear it—I'll get them back for this."

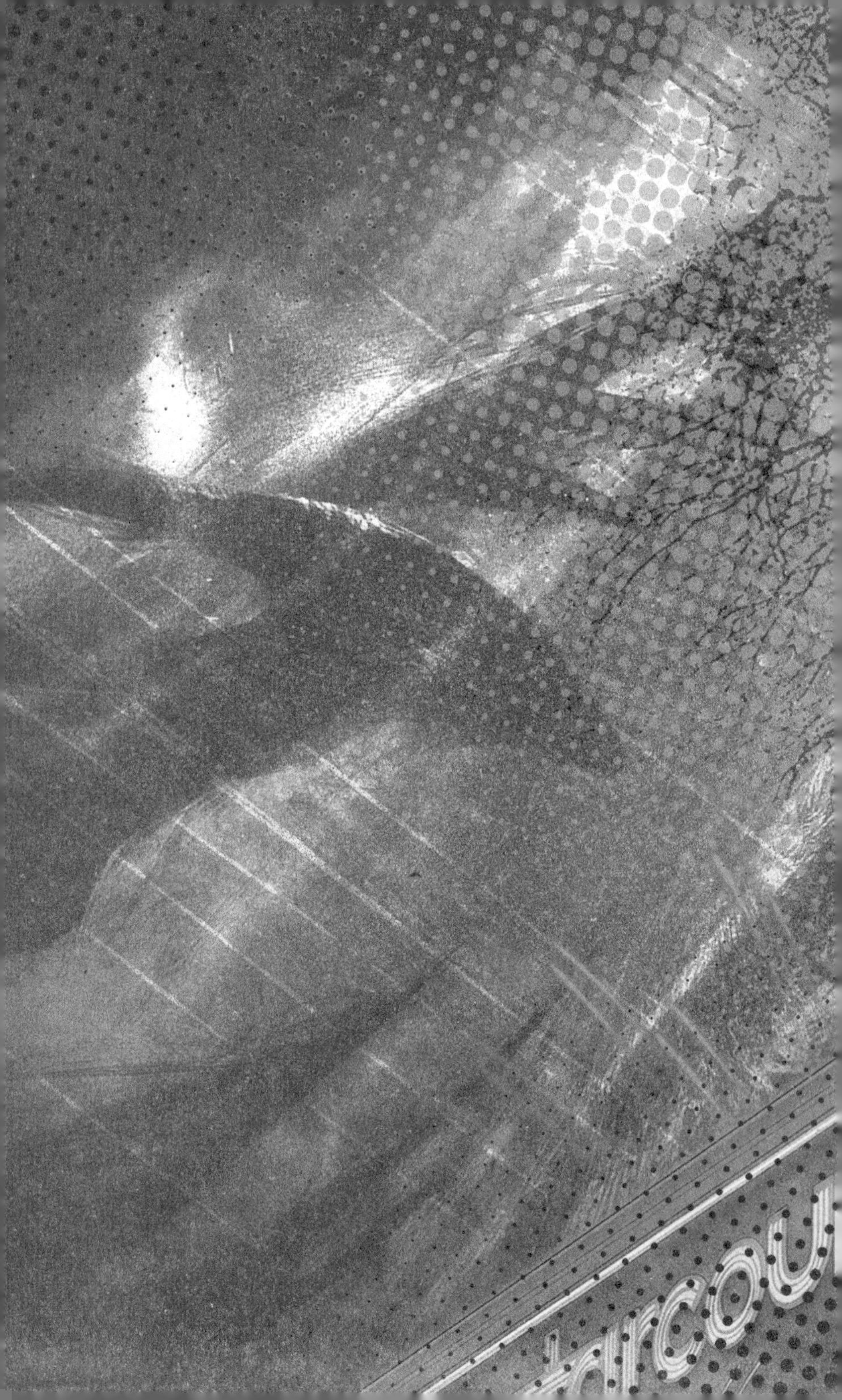

CHAPTER SIX

"Ladies first," Mike joked, holding the basement door open for El and Max. "Wait your turn," he added, locking his arm to block Dustin and Lucas.

El flashed a coy smile, sidestepping them and climbing down the creaky stairs. The rest followed after her.

"Don't let the door hit your ass on the way down," Mike quipped, darting in front of Dustin at the last second.

The door swung shut to bash him. "Child's play," he said, catching it, but not before it smacked him on the butt.

They all clambered down into the cozy, subterranean space, the home of many of their best and most harrowing adventures, even if many of them were imagined over a dice-based role-playing game.

Mike's basement was a perfect expression of teenage chaos, its musty carpet and wood-paneled walls soaked in the scent of stale Doritos and spilled Mountain Dew. Slanted beams of late afternoon sun pierced the high, narrow windows, glinting off a battered coffee table. Dustin wasted no time, procuring tools, clamps, and epoxy tubes, and getting to work on the splintered halves of Max's skateboard with Lucas's help.

The sagging couch groaned under Mike's weight as he sprawled across it, while Lucas and Dustin crouched over the table, bickering over the board's repair. El sat cross-legged on the floor, her neon shirt a bright splash against the drab carpet, her eyes jumping between her friends and the shadows lurking in the corners. Will hovered near a bookshelf, clutching a worn *Dungeons & Dragons Monster Manual,* his fingers tracing the faded dragon on its cover.

Meanwhile, Max paced, her arcade anger still sizzling through her. "Can you fix it?" she asked, her nerves flaring at the sight of her broken board on the table.

"Don't question a genius doctor in the middle of surgery!" Dustin said. "And stop pacing like that. It's making me nervous. I might slip and make a mistake . . ."

Max ground to a halt but wrung her hands, watching Dustin work with the delicate shards of her prized deck.

"Okay, genius," Lucas said, holding up a cracked piece, his tone thick with doubt. He fiddled with the tube of glue.

"You sure this epoxy's gonna hold? It looks like my mom's craft glue."

Dustin adjusted his trucker hat, flashing a smug grin. "Oh ye of little faith. This is industrial-grade, swiped from my garage. It'll make this board tougher than a tarrasque," he said, referring to the monster that usually ended D&D campaigns. "And stop messing with it! Oh, and if you get it on your fingers, they'll stay glued together . . . forever. You'll be a freak."

Lucas yelped and dropped the tube. Dustin glared at him, then grabbed it.

He squeezed a bead of epoxy onto the wood, spread it with a Popsicle stick, then grabbed a magnifying glass and positioned the splinters with tweezers, aligning them like a jigsaw puzzle.

"Trust in Dustin, and Dustin shall deliver," he went on as he worked.

Max snorted, crossing her arms. "Well, you'd better deliver! That board's my lifeline. If it snaps again, you're toast."

"No pressure, huh?" Dustin muttered, but his eyes sparkled with confidence.

Meanwhile, across the room, Mike leaned down, digging under the couch until he unearthed something and yanked it out. He blew the dust off the cover, revealing his 1984–1985 Hawkins Middle School yearbook with the tiger mascot embossed on the cover.

"Check it out," he said, dropping it on the table with

a thud. "I've got something that will cheer you up. Last year's memories. Everyone's signing mine before summer scatters us."

Will perked up, setting the D&D manual down. "Your yearbook? Sweet. I'll grab markers." He darted to a bookshelf cluttered with model spaceships, books, and random junk, returning with a fistful of pens.

"What's a . . . *yearbook*?" El asked, her face twisted up with confusion.

"Oh right," Mike said. "Why would you know that? It's like this book of pictures and memories collected from the whole school year."

He flipped it open to the class pictures, each kid posed awkwardly in peak fashion, crimped bangs and bowl cuts, braces and missing teeth galore.

"See here . . ." Mike said, pointing to the pictures. "Every student gets a picture, and they're organized by class."

El studied them, taking in each face. "Everyone gets a . . . picture?"

Mike nodded. "Exactly! We have picture day. It's kind of lame, but it gets you out of class for a few hours."

"Where's mine?" El asked, tapping the glossy pages.

"Right, you have to go to school to qualify. Otherwise . . ." He trailed off.

Max rolled her eyes, flopping onto the couch beside Mike and breaking up the tension. "Yearbook? Really? That's your plan to cheer us up after those burnouts trashed my board? Lame."

"Uh, it's tradition," Mike shot back, flipping open the book. "And it's hilarious. Look—Lucas, what's with the sweater vest on picture day?"

Lucas groaned, snatching the yearbook away. A grainy photo showed him in a mustard-yellow sweater vest, his expression pained. "Hey, my mom made me wear it! Said it made me look *distinguished.*"

"Dude, you look like a golf club reject," Dustin cackled, dodging Lucas's playful shove.

El watched, a smile tugging at her lips as the group passed Mike's yearbook around, their laughter bouncing off the walls. The pages of candid shots flipped by—kids laughing in the cafeteria, a science fair with lopsided volcanoes, a dodgeball game frozen mid-throw. Her fingers brushed the glossy pages, but the images felt alien, like glimpses into a life she'd never lived. No yearbook bore her name; no photo captured her face. She'd been a ghost at Hawkins Middle, hidden while her friends built these memories.

"El, you okay?" Mike asked, his voice soft, catching her hesitation.

She shrugged, her voice barely audible. "I don't . . . have one. A yearbook. Or any pictures . . ."

The group paused, the air shifting. Max stopped pacing, her expression softening. Lucas set down the epoxy, and Dustin glanced up, his bravado fading. Will fidgeted, as if her isolation echoed his own.

Mike's eyes lit up. "Wait, hold on!"

He flipped through the yearbook, fingers frantic, until he

landed on "Snow Ball '84." There, in a blurry corner, was Eleven—her curls loose, her pink dress glowing under the gym's twinkling lights, her hand in Mike's as they danced. Jonathan Byers's camera had caught her, a fleeting shadow, her face half obscured but unmistakable.

"See? Look . . . you're in here, too," Mike said, pointing. "Snow Ball. Best night ever."

El leaned closer, her heart twisting. The grainy image was her—proof she'd existed in their world, if only for a moment. But it hardly counted. A blurry snapshot wasn't a yearbook, wasn't a record of shared lunches or classes. It was a stolen fragment, not a life.

"It's . . . something," she said, forcing a smile, her voice wavering.

Mike squeezed her hand, his touch warm. "We'll get you in next year's, El. Front and center. All of us. Promise."

She nodded, wanting to believe him, but the ache lingered, a reminder of the lab, the Upside Down, Hopper's rules—all the barriers that stole her chance at normalcy. She couldn't risk going to public school in Hawkins.

They might find her.

Will cleared his throat, holding up the *Monster Manual*. "Uh, maybe we could play a quick D&D campaign? You know, to chill after . . . everything."

Max groaned, snatching the manual and tossing it onto the couch.

"We've got real-world problems—like sneaking El into the Slumber Fest this weekend."

Will's face fell, but he rallied, his voice tinged with excitement. "Come on, Max, hear me out. Maybe you can play! Usually we don't let girls. That rule was ratified mostly to keep Holly, Mike's little sister, from bugging us. But when I'm the dungeon master, I'll allow it. I've got this killer campaign with the Mind Flayer."

Dustin's eyes widened, his epoxy forgotten. He jerked his head around.

"The Mind Flayer? Dude, that's hardcore."

Lucas leaned in, intrigued. "Yeah, it's got those freaky shadow tendrils. It can possess you, make you do whatever it wants. You can't fight it head-on—takes serious strategy to defeat Flayers."

Mike nodded. "Total nightmare fuel. I'll give you credit, Will the Wise. That does sound like a killer campaign."

El's skin prickled, the description hitting too close to her nightmares—the lab, the void, the Demogorgon's maw. She glanced at Will, whose eyes gleamed with a mix of excitement and something darker.

Max rolled her eyes, unimpressed. "Sounds like a total snooze fest. Mind Flayer, really? Can we focus, please? Slumber Fest isn't gonna plan itself."

Will deflated, stuffing his hands in his pockets, but El caught the hurt in his eyes and patted his hand. She knew D&D was his refuge, just like Max's skateboard or the arcade's glow.

"Slumber Fest," Max said, clapping to refocus the group. "This Saturday. *Gremlins, Ghostbusters,* ice cream, and a fifty-buck prize. Swear it! We're all going. Nobody gets left behind."

Lucas raised an eyebrow. "Sounds awesome, but how? You said it yourself." He nodded to El. "Hopper's got her on CIA-level lockdown."

Dustin nodded, setting down the repaired skateboard, its wood now braced with metal strips and gleaming with fresh epoxy. "Yeah, her dad's a cop. The scary kind. He's got, like, a sixth sense for trouble."

"You can say that again," Mike said with a wince. "I dread going over there—" he started, but El pinched him.

"Ouch!" he yelped, grabbing his arm. "Uh, I mean, I *love* going over there for you," he rephrased, softening her with a kiss and drawing groans from the group. "But Hopper's always watching us through the slit in her door and yelling . . . *Is that three inches? Hey, that better be three inches!* I bet next time, he even takes the tape measure out."

"He's just overprotective," Will offered. "Because of everything . . . I mean, I love my mom. But ever since I came back, she's always hovering over me, worried about something."

His words hit the group hard, and a somber tone descended, reminding them of the real horrors they'd faced, not just imagined ones like in Dungeons & Dragons. Will set the *Monster Manual* down gently. The red dragon on the cover stared back at them menacingly.

"Done!" Dustin announced, holding up the board with a flourish. "Good as new! Reinforced with these braces—see? Those burnouts won't snap it again."

Max's eyes widened, her anger melting into relief. "Damn, Henderson, you're a wizard!"

She grabbed the board, running her fingers over the smooth, reinforced wood, then impulsively hugged him and kissed his cheek, quick and fierce.

Dustin's face turned beet red, his arms flailing. "Uh, okay, wow, you're welcome!"

Lucas glared at them. "Two times in one day, really? Is this payback? It's like you're trying to make me jealous."

Max just smirked, while Dustin turned redder. Mike snickered, nudging Will. "See that? Wanna bet? He's definitely getting a camp girlfriend."

"Double or nothing?" Will said.

Mike nodded, pinky shaking. "Winner gets to be dungeon master."

"Shut up, Lucas!" Dustin sputtered, pushing Max away gently. "This is purely professional craftsmanship appreciation! It means nothing."

Max laughed, setting the board down. "Whatever you say. You saved my summer." She turned to El, all business now. "Back to the plan. Slumber Fest. Here's how we do it."

She paced the basement, sneakers scuffing the carpet, as the group leaned in. "Listen up, here's my foolproof plan. El, you tell Hopper you're spending the night at my place. A girls' sleepover, got it? Totally innocent. He'll have no choice but to go for it. If he starts doing that thing where he groans and objects, just hit him with a heavy Dad guilt trip."

"Dad guilt trip?" El asked.

"Oh, Dad, I love you so much, but you never let me go anywhere," Max said, jutting her lower lip out and looking pathetic. *"Please, Daddy, pretty please."*

"Wow, she's good," Mike said, elbowing Lucas. "Even I feel guilty about not letting her go . . ."

"Exactly!" Max said, snapping back to normal. "It's totally foolproof, like I said. Then we sneak out from my place to the mall, hit the Slumber Fest, and get you back home by morning. The sleepover-turned-sneak-out is a classic move! Trust me, it never fails. What Hopper doesn't know can't hurt him."

El's stomach twisted, excitement clashing with fear. "A sleepover? At your house? Just . . . girls?"

"Yup," Max said, nodding. "Because if he thinks Mike will be there, no way in hell he'll go for it. But he can't object to me, right? My mom's working a double shift Saturday. The trailer's ours. Then we convince Billy to give us a ride to Starcourt—and party all night."

Will fidgeted, twisting his shirt hem. "What if we get busted? Hopper's intense. Like, scary intense."

Lucas nodded, his brow furrowing. "Yeah, he's got Spidey sense. He can tell if you're lying. That's like his job."

Mike snorted. "Exactly! Try sneaking past a cop who's *also* your girlfriend's dad. It's a whole new level of terror."

El bit her lip, picturing Hopper's stern face—his mustache fidgeting, his voice booming, *Stay put—or else!*

Lying to him made her chest tight, but the Slumber Fest—movies, ice cream, Mike's hand in hers—was too tempting. She'd been caged too long, first in the lab, now in the cabin. This was her chance to live, to be a real teen.

"I want to go," she said, her voice firm despite her worries. "I'll do it."

Max grinned, high-fiving her. "That's my girl! Just stick to the plan, okay? A sleepover at my house, got it? That's it. The less you say, the better. With lies, you have to keep it simple. You're not missing Slumber Fest, and that's final."

Mike squeezed El's hand, his eyes shining. "We'll make it work, El. All of us. Best night ever."

Dustin groaned, slumping onto the couch. "Why does science camp start now? I'm missing *Gremlins, Ghostbusters,* and a scavenger hunt? A whole night at the mall? I'd kill for that prize money."

Lucas smirked, tossing a couch pillow at him. "We'll spend it for you. Maybe buy you a new hat—something less hideous than that monstrosity."

"Hideous?" Dustin clutched his trucker hat, feigning offense. "This is a classic! It's my signature. Chicks dig it."

Max rolled her eyes. "Sure, Henderson. Keep dreaming."

The group laughed, the tension easing, but El's focus drifted to Will, who stood by the bookshelf, rubbing the back of his neck. His haunted look hadn't faded, and the Mind Flayer talk lingered in her mind, an uneasy echo of her nightmares. She wanted to ask if he felt the Upside Down's shadow, if he still dreamed of it, but the words stuck.

Mike flipped open his yearbook to the signing page, passing it to Lucas.

"Your turn, man. Sign something epic. No pressure, but make it better than Dustin's 'Stay cool, loser.' "

Dustin gasped, clutching his chest. "That was poetry! You're jealous of my wit."

Lucas grinned, scribbling a message, then handed it to Max. She snorted, adding her own in bold, messy letters, then passed it to Will. He hesitated, his marker hovering, before writing something short and passing it to El.

She stared at the blank space, her heart sinking. What could she write? She barely understood yearbooks, let alone what to say. Plus, her writing skills weren't as good as her friends'. Insecurity flared, but this was for Mike. She had to come up with something. She bit her lower lip, thinking hard.

Glancing at the Snow Ball photo—her blurry figure a ghost—she scribbled underneath it in blocky print:

To Mike, thanks for the dance. El.

It felt small and unworthy of the yearbook, but Mike's smile warmed her.

As the group bantered, signing the yearbook and tossing insults, Max pulled El aside, lowering her voice. "You sure about this? Hopper's not easy to fool. One slip, and we're toast."

El nodded, her jaw tightening. "I'm sure. I want . . . a real summer. With you. With everyone. *Daddy, please . . .* " she said, imitating Max's little act.

Max's grin returned, fierce. "Then we're doing this. Sleepover at my place, Slumber Fest at the mall, back before Hopper's morning coffee. Foolproof."

The group gathered around the repaired skateboard, admiring Dustin's work, their voices overlapping—movie quotes, scavenger hunt strategies, splitting the prize money, and wishing Dustin farewell before camp. El felt hope surge, the basement's warmth a promise. Summer felt within reach, a glittering possibility beyond the cabin's walls. It was a totally foolproof plan.

Or was it . . .

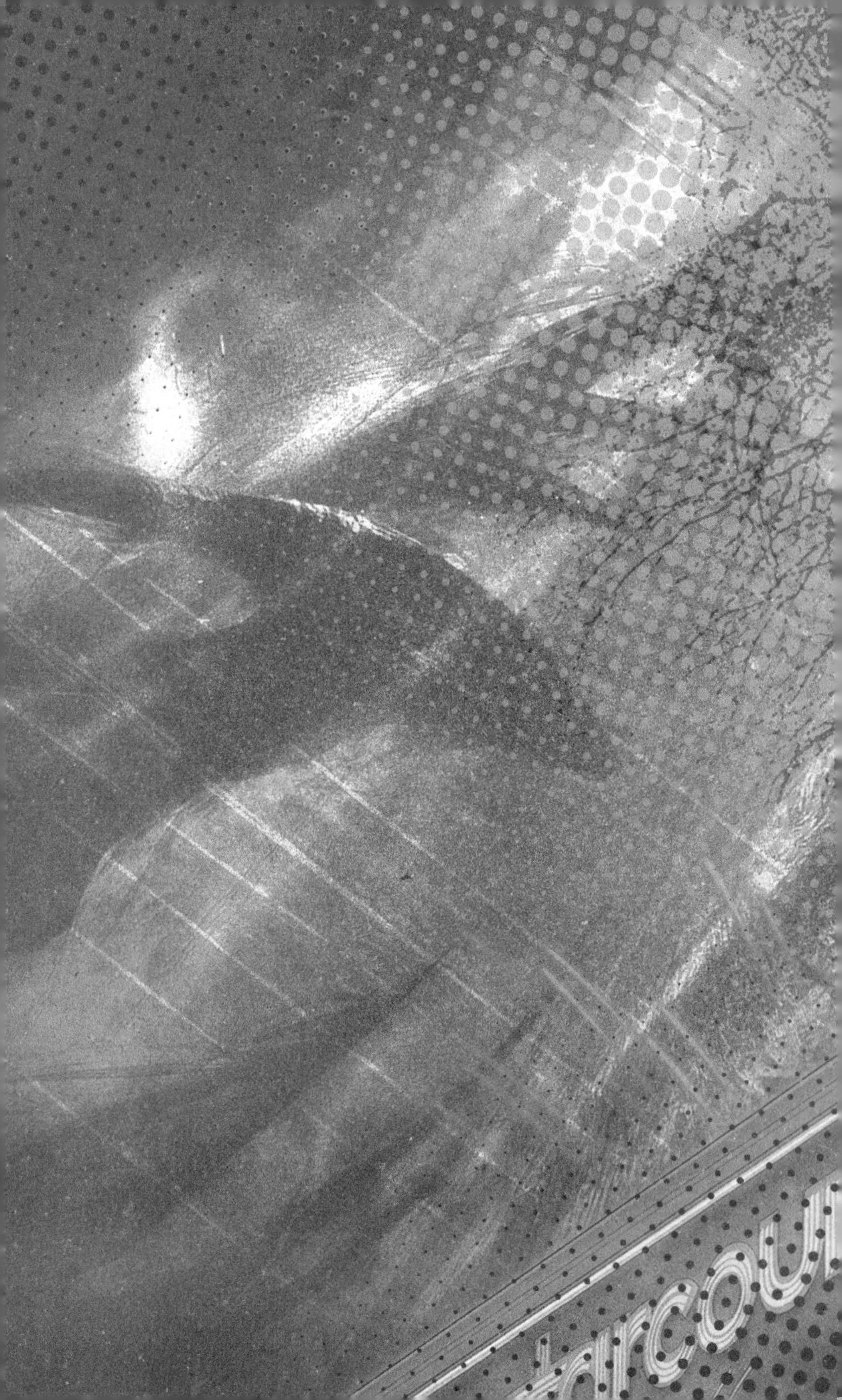

CHAPTER SEVEN

James Hopper screeched up to his cabin as the sun was setting, his truck kicking up dust and rubble. It had been a long day patrolling Hawkins. Some punk kid had wreaked havoc, driving recklessly through downtown, which had led to a high-speed chase. The worst part? The perp outran Hopper in his muscle car, pulling some fancy moves and losing him on the back roads.

The reminder sullied his mood, turning him grumpier than normal.

And he was already pretty damn grumpy on a regular basis.

He jerked the truck into park with a little more force than needed, then switched off the engine. The beast rumbled and fell silent. He caught sight of a shadow rustling the curtains.

Eleven.

That kid was his soft spot. He felt his mood improving. For a moment, a stab of guilt hit him for keeping his surrogate daughter—officially known as *Jane Hopper*—locked up inside when all the kids, including her friends, were out on summer break, doing . . . well . . .

Regular kid stuff. Whatever that was.

The truth was Hopper didn't exactly know what kids her age did for fun. He only knew what they did to get in trouble, which was when he usually got called in. Joyce tried to help coach him on being a more understanding parental figure. Especially when it came to . . .

Mike and El.

Ugh, even thinking about that made anger surge in his gut. His surly mood returned full force. It was bad enough that El had a boyfriend, but why did it have to be that Mike kid? Hopper didn't trust him. But truthfully, he didn't trust any boys. Because he'd once been a boy.

And he *knew* boys.

He knew how they thought. He knew what they wanted. And most of all, he knew they couldn't be trusted. Worse yet, ever since the Snow Ball, El and Mike were always . . . making out.

And he worried about what else they might get up to, especially if he wasn't around and able to enforce the *three-inch rule*. Despite his earlier guilt, that reminder reinforced his summer lockdown plans for his daughter. His job, above all else, was to keep her safe and out of harm's way, whether that meant protecting her from the bad men who hunted her from the lab, the ravenous monsters that lurked in the Upside Down trying to claw their way into their world . . .

Or Mike Wheeler.

Truth be told, that kid was the bigger threat lately.

Determination settled over him, propelling him forward. He hitched his pants up, his jacket catching on his sidearm, climbed out of the truck, then trudged up the porch and strode through the front door. It slapped shut behind him against the coming dusk. He stomped into his family cabin, his boots thudding against the creaky floorboards, then shrugged off his sheriff's jacket, his badge glinting as he hung it on a hook. He moved to the gun safe by his bedroom door, his movements deliberate, unlocking it with a soft click and sliding his revolver inside.

El waited by the sagging couch, a jumble of nerves, her heart pounding as she steeled herself for the fight ahead.

"What's up, kid?" he asked, his voice gruff but tired, and loosened his tie. "You're hovering like you *want* something."

El swallowed, her throat tight. "Daddy, please. I want to go to a sleepover. At Max's house. Tomorrow."

It didn't come out right, the way Max showed her, but instead was stilted and stiff. Hopper froze, one eyebrow arching so high it nearly vanished under his hat.

"A sleepover? At Max's? Tomorrow?" His tone dripped

with skepticism. He crossed his arms, his broad frame filling the doorway. "You're not old enough. Maybe when you're eighteen we can discuss it."

El's jaw tightened, frustration flaring hot in her chest. She stomped over to her bedroom and returned with an armful of magazines. She thrust the first one forward, flipping open the issue of *Seventeen* to a dog-eared page.

A photo showed a gaggle of tween girls at a slumber party, sprawled on sleeping bags, giggling over popcorn and nail polish, their brightly colored scrunchies glowing under fairy lights. Her eyes pleaded, wide and desperate, her expression screaming, *Please!*

Hopper glanced at the photo, his scowl deepening. "Magazines? That's your argument?" He rubbed his temples, muttering, "Joyce and her damn advice and shopping trips."

"Look at it," El insisted, her voice rising. "Friends. Fun. Summer. Sleepovers." She jabbed a finger at the photo, her curls bouncing with the force of her conviction. "Please, I want this."

Hopper's eyes narrowed. "Just girls, right? Because if I find out Mike's there—" His voice dropped to a low, menacing growl, his overprotective streak rearing up like a bear. "That kid's trouble. I see the way he looks at you. Oh, and he doesn't respect my three-inch rule!"

El's cheeks flushed, but she held her ground, planting her feet.

"Just Max. No boys. I swear." The lie tasted sour, but she pushed through, her frustration boiling over. "You *never* let me out. I'm not your prisoner!"

Hopper started to turn away, waving her off, but El's powers surged, a flicker of rebellion she couldn't contain. With a sharp gesture, she slammed his bedroom door shut—*WHAM!*—the wood rattling in its frame. Hopper spun back, his eyes wide, a mix of shock and irritation flashing across his face.

"Really, El?" he barked, pointing at the door. "We're using powers for teenage tantrums now?"

She crossed her arms, mirroring his stance, her chin jutting out. "You have to listen. I'm not a kid anymore. I can handle this."

Hopper groaned, dragging a hand through his hair, his tough exterior cracking under her stubborn glare.

"You're gonna be the death of me, you know that?" He paced, muttering, "If it were up to me, I'd keep you locked up till you're thirty. Safer that way."

El didn't budge, her eyes locked on his, pleading and fierce. The magazines trembled in her hands.

"Please, Dad. Just one night."

The words—*Please, Dad*—hit him like a punch, softening his scowl. She did it right this time, Max's foolproof method.

He sighed, his shoulders sagging, and leaned against the wall.

"Really? Playing the *please Dad* card? Where'd you learn that little trick?"

El blushed but couldn't admit to the plan. He scrubbed his face, muttering, "Fine. One night. Sleepover with Max.

But you're back first thing in the morning. Got it? No funny business."

El's face lit up, a yelp of joy bursting from her as she dropped the magazines and threw her arms around him.

"Thank you, Dad! Thank you!"

Her hug was fierce, her curls tickling his chin, and Hopper's gruff exterior melted, his arms wrapping around her in a reluctant embrace.

"Yeah, yeah," he grumbled, patting her shoulder. "Don't make me regret this." He pulled back, his expression turning serious. "Town's been strange lately—stay safe. I'm working the night shift tomorrow; Callahan called out sick. I'll drive you to Max's before work."

El's stomach twisted, her excitement dimming. She remembered Hopper chasing after Billy's Camaro, the squeal of tires and flashing lights. If he saw Billy at Max's trailer, he might change his mind, lock her back in the cabin.

But Hopper's face was set with no room for negotiation. She had no choice.

"Okay," she said, nodding quickly before he could change his mind.

Hopper grunted, satisfied, and headed to his room, the door creaking open. "Okay, get packing. And no powers when you're out of the cabin unless it's an emergency, you hear me?"

El nodded, already halfway to her room, her heart racing with a mix of triumph and nerves. She'd won—for now. But the plan hinged on Hopper not sniffing out the truth. She shut her door, the tiny space a mess of crumpled quilts and scattered Eggo boxes, and grabbed her backpack. She stuffed in a change of clothes, her toothbrush, and a flashlight, her hands trembling with anticipation.

Then she paused, an idea sparking. She needed to warn Max—and make sure the plan was solid, without tipping off Hopper. Sitting cross-legged on her bed, she pulled a black scarf from her drawer and tied it over her eyes, the fabric cool against her skin.

She took a deep breath, focusing, her mind reaching out into the void. The world faded, replaced by a cold, inky blackness, her powers humming as she zeroed in on a figure slumped on a bed, surrounded by the faint glow of fairy lights. She focused harder. Not even the trickle of blood dripping from her nostril could distract her from this task.

She just hoped this worked. Or their summer plans were over before they even had a chance to get started.

▶

Max's trailer bedroom was a cramped fortress of rebellion, its walls plastered with skateboard stickers and torn-out magazine pages of Madonna and Cyndi Lauper.

The air was thick with the chemical tang of nail polish and the distant reek of Billy's Marlboros seeping through the thin walls. Outside her door, Billy's stereo blared Metallica's "Ride the Lightning," the pounding drums and screeching guitars rattling the trailer's flimsy frame.

"Hey, loser, turn it down!" she yelled, banging on his bedroom door.

He didn't respond.

Just cranked up the heavy metal louder. The racket was deafening.

"Asshole," Max groaned as she slumped against the window frame and cranked up her Walkman.

The music was her escape, a shield against Billy's chaos and the suffocating weight of her home life. She needed the Slumber Fest as much as El did—a night of movies, ice cream, and freedom, far from the trailer's gloom. Her lips curved in a faint smile as she imagined the scavenger hunt, and the fifty-buck prize. That was more money than she'd ever seen.

"It's a fortune . . ." she whispered.

Max gazed out into the dusk at the empty gravel lot and Billy's Camaro parked crookedly outside. The lousy parking job seemed to fit with the dilapidated trailer that also rested crookedly on its foundation.

Rats darted out from under Billy's car.

"Yuck, rodents," Max said, watching the vermin cross the yard and stream into the storm drain across the street, moving together strangely in sync.

She shivered and yanked off her headphones, thinking she'd heard a rat, afraid she'd find one in her room.

Nothing moved. Nothing squeaked.

Then her walkie-talkie squawked.

Relief washed over her as she reached for the radio.

"Hello?"

El's small voice cut through the static. "Slumber Fest . . . tomorrow night . . . sleepover . . . Hopper said YES!"

"That's awesome," Max replied.

They signed off and Max put her headphones on. Kate Bush's voice surged back, clear and triumphant, drowning out Billy's metal racket. Max exhaled, a grin slowly spreading across her face. The plan was on.

But then she frowned. *The Billy issue.*

Well, she was good at solving stepbrother problems. She'd been doing it practically her whole life. She'd just have to find an excuse to get him away from the trailer.

Then it dawned on her. She remembered Hopper chasing him. Billy had evaded the cops . . . for now. But slipping that the chief of police would be swinging by their trailer tomorrow should do the trick. He'd screech out of here in his car faster than a bat out of hell.

After all, he didn't want to get busted.

Max flopped back on her bed, cranking the Walkman's volume, the music a defiant anthem against her miserable home life. Billy's stereo thumped, his laughter grating as he shouted something to a friend who had pulled up outside, but Max didn't care.

Not even Billy's annoying antics could ruin her mood now. Slumber Fest was her ticket out, a chance to seize the summer she and El both craved—a night of rebellion, laughter, and sticking it to the world. It had officially been decided . . .

Slumber Fest was on.

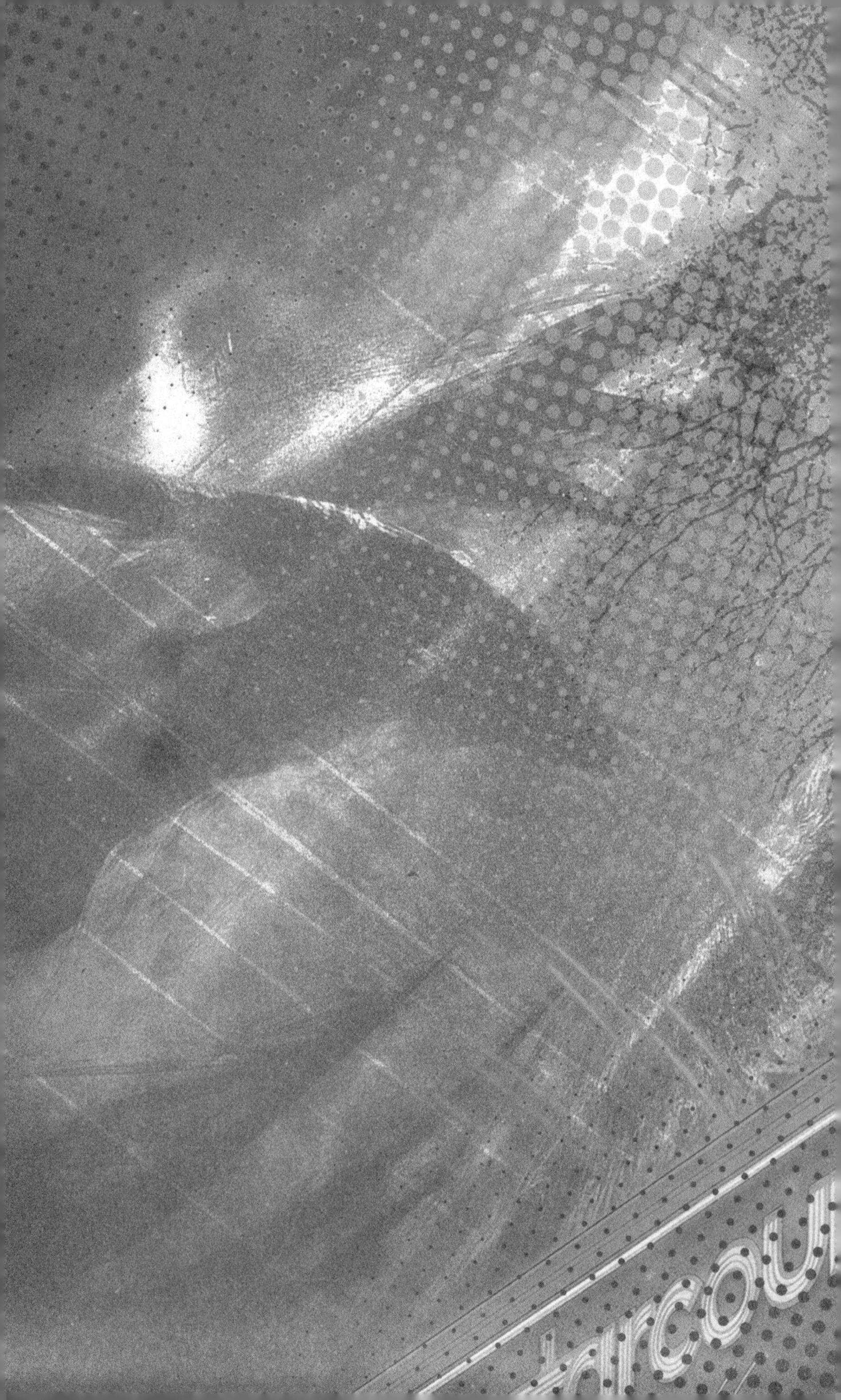

CHAPTER EIGHT

"Pedal to the metal!" Billy Hargrove said, cranking up the car radio. He tore down Hawkins's back roads, the tires screeching against the asphalt. He wasn't alone in his muscle car.

"Slow down!" Max yelped from her shotgun spot, clinging to the armrest handle while he swung the car around a sharp curve, emitting more squeals and plumes of exhaust—and sending Eleven sliding across the back seat into the door.

Max glanced back at her friend. El looked pretty freaked out. She wasn't used to Billy's psychotic driving.

"My car only goes one speed," Billy said with a smirk. "And that's . . . RDF."

"What's RDF?" Max asked.

Billy grinned, jamming the accelerator and rocketing them down the road. "Really *damn* fast."

"Well, your RDF is going to get us RDD—really *damn* dead—if you don't slow down already," Max shot back.

That only made Billy cackle. "Ha, you're the one who *asked* me for a ride, dumbass," he said, jerking the steering wheel the other way. "Plus, it's payback—for having the chief of police come by our home today. You're such a narc—"

"Am not!" Max snapped as they swung the other way.

"Are too!" Billy replied.

"What's a . . . narc?" El asked, trying to keep up with their sibling banter.

She huddled in the back seat, her hoodie pulled low over her curls, her heart pounding with a mix of exhilaration and dread. The air was thick with the scent of Billy's cologne, cigarette smoke, and the faint tang of motor oil, the windows cracked just enough to let in the humid evening breeze. It was almost seven o'clock.

Hopper had dropped her off about an hour ago before he left for his night shift, and thankfully Billy had hidden his blue Camaro in the woods behind their trailer so Hopper didn't spot it. That had saved her—and their plan—to sneak out to Slumber Fest under the guise of a girls' sleepover with Max.

Abruptly, Billy swerved around another curve, the car fishtailing.

"Keep this up, you're gonna get busted," Max grumbled.

"How many speeding tickets do you have? Hopper's on duty tonight. I'll bet he's gunning for you after your escape act yesterday."

Billy's laugh was sharp, his mullet swaying as he jerked the wheel, screeching through a red light and making an illegal right turn.

"Ha, fat chance! He has to catch me first. Nobody can match my vehicular motor skills. I'm the best around." His aviators glinted in the rearview mirror, his smirk cocky as he pressed the gas even harder, the speedometer climbing.

"The *best* at making your passengers wanna hurl," Max muttered, rolling her eyes. She glanced at El, who clutched her backpack in the back seat, her knuckles white. "You okay back there?"

El nodded, her throat tight, but her stomach churned with every lurch of the car. Billy's driving was a nightmare—and worse, risked drawing attention from the exact person she most needed to avoid—Hopper. He'd dropped her off at Max's trailer with a stern warning: *Back by morning, kid. No funny business.* If he spotted her now, sneaking into Starcourt, the Slumber Fest would be over before it began. She sank lower, the hoodie's shadow hiding her face.

Billy's mood soured, his grip tightening on the wheel. "Still pissed I had to clear out for your little sleepover stunt," he growled, shooting Max a glare. "Making me dodge the damn chief of police? Not cool, Maxine."

Max smirked, unfazed. "Well, it could be worse. Try

having the chief of police as your father."

She nudged her chin toward El, who giggled despite her nerves.

Billy snorted, shaking his head. "Yeah, tough break, kid. Hopper's a real hardass." He cranked the stereo, Metallica blasting through the speakers, drowning out further argument.

A few minutes later, the Camaro roared into Starcourt Mall's sprawling parking lot, the neon-lit complex looming like a beacon against the twilight. The lot buzzed with activity—minivans and station wagons disgorged gaggles of kids clutching sleeping bags, their laughter mingling with the hum of cicadas. Older teens piled out of beater cars, their radios blaring Journey and Madonna, while mall cops in crisp uniforms patrolled the perimeter, walkie-talkies crackling.

El spotted a familiar car—Joyce's Pinto, pulling up near the entrance. Will climbed out from the back seat, his backpack slung over one shoulder. Joyce fussed, shoving a second backpack stuffed with snacks into his arms, her voice carrying. "You call me if you need anything, okay?"

Will waved her off, his smile strained. But El recognized how Joyce acted—overprotective. Just like Hopper.

Will's older brother Jonathan emerged from the front passenger seat, his camera with the zoom lens dangling from his neck, ready to snap shots of Slumber Fest for the *Hawkins Post*.

El ducked lower in the back seat, her hoodie a shield against prying eyes.

"If Joyce sees me, she might tell Hopper," she whispered, her voice tight.

Max nodded, her hand on the door handle, ready to bolt. "Get ready . . ."

The Camaro swung toward the mall's front entrance, its sign blazing—STARCOURT MALL—a kaleidoscope of '80s excess. El expected Billy to slow down, drop them off, and peel out, but he didn't. Instead, he roared into a parking spot, the tires squealing as he nearly plowed into Mike and Lucas, who leapt back, clutching their sleeping bags. Mike's eyes widened, his dark hair flopping as he shouted, "Watch it, jerk!"

"What the hell, Billy?" Max hissed, her face paling. "You're supposed to drop us off and leave!"

Billy killed the engine, his smirk returning as he leaned back, one arm draped over the seat.

"Think Slumber Fest is just for kids?" he drawled, his attention drifting to a trio of high school girls strutting by, their perms bouncing, neon off-shoulder shirts displaying their perky curves. Their tanned legs gleamed from under their pleated shorts, scrunchy socks peeking from white Keds.

Billy let out a shrill whistle through the rolled-down window, running a hand through his mullet and flexing his biceps against his tight tank top.

The girls giggled, tossing flirtatious glances, while he posed in the Camaro, all swagger.

Max's jaw dropped open, the horror washing over her.

"You're crashing Slumber Fest? That's nightmare fodder!"

She grabbed El's hand, yanking her out of the car. "Come on, El, let's go before I puke."

El scrambled out, her backpack bouncing, but her heart soared as she spotted Mike. She ran to him, her hoodie falling back, and threw her arms around his neck. He hugged her tight, lifting her off the ground, his sleeping bag dropping; then he kissed her, soft and quick, his lips warm against hers.

"You made it," he whispered, his grin infectious. "Trust me, this is gonna be the best night ever. I promise."

El kissed him back, her cheeks flushing, the mall's chaos fading for a moment.

Max groaned and rolled her eyes, exchanging an annoyed look with Lucas, who'd joined them with Will.

"This all night?" she muttered, gesturing at the smooching couple.

Lucas smirked, shrugging. "Guess so. At least they're happy. You know, we used to be happy. Remember?"

Max frowned. "Don't. Even. Try. It. We are so *not* getting back together."

"Really, you sure?" Lucas said, his eyes big and brown and pleading. "Just one more chance? Come on, Max—"

"I'm not falling for your whole wounded puppy dog act again," Max said, crossing her arms to repel him.

"Come on, you love it—admit it," Lucas said, looking more pitiful now. He fluttered his eyes at her with their long lashes, pushing his lips together.

"Fool me once," she said. "And you've fooled me three

times. It's over. I dumped your ass . . . for a reason!"

Lucas grabbed at his heart and flopped back dramatically. "Shot through the heart," he sang out.

"Savage," Mike said with a smirk. "But good Bon Jovi reference."

Will fidgeted, his sleeping bag slung low, his eyes darting to the mall's glowing facade. Something was bothering him, though nothing looked amiss in the swarming parking lot.

"Let's just get inside," he said, his voice quiet, rubbing the back of his neck. El caught his haunted look, a mirror of her own unease, but she pushed it down, linking arms with Mike as they grabbed their gear and headed for the entrance. She wasn't letting anything ruin her chance at freedom.

As they crossed the lot, El noticed the mall's rear loading dock, tucked behind a row of dumpsters. A pair of unmarked semi-trucks idled, their engines rumbling, as men in dark coveralls unloaded wooden crates, their movements brisk and secretive. The crates were stamped with unfamiliar symbols, sharp and angular, unlike anything she'd seen. Her pulse quickened, a chill prickling her skin despite the oppressive summer heat.

FLASH! The sky flickered, turning bloodred, the air heavy with the crackle of electricity. Thunder rumbled, low and guttural—and the men's faces twisted into featureless voids. Their heads all jerked in unison—locking onto her.

Suddenly, the crates pulsed, as if alive, their wood splintering apart to reveal writhing shadows within.

El blinked, gasping, but then the vision snapped away.

The sky was golden again, the trucks ordinary, the men just workers unloading deliveries.

Her breath hitched, her hand tightening on Mike's arm. "Did you see that?" she started, but he frowned, confused. He scanned the parking lot.

"See what?" he asked, following her gaze. The loading dock looked totally normal now, the crates stacked neatly, the men chatting over clipboards.

El hesitated, her throat dry. She glanced at Will, who'd frozen midstep, his eyes wide, rubbing his neck again.

His haunted expression met hers, a silent confirmation—he'd seen it too. The crackle of lightning, the faceless men, the shadowy tendrils. The disconcerting moment lingered between them.

But El shook her head, forcing a smile. She wouldn't let these echoes of the Upside Down and the trauma of the past ruin this special night—with Mike, with her friends. And that's all it was, she reminded herself firmly, visions from the past. She'd used her powers to close the gate. No portal existed between this world and the Upside Down and its horrors anymore.

And it would stay that way.

She would make sure of it.

El broke eye contact with Will and tugged Mike toward the entrance.

The Starcourt Mall loomed before them in all its glory and its promises of fun. The exterior sported a flashy Starcourt logo in bold, triangular, futuristic font. Out front, the massive parking lot hummed with energy, kids shrieking as they raced toward the doors, their sleeping bags bouncing, while mall cops barked orders that mostly fell on deaf ears.

The group reached the entrance, their sneakers squeaking on the polished concrete. Two mall cops stood guard, their polyester uniforms straining over beer bellies, their lips pursing as they checked a clipboard.

Unlike a typical night, when Starcourt would be closing, the Slumber Fest was kicking off at seven p.m. sharp. A banner overhead read: *Teen Slumber Fest! Gremlins & Ghostbusters! Scavenger Hunt! Stay Locked in 'Til Dawn!*

The cops waved kids through, and El felt a thrill as she stepped closer to the doors, the mall's cool air washing over her.

Max led the way, her repaired skateboard tucked under her arm, her grin fierce. She glanced back. "This is it, guys. Movies, ice cream, fifty bucks on the line! We're winning this thing."

Lucas nodded, his eyes gleaming, while Mike squeezed El's hand, his excitement contagious. Will trailed behind them, glancing at the shadows, but he forced a smile, clutching his sleeping bag tighter.

The glass doors slid open automatically for guests, revealing the mall's dazzling interior—marble floors, escalators humming, two whole levels of shops, neon lights casting a surreal glow. El's breath caught in her throat at her first sight of this modern bastion of capitalism. The whole place vibrated with kinetic energy, a sensory overload that made her heart race. Kids swarmed the atrium, their laughter echoing off the atrium's glass ceiling, while a DJ booth with huge speakers blared hit music, the beat pulsing through the crowd.

Ahead of them, Billy slipped through the sliding doors after the trio of high school girls. Max groaned and rolled her eyes. She caught El's attention.

"Ugh, told ya! So lame. Why does he have to crash our party?"

El giggled at their antics. Billy was a troublemaker, but he also flirted with an exhilarating type of freedom that she'd never known, breaking the rules and speeding all over town, cops be damned. And tonight, El felt closer to his way of living, for she was a rule breaker, too. And there was something else they had in common—they were both avoiding the chief of police.

Or else their nights would end faster than they got here in his Camaro.

The mall cops barked a final order. "Last call! Doors locking in five! They won't reopen until tomorrow morning."

They began herding stragglers inside, their keys jangling. El's group slipped through, their backpacks bouncing, and the doors slid shut behind them with a heavy *thud*.

A few minutes later, the locks clicked, a sharp, final sound that echoed through the air. The cops secured the entrance, sealing the mall for the night.

El froze, a chill creeping up her spine. The mall's happy

facade felt suddenly imposing, the locked doors a barrier as much as a thrill. She flashed back to the vision she'd had outside in the parking lot—the faceless men on the loading dock with the mysterious crates.

She glanced at Will, whose haunted eyes mirrored her own, but Mike's hand in hers grounded her, his voice bright. "We made it, El. Best night ever."

Meanwhile, Max pumped her fist, leading the charge into the atrium. "Let's do this!" she said, her voice swallowed by the mall's din. But thoughts echoed through El's head as the doors shut and locked behind them.

For better or worse, they were locked in for the night.

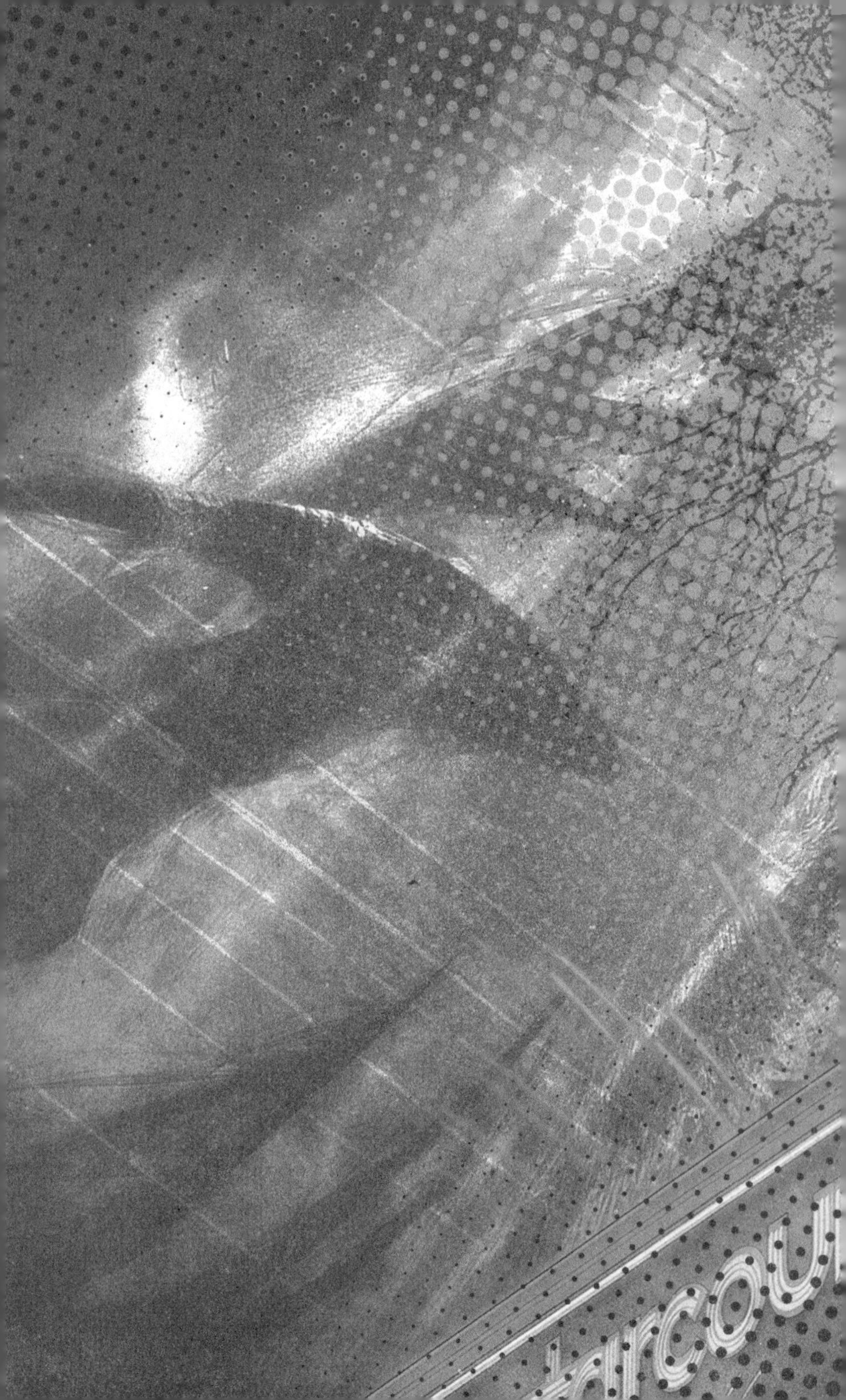

CHAPTER NINE

"Hurry up, slackers!" Max led the charge into Starcourt, her repaired skateboard tucked under her arm, her red ponytail swinging behind her. "Let's get tickets before the line's a mile long," she said, dodging a kid clutching a sleeping bag.

Lucas nodded, his eyes scanning the crowded atrium packed with kids and teens, while Will trailed behind, his backpack stuffed with Joyce's snacks and his D&D gear, his gaze flickering to the shadows pooling in the mall's corners. Bringing up the rear, El and Mike stuck together, holding hands.

At the edge of the atrium stood a folding table under a spotlight, where Mike's older sister Nancy collected ticket money, her summer gig before her newspaper job kicked in. Her hair was teased high, the paper on her clipboard crisp as she called out, "Line up in an orderly fashion! Five bucks each! No pushing!"

Two kids shoved each other to get closer anyway, drawing her ire. "I said, no pushing!" she barked, and they froze, sheepishly offering crumpled five-dollar bills.

Nancy's eyes flicked up, spotting El among the group. Her brow furrowed, clipboard lowering. "El? What are you doing here?" she asked, her voice sharp with concern, as she stepped around the table.

El froze, her heart pounding, powers tingling. "I . . . want fun," she said, her words halting, eyes darting to Mike.

Mike stepped forward, his voice low but urgent. "Nancy, please, don't tell Hopper. Just for tonight, let El have this—one normal night with us, like everyone else." He gestured to the crowded atrium, kids laughing and jostling. "She deserves it."

Nancy crossed her arms, her gaze softening but hesitant. She lowered her voice to a whisper. "Mike, you know it's risky. Hopper's rules are there for a reason—if those government suits are still out there . . ."

"I know," Mike said, his tone pleading, eyes wide. "But we'll keep her safe, I swear. She's with us. Just . . . let her be a kid for once. Please, Nance."

El nodded, her voice small. "Normal . . . please."

"Yeah, and you'll be here the whole time, looking out for us," Mike rushed to add, trading a glance with El. "What could go wrong? Please . . . pretty please!"

Nancy sighed, rubbing her temple and glancing at

the crowd, then back at El's hopeful face. "Fine," she said reluctantly, her voice low. "But you stick with the group, and you get her home before Hopper notices. If anything goes wrong, Mike, it's on you."

Mike grinned, relief flooding his face. "Thanks, Nancy. You're the best."

"Don't make me regret this," Nancy muttered, shaking her head as she returned to her table, scribbling on her clipboard with a tense grip.

Mr. Clarke, Hawkins Middle's science teacher, stood nearby at another folding table, prepping scavenger hunt packets, his bow tie askew as he sorted clue cards. Jonathan Byers circled the crowd, his camera clicking, snapping shots of the Slumber Fest for the *Hawkins Post*, his zoom lens catching every grin and scuffle.

El's group joined the ticket line, weaving past a Waldenbooks display of Stephen King's shiny new trade paperbacks for *Christine* and *Pet Sematary* and a RadioShack blasting a boom box ad. Each of them pulled out their five-dollar bills. El's excitement faltered as she patted her pockets—empty.

"I . . . don't have money," she whispered to Mike, panic rising, her cheeks flushing.

Mike squeezed her hand, his voice chivalrous. "I've got you. No worries." He dug into his jeans, pulling out more crumpled bills, but his face fell as he counted. "Dang, I'm a buck short."

Lucas quickly fished in his pockets, only producing lint

and a single, dingy penny. "Uh, does this help?"

Max looked closer, then shook her head. "That's a Canadian penny."

"Really? How can you tell?" Lucas said, squinting at the copper coin.

Max didn't have anything to offer either. She turned her pockets inside out. "Ugh, sorry, El. I spent my extra cash on our bus ride yesterday."

Will searched his pockets and found a few coins. They were still short. The line shuffled forward. If she couldn't pay, El would have to leave. A dark mood fell over their group.

Her eyes darted to the atrium's fountain, its water glinting with coins tossed for wishes. An idea sparked. "Wait, I've got this," she whispered. She nodded to Max, who grinned, catching onto her plan.

"Hey, Nancy . . . Mr. Clarke!" Max called, waving wildly to get their attention and distract them. "Quick question about the scavenger hunt!"

She dragged Lucas and Will into a loud, fake argument about obscure clue rules, their voices drowning out the crowd. Mike joined in, asking Nancy about prize details and fine-print clauses, his gestures exaggerated.

While they were distracted, El whipped around toward the fountain, burbling next to the atrium. She focused, her powers humming. She raised a hand, subtle, her fingers twitching.

Coins in the fountain quivered in the water, then rose, glinting under the lights, and floated silently into her palm. Quarters, dimes, a few nickels—enough. Each had been tossed in there for a wish that now granted her wish. A trickle of blood seeped from her nostril, but she wiped it away with a grin, stuffing the coins into Mike's hand.

"Uh, problem solved!" Mike said, signaling for everyone to break off their incessant questions and chill out.

"Don't you mean, question answered?" Mr. Clarke said, suspicious.

"Uh, exactly," Lucas cut in, covering for him. "That's what he meant."

Mike handed the coins along with the wad of cash to Nancy, who barely looked up, scribbling their names on tickets. "Five for the Slumber Fest, plus Midnight Scavenger Hunt entries," she said, passing them stubs and neon wristbands. "Don't lose these."

El's heart soared as they slipped on the wristbands, the plastic shimmering under the lights. *They were in.*

Clutching their belongings, the group strolled farther into the atrium, passing a sensory overload of shops. Time-Out Arcade pulsed with *Pac-Man* beeps. The machines looked newer and shinier than the dingy innards of the Palace Arcade. No wonder downtown Hawkins was losing business to the new mall.

Teens swarmed Spencer's, giggling over lava lamps and kitschy gifts, while Orange Julius blended frothy drinks, the air tangy with citrus. They passed movie posters outside the theater entrance, *Gremlins*' Gizmo chirping adorably, *Ghostbusters*' Stay Puft Marshmallow Man looming. Lucas punched Mike's arm, grinning. "Who ya gonna call?"

"Ghostbusters!" Mike shot back, mimicking a proton pack.

Will joined in, quieter, "Don't cross the streams!"

El frowned, the references sailing over her head, her outsider status stinging. Mike caught her expression and said softly, "Hey, that's why we're here, El. So you can see the movies, get the jokes. It's gonna be awesome."

Lucas leapt at her, arms flailing. "Boo! Don't get me wet or feed me after midnight!"

El rolled her eyes, a smile breaking through. "And they think *I'm* weird."

The group reached the atrium's center, where kids staked out spots under the big screen that had been erected for the special event. Lucas, ever strategic, pulled out a protractor from his backpack, muttering about angles. "Geometry, people. We need the ideal view—forty-five degrees from the screen, no heads blocking us."

Lucas paced out a prime spot near the fountain and waved them over. "Here! Perfect sightline."

They dropped their sleeping bags, claiming the space. Will unzipped his backpack, revealing Joyce's treats—Twinkies, Doritos, and a box of Cracker Jack. He shook the box, fishing out a decoder ring, its plastic glinting.

"Score," he said, slipping it on, his grin rare and bright.

El hesitated, realizing she didn't have a sleeping bag. But Mike patted his spot, his *Star Wars* sleeping bag unzipped wide. "Share mine. Plenty of room."

They snuggled in together. Mike snuck a kiss, planting it on her lips.

Max groaned, flopping onto her bag. "Gross. Save it for the next Snow Ball."

Lucas rolled his eyes, but El smirked, her powers tingling. With a subtle flick of her wrist, a handful of Will's caramel popcorn levitated, pelting Max and Lucas. They yelped, swatting the air, then burst into hysterical laughter.

"Nice aim, El!" Will said, tossing her a Twinkie. She ripped it open, finishing the pastry off in a few big bites. Frosting decorated her nose, so Mike leaned over and kissed it off, making her giggle.

They settled into their spot, taking in the scene around them. The atrium buzzed like a glowing hive as kids flitted around. Sleeping bags with an array of characters and products, from My Little Pony to He-Man to Kool-Aid, littered the marble floor, their corners curling under the stampede of teens.

Overhead, the massive screen hung from the second-floor railing, its edges swaying slightly, a projector waiting in the shadows ready to blast *Gremlins* and *Ghostbusters* for the movie doubleheader. Bright signs from the stores cast a surreal glow over everything.

DJ Rick, a lanky guy in a shiny jacket, spun records from a booth, his voice booming over the mic. "All right, Hawkins teens, let's crank this party to eleven!" He hit a few buttons and a catchy beat—"You're the Best," the *Karate Kid* theme song—thumped out.

Max looked up, then frowned, spotting Billy across the atrium, lounging near the Gap and flirting with the trio of high school girls from the parking lot. His mullet gleamed, his tank top tight as he pulled a silver flask from his jeans, offering it with a smirk.

The girls giggled and blushed, glancing around before sipping from his flask, their neon scrunchies bobbing.

He caught Max watching and his eyes narrowed.

Buzz off! he mouthed, dragging a finger across his neck. *Or else!*

Max scowled, muttering, "Why does my dysfunctional family follow me everywhere? They always have to ruin everything."

El patted her arm, her voice soft. "Maybe he will get bored and go away." One of the girls giggled and touched his arm.

"Fat chance with that eye candy." Max sighed dejectedly. "I've got a bad feeling. He's not going anywhere."

"Well, at least he's distracted," Lucas offered. "And you've got us, right?"

Max snorted, but her tension eased. Lucas was right. Her friends were a powerful shield protecting her from her family issues. They sprawled back on their sleeping bags, passing snacks, the atrium's energy wrapping them in a warm glow. Everything felt perfect.

A few minutes later, Steve Harrington and Robin Buckley trudged by in their rumpled sailor uniforms, their expressions sour. They were heading for the escalators to the second level. Steve's hair was still perfect, but his eyes screamed exhaustion.

Spotting him, Lucas and Mike waved dramatically and gestured to Steve.

Robin nudged him, pointing to the group. "Dingus, looks like your kids are here. How many do you have?"

Steve groaned, waving her off. "Not my kids, Robin. I'm just their . . . babysitter, okay?" He glanced at Mike, trying to look grumpy, but couldn't stop himself from smiling. "Don't make my night harder," he called out.

Mike grinned, saluting. "Aye, aye, Captain Hair!"

"Hey, where's Dustin?" Steve asked, scanning them and coming up short. "Don't tell me he got a life."

"Ha, not exactly," Mike said. "He went to Camp Know Where."

Steve frowned. "Camp . . . what?"

"Not, camp *what*—Camp Know *Where,*" Mike replied. "It's a science summer camp."

"He left this morning," Lucas added, then he lowered his voice, confidingly. "He said he's going for the science, but I think he's looking for a girlfriend."

"Yeah, he's probably charming someone right now," Mike said. "Bet she's totally into his computer knowledge and *Star Wars* trivia."

Steve grinned triumphantly. "That little guy! I knew it! Look, I taught that kid everything he knows. I'll bet he's using all my slick moves. Those campers won't know what hit them—"

"Slick moves?" Robin said, arching her eyebrow. "Is

that why you keep striking out? I'm keeping score on this whiteboard . . . It's not looking good."

"Shhh," Steve said, hissing in a low voice. "Don't ruin my street cred."

Robin rolled her eyes, adjusting her sailor hat. "Come on, Harrington. We're late. Overtime's gonna kill us, but at least we get paid double to dish out double scoops," she added with a wink.

They headed toward the escalator that carried them to the second-level food court. El watched them ascending the escalator and sliding behind the Scoops Ahoy counter with its nautical stripes and sailor-hatted staff dishing out sundaes.

So, that was what Max meant by . . . boat ice cream, she thought, smiling.

With each little revelation, she felt more like a normal teen having a normal teen summer. Everything else was just icing on the cake—or more like, the cherries on top of the ice cream sundae.

Mr. Clarke's voice crackled over a PA system, cutting through the din. "Attention, Slumber Fest teens! Settle down! *Gremlins* starts in five minutes, followed by the Starcourt Scavenger Hunt; then the midnight screening of *Ghostbusters* kicks off after! Grab your spots, and no roughhousing!"

Cheers rang out, filling the air with an electric buzz of anticipation. Gooseflesh pricked El's skin as her heart thumped faster. She didn't know much about *Gremlins,* just the silly jokes the boys traded, but she was excited finally to learn what all the fuss was about.

The crowd quieted, kids sprawling on sleeping bags, waiting for the projector to whir to life. El leaned into Mike, his arm around her, the sleeping bag soft beneath them. Max crunched Doritos, Lucas angled his head for his "perfect view," and Will fiddled with his decoder ring, his smile lingering.

The lights dimmed, the atrium hushing, anticipation thick.

For a moment, everything was perfect. *Almost too perfect.* But then, a shadow fell over them—three shadows, to be exact, sharp and menacing.

El's breath caught, her powers tingling. She looked up, her heart sinking when she saw them.

The bullies—Kyle, Becks, and Danny—loomed over them, their smirks vicious, their wristbands glinting.

"Well, lookee here," Kyle drawled, his voice dripping with malice.

"What are *you* doing here?" Max said, whipping her head around. Instinctively, she grabbed her newly repaired skateboard and clutched it tightly.

Kyle leered closer, the light catching on his chipped tooth. "And don't get excited for that Starcourt scavenger hunt. You're not going to win anything, losers!"

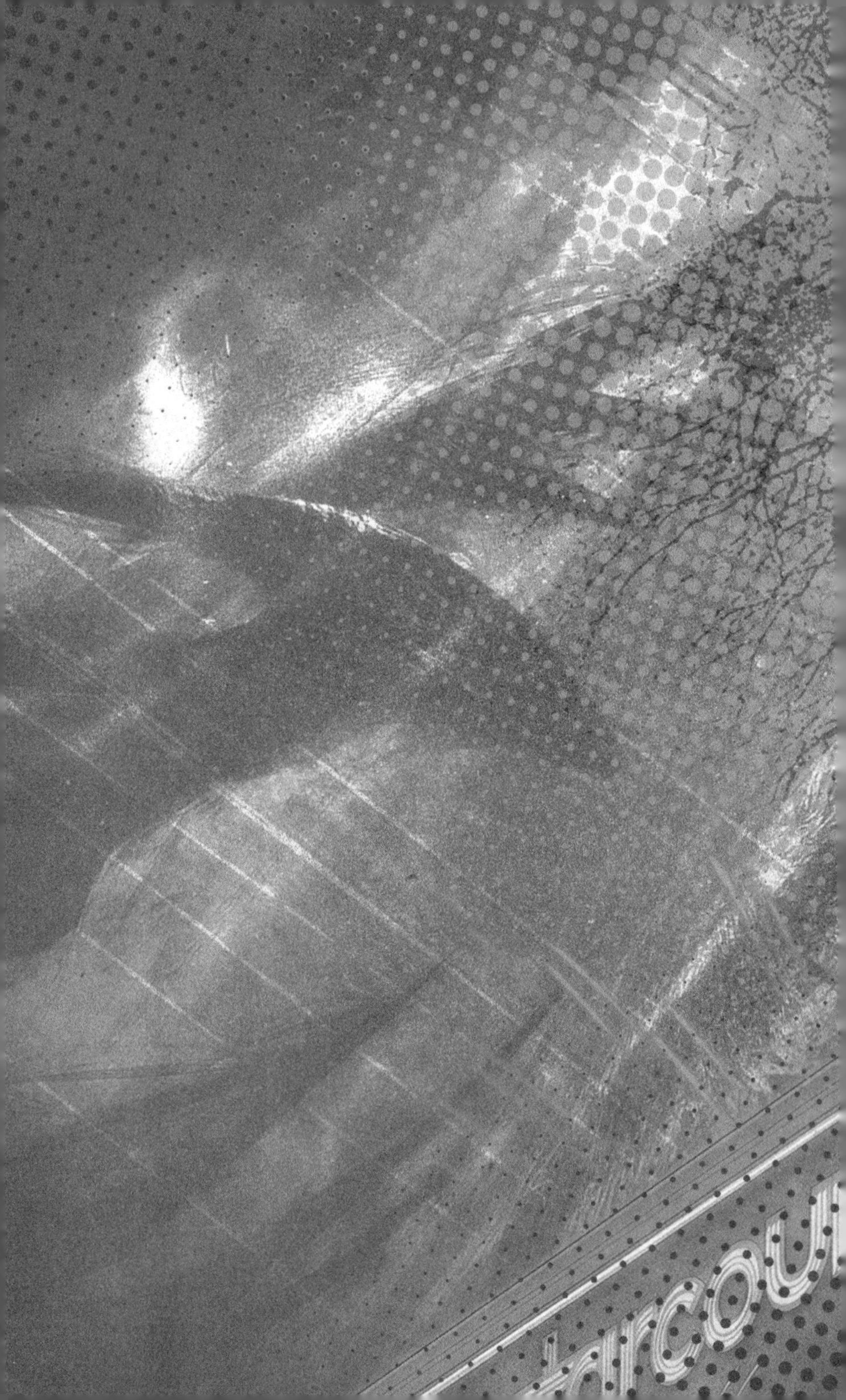

CHAPTER TEN

Kyle, Becks, and Danny stood over Max, El, and their group in the atrium. Kyle's greasy mullet looked even greasier today. He flashed a menacing grin, displaying his chipped tooth.

"Dweebs, time to crash your party," Becks said, blowing her frizzy bangs back and cackling, while Danny cracked his knuckles, his buzz-cut-topped head gleaming under the lights in the atrium. They hadn't forgotten about the run-in yesterday in downtown Hawkins. Even worse, they'd seen the Slumber Fest flyer and decided to crash the party.

Kyle kicked Mike's *Star Wars* sleeping bag. "Ready to *lose,* losers?" he taunted, his voice dripping with malice.

Max leapt up, her skateboard raised.

"Back off, Kyle, or you'll regret it," she snarled, her eyes blazing. She stepped forward, unafraid, her sneakers planted firm. El jumped up and stood beside her, her heart pounding. She stared down the bullies, her jaw tight, her powers humming beneath her skin.

Kyle's smirk widened, his glare locking on her.

"Two *girls* and a bunch of *nerds*? What you gonna do about it?" he drawled, kicking Lucas's sleeping bag next, scattering Will's Cracker Jack.

"Oh no, not *these* guys again," Mike muttered, face-palming himself dramatically. "God, I hate burnouts."

"Totally. They're the worst kind of bullies," Will agreed. "These wastoids make Troy look almost friendly."

"Yeah, he's like Troy *squared,*" Lucas agreed, looking equally distraught.

"Really?" Mike said. "You're just reinforcing their *nerd* accusation."

"Don't look at me!" Lucas said. "I own it. Somebody should get these guys a thesaurus. *Lose . . . losers,* really?"

Meanwhile, El's hands clenched into fists. The lights overhead flickered, a sharp buzz cutting through the atrium's din. Kyle's taunt was a match to her fuse—she wasn't letting these stooges ruin their night.

Her powers surged, a wildfire she could barely contain, and that was when bullies weren't picking on her friends. The air sizzled with her anger. The lights flickered again, drawing attention now. A hush fell over the atrium.

Mike grabbed her arm, his voice low, urgent. "El, don't . . .

he's not worth it. We don't wanna get kicked out . . ."

His eyes darted to the mall cops patrolling the atrium's edges, polyester uniforms straining as they scanned the crowd. But El was locked onto Kyle.

She gritted her teeth. The power surged, stronger this time, and darkness fell over the mall, shorting the power. The emergency strobe lights kicked on, casting a strange glow over the mall. A trickle of blood dripped from her nose. She tasted blood on her lips.

"Freak, are you doing this?" Kyle hissed, looking slightly afraid.

"She's crazy! Just look at her," Becks said, pointing to the blood on El's face.

"The hell?" Danny said, slow to catch on. He whipped around, looking scared. "What happened to the lights . . . ?"

They flickered again. The atrium flashed with the unnatural light.

"Everyone, stay calm." Mr. Clarke's voice echoed from the PA system. "Don't panic. Just sit tight. We'll get the power back on soon."

Boos rang out from the crowd. "Hey, what happened to *Gremlins*?" someone yelled, sounding upset.

"Yeah, we paid five whole bucks for this junk!" yelled another angry kid, followed by a chorus of more boos.

The crowd was growing restless. Someone threw some popcorn at Mr. Clarke and Nancy, who were busy conferring with the mall cops.

Another big flicker of lights as El focused on the bullies.

She raised her hand, preparing to direct her powers at Kyle.

El's breath hitched, Hopper's warning echoing: *No funny business.*

If he caught her using her powers—or worse, fighting—she'd be back in the cabin, locked away for good. But the bullies' smirks fueled her rage.

The lights flickered again, harsher, casting jagged shadows across the sleeping bags and unsettling the crowd.

Mr. Clarke crawled over near the projector, fiddling with the power cord, muttering, "Maybe this will help?"

El's fingers quivered, the urge to fling the bullies across the atrium overwhelming. Just one push—*one flick of her wrist*—and they'd crash into the fountain, coins scattering like her wish for freedom. But Mike's hand tightened, grounding her, his eyes pleading. She took a shaky breath, forcing her powers down, the blood dripping slower.

Suddenly, the lights stabilized and—with an electrical *pop*—kicked back on.

The emergency strobes cut off as the overhead fluorescents and storefront signs all came back to life. The tension immediately dissipated from the crowd.

"Way to go, Mr. Clarke," a kid yelled at the teacher.

"Did I do that . . . ?" Mr. Clarke straightened up from the power strip.

A round of applause broke out. Slumber Fest was back in business.

Even Billy let out a *whoop* from where he was lounging near the Gap with the high school girls. "Party on!" he yelled.

Under the glare of the bright lights, Kyle and his crew backed off. Kyle yelled over the thunderous applause, "Don't think this is over! You'd better watch your backs, losers!"

His voice carried, sharp and mean, before they vanished into the mall.

El exhaled, her shoulders sagging, the blood at her nose drying.

Mike smiled and handed her a tissue from Will's overpacked bag of supplies.

"Thanks," El said, blushing but secretly thrilled. She took the tissue, wiping away the blood from her face—and the bad taste of that altercation—and sank onto Mike's sleeping bag, his long arms wrapping around her.

Suddenly, the atrium plunged into darkness, the lights snuffing out with a sharp *pop.* Kids gasped, their voices rising in a chaotic swell, sleeping bags rustling as they fumbled for flashlights.

"Don't look at me," El said, throwing her hands up. "I didn't do it this time."

They all laughed, realizing that this wasn't some unnatural occurrence.

"Get ready—it's showtime," Lucas said, his voice tense with excitement.

The screen flickered to life, the opening scene for *Gremlins* rolling, the eerie score cutting through the dark. The projector's glow cast monstrous shadows, while Gizmo's chirp provided a surreal counterpoint to the tension. The atrium settled as kids sprawled out, their whispers fading under the movie's ominous hum.

El snuggled into Mike, the sleeping bag soft, his warmth a welcome comfort. They'd never had a whole night together, just stolen moments in her bedroom under Hopper's careful watch, yelling at them over and over—*three inches!*

She watched the movie, everything new to her. El wasn't sure what was supposed to be scary about it yet—a mysterious shop on a dark night felt tame compared to her real life, the lab's sterile horror and the Upside Down's claws still vivid in her mind.

Max flopped beside them, her skateboard propped against her bag. She started stress eating some Doritos, triggered by the bullies, but also by El and Mike's snuggling and kissing, her recent breakup looming in her mind.

Lucas leaned in, his voice teasing, his eyes on the screen where Gizmo peeked out from a box. "El's kinda like Gizmo, right? Remember when you found her, Mike? Crazy powers and all . . ."

Mike grinned, kissing El's forehead, his lips soft. "But she's way cuter."

El blushed, her heart fluttering, the movie's glow painting her cheeks pink.

Lucas smirked, tossing a Twinkie at Mike that he'd pilfered from Will's bag. "I dunno, dude. Gizmo's pretty damn cute."

Mike caught the Twinkie, laughing. "You like 'em furry, huh?" he shot back, dodging a playful punch from Lucas.

"You're just jealous Gizmo's got better hair than you," Lucas joked.

Max snorted at their antics, trading a look with El. "Ha, Lucas can have Gizmo. He's single . . . for a reason."

Lucas propped himself up, his grin sly, scooting closer to Max.

"Come on, Max. You know you miss me. Admit it already! Just one more chance?" His puppy-dog eyes gleamed, his lashes fluttering, but Max shoved him away, her Doritos scattering.

"Not happening, Lucas," she said, her tone firm but her lips fidgeting, betraying a flicker of amusement. "You're worse than a gremlin fed after midnight. And harder to repel."

"Ouch, that stings." Lucas clutched his chest. He flopped back dramatically, drawing a laugh from Will.

El giggled. The movie was both scary and funny at the same time, a combination she hadn't encountered yet. But she supposed that was how life was, too. Filled with untold horrors, but also lighter moments, especially when you weren't alone to face the darkness.

Her attention drifted across the atrium. Billy still hung near the Gap, his arm around one of the high school girls, their lips locked in a sloppy make-out session, her scrunchie bobbing.

Max followed El's stare, her mood souring and jaw tightening.

"Ugh, why does he have to be so terrible?" she muttered, tossing a Dorito in his general direction. "And ruin everything?"

El shook her head. She spoke softly, "Not worth it."

"Easy for you to say," Max griped, watching him give

the girl a hickey on her neck. "You're not related to that walking petri dish. But I guess you're right—I can't let him ruin my night."

"*Our* night," El said with a smile.

Max sighed, nodding, but her eyes flickered with frustration, the weight of her toxic homelife dragging at her.

The movie continued playing, Gizmo's adorable chirps giving way to the gremlins' chaos as they wreaked havoc, their cackles echoing through the atrium. Kids gasped and laughed, sometimes at the same time, but El's attention snagged on the bullies, lurking near the escalators to the food court.

Kyle, Becks, and Danny cornered a younger kid, maybe twelve. Kyle snatched the kid's ice cream sundae, its cherry tumbling to the floor, and smirked. "What you gonna do about it, kid? Go cry to your mommy!"

Becks cackled, shoving the kid, while Danny loomed, his fists ready.

The kid's eyes welled up, his sundae splattering on the marble floor, the cherry rolling pitifully.

El's fists clenched, her powers tingling, but Mike's hand on hers stopped her. "Not now," he whispered, nodding toward the mall cops circling closer, their walkie-talkies buzzing. "We'll deal with them later."

Lucas leaned in, his voice low. "They're jerks, but Mike's right. We can't start a fight here. Hopper'd be on us in ten seconds flat."

Max's eyes narrowed, her grip on her skateboard tightening. "They're not getting away with this," she muttered, her voice fierce. "Not tonight."

Will stayed quiet, his decoder ring catching the light. El caught his unease, a mirror of her own, but she pushed it down, refocusing on the movie. Gizmo cooed onscreen, his big eyes wide, and the group's banter sparked again.

"See, El, Gizmo's got rules, just like you," Mike teased, grinning. "Don't get you mad, or you'll fry the whole mall."

El smirked, tossing a piece of popcorn at him, drawing laughs from the group. Mike pulled her closer, his arm around her shoulders.

"Ignore the haters. You're perfect," he whispered, kissing her cheek, his breath warm against her skin.

Max groaned, flopping back. "You two are gonna make me puke worse than Billy's make-out session."

Lucas seized the moment, scooting closer to Max. "You know, I could be your Gizmo. Loyal, cute, no feeding after midnight required."

Max shoved him, but her laugh betrayed her. "Yeah right. You're about as loyal as a gremlin. Nice try."

But as *Gremlins* hit its climax—gremlins exploding in microwaves, melting in sunlight—Max watched Kyle's crew, now sprawled near Waldenbooks, passing a stolen bag of Twizzlers, their laughs grating.

Billy was still tangled with the high school girl, their make-out session drawing annoyed glances from nearby kids. The mall cops patrolled closer, their eyes narrowing, but they hadn't noticed the bullies' antics yet.

Max leaned toward El, her voice low. "I just hope we win

the scavenger hunt. Those morons aren't gonna play fair."

"Don't worry," El said in a determined voice. "I'm not letting them beat us again."

The screen flickered and then went to black after the *Gremlins* credits rolled. The crowd erupted in cheers and chatter. Mr. Clarke's voice crackled over the PA system.

"Attention, Slumber Fest teens! Intermission time!" Mr. Clarke announced. "The food court is staying open late for our special event. We'll regroup in thirty minutes for the first annual Starcourt Scavenger Hunt!"

Nancy's voice cut in, taking over. "One entry per team! Make sure you have your wristbands that we handed out at the door. Don't miss out on the prize—a fifty-dollar gift certificate."

The atrium buzzed over the prize—fifty *whole* dollars—kids scrambling to form teams, but El stayed focused on Kyle's crew and winning the hunt. She had her game face on.

The night was far from over, and the real fight was just beginning.

CHAPTER ELEVEN

"That was . . . *awesome*!" Lucas cheered as the movie screening adjourned for the intermission, punching the air, his eyes bright. "Gremlins in the microwave? Boom! Total carnage!"

Mike grinned, tossing a stray popcorn kernel at him. "Yeah, but Gizmo stole the show. Right, El? He's cuter than Lucas, at least."

El giggled, her curls tickling Mike's chin. "Way cuter," she teased, dodging Lucas's mock glare.

Lucas clutched his chest. "Betrayed! By my own crew!"

Max snorted, kicking his sneaker. "Get over it, Lucas! Gizmo's got you beat. And he doesn't fart nacho cheese."

Will laughed, a rare spark in his eyes, but it faded as he glanced at the atrium's shadows, his fingers twisting the decoder ring. "The gremlins were creepy, though," he said softly. "Kinda reminded me of . . . you know."

The group quieted, El catching his haunted look. *The Upside Down.* It clung to Will, a ghost they all felt. She squeezed Mike's hand, her own unease stirring—the vision of faceless men at the loading dock, the crates pulsing with shadows. But she pushed it down, refusing to let it ruin their night.

Mr. Clarke's PA system boomed, his voice slicing through the chaos.

"Attention, Slumber Fest teens! This is your final warning! Intermission time! Scavenger hunt starts in thirty minutes—so don't wander too far!"

The crowd dispersed with kids scrambling toward the escalators, their sneakers squeaking on the marble floors. Mall cops barked orders, their walkie-talkies buzzing, but the teens ignored them, racing for the food court's neon-lit promise of sundaes and fries.

Max leapt up, her skateboard tucked under her arm. "Come on, let's move before the line's a mile long," she said, weaving through the sleeping bags. "I need sugar after those bullies."

Lucas nodded, jumping up and brushing Doritos dust off his shirt.

"Yeah, Kyle's crew better not show their faces again. I'm ready to take 'em down." He flexed his fists but looked silly rather than threatening.

Everyone laughed at the display.

"Ha, sure you are," Max said, rolling her eyes. "Just like last time . . ."

They left their sleeping bags to hold their spot in the atrium for the next flick and hurried toward the escalators, cutting ahead of other kids to board.

"Hey, fools, hurry up—ice cream time!" Lucas said, leading them through the mall.

"Don't you mean, 'Ahoy, matey'?" Mike said, slipping into a pirate accent. "Time to set sail for some ice cream."

"Boat ice cream," El repeated, feeling better now that she got the joke.

"Just don't eat too fast—or you'll get brain freeze," Mike said, teasing her. He sucked his cheeks in and grabbed his head, imitating the painful cold rush.

El giggled, and they linked hands, continuing to weave through the mall toward the escalators to the second-floor food court. The air hummed with excitement as the mall stayed open for the special late-night Slumber Fest. Sneakers squeaked over the marble floors with kids swarming the shops.

Luckily, Kyle and his bullies seemed to have faded into the background after their altercation in the atrium.

"Maybe they dipped," Max said, scanning the crowded mall. Her voice was hopeful, but El frowned.

"Maybe," she hedged. "But I don't think so. I can still *sense* them . . ."

A chill emanated from El's spine, spreading through her body, kind of like the brain freeze Mike imitated. Only instead of the promise of a sweet treat, it indicated Kyle was lurking nearby.

Max caught the look on El's face and pressed her lips together. "Well, hopefully they learned their lesson."

"Fat chance of that," Mike interjected. "Remember Troy? This is his cousin's crew. They're way worse!"

"I can protect us," El started, her voice halting, but Mike gave her a look.

"We'll find a way, but no powers, okay?" he whispered, his eyes teasing but serious, nodding toward the mall cops patrolling nearby. "Hopper's on duty, remember?"

Anger flashed on Max's face. "Mike, you know she's her own person, right? She can make her own decisions."

"Of course," Mike said, backing off. "I'm just trying to look out for her."

"More like, tell her what to do," Max shot back, glaring at him. "El can take care of herself—she always has."

"Please stop," El said, stuck between two of her favorite people.

"Sorry, El," Mike said sheepishly. "I just care about you. That's all . . ."

He reached for her hand and squeezed it tight, pulling her closer and drawing a dramatic huff from Max.

El appeared torn—between her friend's assertion that she should be more independent and Mike's overprotectiveness, which felt familiar and safe, probably because it reminded her of Hopper. And Papa before that . . .

All these men trying to *protect* her.

From what?

Herself, she realized. The biggest threat that existed in this world. Could she handle problems without using her powers? She had to resist dunking Kyle and his crew in the mall fountain earlier. Something she still regretted a little.

But Mike was right. Hopper was on duty tonight. Her eyes darted to the mall cops patrolling the periphery with their walkie-talkies. If pandemonium broke out at Slumber Fest, the mall cops would probably call the *real* cops.

And El's night would be over. She would control herself—she could do it. At least, that's what she told herself. But doubt lingered anyway, pooling around her heart like poison.

They wandered through the mall. The atrium's glass ceiling reflected the lights and signs. Escalators hummed and shops pulsed with life. Teens swarmed Spencer's, pointing at the glow-in-the-dark posters and lava lamps, while the Time-Out Arcade beeped flashy games.

They reached the food court and headed for the nautical-themed Scoops Ahoy counter, mobbed with kids. Steve and Robin, in their rumpled sailor hats, scooped ice cream at breakneck speed. Steve's hair appeared to defy gravity despite the frozen treat frenzy. The air was thick with the sweet scent of waffle cones, making their mouths water.

But as the group inched forward and patted their pockets, their faces fell.

"Uh, guys?" Lucas said, turning his pockets inside out, lint fluttering to the floor. "We forgot a crucial detail. We spent our last bucks on the tickets."

Max groaned, checking her jeans. "He's right! How did we forget that?"

Mike dug through his wallet, producing a Scoops Ahoy buy-one-get-one coupon.

"Damn, this won't help if we can't buy one to begin with," he muttered, glancing at El, who shrugged, her cheeks flushing. She'd never had money—Hopper's cabin wasn't exactly a piggy-bank haven.

"Yeah, where is Dustin when you need him?" Lucas moaned. "Steve is like his hookup. We'd score free ice cream."

Max sighed. "What are we gonna do?"

"Yeah, we have a Class 1 Ice Cream emergency," Lucas said, his stomach growling painfully. He looked forlorn.

They all stared longingly at the Scoops Ahoy counter, watching Steve and Robin dish out more cones and sundaes.

"Don't worry, Mom's got us covered," Will said, patting the backpack filled with snacks.

"There's more? I thought we scarfed it all already during the movie," Mike said, his eyes bugging out at the haul.

"Wow, Joyce is the real MVP," Max said, her mood lifting. "Who needs ice cream when we've got this?"

The group cheered, diving into the snacks, their laughter echoing as they sprawled near the food court's edge, passing a bag of M&M's around.

Lucas nodded, stuffing his face with Doritos. "Yeah, but I'm still dreaming of a Scoops Ahoy sundae. Extra cherries."

El smiled, but her attention drifted, snagging on a

storefront across the mall's second level. Flash Studio. The photo studio was closed but the display window glowed, lit up with a litany of posed photos—teens with permed blowouts and crimped hair, brightly colored eyeshadow in teals and purples, and feathered bangs, their smiles frozen in soft-focus glory. One girl posed with a sequined scarf in a pink, glittery dress, her hair a towering masterpiece; another leaned against a velvet backdrop, her lips glossy pink.

The images reminded her of the effortless glamour in the *Seventeen* magazines El pored over in the cabin, a world she craved but never touched. She also remembered Mike's yearbook and the blurry picture of her in the background, but no class picture.

El drifted away from their group, hypnotized by the studio, drawn to the display window. She stopped in front of the portraits, her own reflection superimposed over them. But rather than vibrant and glamorous, her visage looked drab and colorless. She reached up, her fingers brushing her curls.

She imagined them teased high, sprayed stiff with hair spray, her face framed by a blowout like the girls in the photos with glittery backdrops—a snapshot of a summer she could keep forever. She let her fingers fall away, and her hair flopped back down. Her heart ached, the longing sharp and raw.

Mike noticed, joining her by the studio. "Hey, what's up?" he asked, his voice soft.

The others trailed behind him, munching snacks, their

banter fading as they saw the display. El touched the glass, her reflection warping slightly.

"Pictures," she said, her voice quiet. She pointed to the flashy display with the portraits. "Like . . . in the magazines. Or yearbooks. I want . . . that."

Max raised an eyebrow, swallowing a Twinkie bite. "Flash Studio? Really? You wanna look like a poodle exploded on your head?"

El frowned, her cheeks flushing, but she didn't back down. "It's . . . pretty."

Lucas squinted at the display, then pointed to a price sign taped to the window: BASIC PACKAGE—$49.99.

He whistled low. "Damn, that's steep. Who can afford that? Almost as much as the scavenger hunt prize."

El's eyes lit up, a spark of hope flaring. "But if we won . . ." she started, turning to the group. "The fifty dollars. We could get pictures."

Will shifted, his decoder ring glinting as he fidgeted. "Ugh, I hate taking pictures," he muttered, his voice barely audible. "Mom's got enough of me in that stupid sweater she knitted for me."

Lucas grinned, tossing an M&M in the air and catching it in his mouth.

"Are you crazy? Fifty bucks? We could have an ice cream and arcade day! Quarters for days, man!"

Will perked up, his unease fading. "Or all-day movie fest! *Back to the Future*'s coming out soon. We could hit every screening. It would be epic!"

Mike hesitated, his loyalty torn. He glanced at El, her eyes wide with longing, then at the group's excited faces. "I mean . . . an arcade day sounds kinda awesome," he admitted, running his hand through his mop of curls. "Or movies. But if you really want it . . ."

Max shrugged, popping another M&M. "Sorry, but I'm with the guys. That's all more fun than posing for cheesy photos. I could get skater gear at Spencer's. No offense, El. I'm sure we can find another way to get photos—that doesn't cost an arm and a leg."

El's face fell, her fingers dropping from the glass. She tore her gaze away. The group's excitement for arcades and movies and skater swag drowned out her quiet dream. She forced a smile, not wanting to dampen their mood.

"Okay," she said softly, stepping back. "Whatever you guys want."

Max nudged her, sensing the shift. "Come on, let's keep moving," she said, leading the group toward the escalators, their sneakers squeaking. "We'll crush that scavenger hunt, then decide."

"Okay," El said, but her heart sank anyway, and her photo dreams with it.

The others continued through the mall, their banter reigniting, quoting *Ghostbusters* lines. But El trailed a few feet behind them, reluctant to leave the glamor of Flash Studio.

She sighed, turning to catch up, but something down the narrow hallway that branched off from the mall's main corridor snagged her attention.

Suddenly, the lights flickered, a sharp buzz cutting through the mall's hum. This time, it wasn't her doing.

She snapped her head around. At the corridor's end, near a sign that read EMPLOYEES ONLY, two men in dark coveralls ducked through a heavy door, their movements quick and secretive. One carried a clipboard, the other a flashlight that cast jagged shadows. El's pulse spiked, her powers tingling.

They seemed caught in a heated exchange. A foreign language drifted through the air to her sensitive ears.

What language was that?

She could sense that something was *wrong* about these men. What were they doing here during Slumber Fest?

She took a step forward, squinting.

FLASH! The hallway warped, the air thickening with a crimson haze. The door swung open, revealing a back area—sterile, cold, almost like the lab. Crates lined the walls, their wood splintering, pulsing with writhing shadows.

The men turned, their faces melting into featureless voids, their heads jerking toward her in unison.

A low, guttural hum filled the air, like a machine waking up, and the crates shuddered, tendrils of darkness seeping out and whipping at her.

"No, stop!" El gasped, lurching back, thrusting her hands into the air.

CHAPTER TWELVE

"Help, please, stop!" El started, gasping at the horrific vision.

But then she blinked, and just as suddenly as it had appeared, the vision snapped away. The hallway looked normal, the lights stabilizing, the crimson veil lifting from her eyes.

The EMPLOYEES ONLY door slammed shut with a decisive *THUD,* cutting off her view of the restricted area.

Her breath hitched as she slowly lowered her hands. She shook her head, trying to clear the echo of the lab, the Upside Down. Just a memory, she told herself, like the loading dock vision. The gate was closed. She'd made sure.

A rat scurried past, its oily body darting down the

corridor, vanishing into the shadows. El froze, her skin prickling. The rat's beady eyes flashed in her mind, bubbling into a bloody mass, like the one in the alley downtown. Her stomach twisted.

A voice broke through her fear. "El, you coming?" Mike called.

She jerked her head around. He was halfway to the escalator with the others. The group waited for her, their faces a mix of concern and impatience.

She nodded, forcing her legs to move, but her eyes lingered on the corridor. She rejoined the group, Mike's hand finding hers, steadying her. But a bad feeling lingered in her mind like a warning that she couldn't shake.

Suddenly, Mr. Clarke's PA crackled again, his voice booming through the atrium. "Scavenger Hunt starting! All teams, gather in the atrium—now!"

The mall pulsed with renewed energy, kids racing back to the first floor as they struggled to form teams. Restless chatter and rustling bodies filled the air from kids hyped for the scavenger hunt.

Max pumped her fist, her grin fierce. She gestured for them to hurry. "This is it, guys. Fifty bucks, here we come!"

Lucas nodded, cracking his knuckles. "Kyle's crew's going down. No way they're beating us."

"Don't underestimate nerds," Mike said. "Oh, and girls. Bad idea!"

El forced a smile, her heart still racing from the vision, but Mike squeezed her hand, his excitement contagious, and she pushed the fear down. The scavenger hunt was their chance—not just for the prize, but to prove that she could be more than the girl from the lab, that she belonged.

They made their way down the escalator to the first floor, jostling behind other kids, and reached the atrium. The massive movie screen overhead was dark after *Gremlins,* its projector dormant until the midnight *Ghostbusters* screening, but the mall's central hub buzzed with frenetic energy—the main event was about to begin.

El stood with her group—Mike, Max, Lucas, and Will—near their claimed spot by the fountain, its coins glinting with unspent wishes. Her curls brushed Mike's shoulder as he squeezed her hand, his *Star Wars* sleeping bag crumpled beneath them.

Max clutched her repaired skateboard, ready to deploy it, while Lucas angled for a better view, his Doritos-stained fingers twitching with excitement.

Mr. Clarke, in a corduroy blazer and a bow tie that screamed *science teacher,* climbed onto a folding table at the atrium's center, his microphone crackling. Nancy stood behind the table, clutching her clipboard to record their teams and keep track of the entries.

Mr. Clarke's voice boomed out, cutting through the din. "Attention, Slumber Fest teens! Welcome to the first annual Starcourt Scavenger Hunt!"

Applause erupted, along with excited voices. El's heart raced. Her fingers clenched together impatiently. Max shot her a look and grinned. *We've got this,* she mouthed. *Just stay together!*

"Together," El said back with a determined look, her lips twisting at the corners. "Nobody gets left behind."

"Five clue cards are hidden across the mall," Mr. Clarke continued. "Each leads to the next. The cards hold a riddle you must solve to find the next clue's location. The first team to find a card gets a head start to crack its riddle and hunt for the next one. Late teams, don't worry—return to the registration table, and we'll release clue card copies ten minutes after the first team has claimed it."

Excited whispers broke out around them. El concentrated, learning the rules. Her friends and the other kids had experience with scavenger hunts, but this was all new to her. Clue cards? A riddle she had to solve? That led to the next clue and yet another riddle? She felt relieved to have her friends.

"The first team that figures them all out gets to claim the prize," Mr. Clarke went on in a booming voice. "A fifty-dollar gift certificate to use at Starcourt!"

The crowd erupted, cheers echoing off the glass ceiling. Mr. Clarke passed the microphone to Nancy. A sharp *squeal* erupted, making everyone groan. She banged on it to quiet the feedback.

"Everyone form teams, one entry per group! Wristbands must be visible! Winners report to me!" Her summer gig at the ticket table had morphed into hunt referee, her bossy streak in full force as she scribbled team names, ignoring two kids shoving for position.

El and her friends got to the front and gave her their names. From the corner of her eye, she saw Kyle and his crew lurking. *Bummer.* They hadn't left after all—and worse, they lumbered forward to enter the scavenger hunt.

Once everyone turned their tickets in to Nancy, got glossy maps of the Starcourt Mall, and signed up in teams, including Kyle and his crew, Mr. Clarke raised a neon-green clue card, its edges glowing under the fluorescent lights.

"Are you ready for the first clue, Slumber Fest?" he teased them.

Whoops and cheers broke out; then a hush fell over the atrium. Everyone waited, straining to hear. El clenched Mike's hand for reassurance, while Max gripped her skateboard tighter, knowing it was her secret weapon.

Will whipped his sketchbook out of his backpack, thumbing through darkly disturbing drawings of the Upside Down. El caught sight of them with a shudder—their shared trauma transformed into artistic expression. But then Will flipped to a blank page, and Lucas passed him a marker to write the clue down for their group to study.

"Smart move," Max said with a nod of respect. "Nerds for the win indeed."

"Success is where preparation meets timing," Lucas replied with a grin. He unfurled the large, glossy map of the mall, then slipped in, "Maybe if we win the prize, you'll take me back?"

He batted his eyelashes.

Max snorted. "You're completely incorrigible, do you know that?"

"Yeah, I don't give up," he said. "And I especially don't give up on you. Plus, that's what is going to help us win the scavenger hunt—my tenacity."

"We'll see," Max hedged. "Now stop getting distracted and pay attention."

But the seed of hope was planted. Lucas pumped his fist. "Yes! Now we *have* to win. Listen up, everyone!"

Mr. Clarke leaned into the microphone, reading off the card.

"Clue One!" he announced, his voice dramatic. "Listen carefully: *Set a course for sweet seas of flavor, or risk falling out of the captain's favor.* First team to find the clue card gets a head start! Go!"

The atrium exploded into chaos, kids bolting in every direction, their sneakers squeaking on the marble. Mall cops barked futile orders, their walkie-talkies buzzing, while Jonathan circled with his camera, snapping shots for the *Hawkins Post*. El's group huddled tight with their heads bent together and voices overlapping in a flurry of ideas.

"Captain's favor? Gotta be the arcade!" Lucas said, pointing to the spot on the Starcourt map. "I think there's a game called *Treasure Island*! If you fall out of their favor, you die and game over!"

Lucas dragged his finger across his neck, then stuck his tongue out.

But Will shook his head. "*Treasure Island* is also a book," he said, jabbing at another location. "I bet it's hidden in Waldenbooks."

Mike frowned, running his hand through his hair. "I call foul—you just want to scope for new D&D books."

"Well, think about it—D&D does have a lot of pirates and sailors in the campaigns," Will pushed back. "*The Sinister Secret of Saltmarsh, Danger at Dunwater, The Final Enemy.*" He ticked them off on his fingers, only to get hushed by the group.

Mike's eyes widened with excitement. "Wait, are there any nautical movies out? Maybe it's at the Starcourt theater?"

They continued to argue back and forth with nobody agreeing.

El stayed quiet, her mind racing. The imagery reminded her of something, but what? She searched her memory, trying to summon the answer to the riddle. A kid sauntered by licking an oversized ice cream cone. That sparked an idea. She flashed back to the bus ride to downtown with Max yesterday. Her eyes widened.

"Scoops Ahoy!" she whispered, turning to the group. "The ice cream place. Max said . . . they have *boat* ice cream."

Max snapped her fingers, her grin fierce. "Hell yeah, El! Scoops Ahoy! We're so dumb—how did we miss that? *Set sail on an ocean of flavor*—it's their slogan! The clue card's gotta be hidden up there in the food court!"

"Damn it, El is right," Mike agreed, jumping to his feet.

Max ignored him, dropping her skateboard, its wheels clacking on the tiles, and kicked off, her ponytail bouncing. "Let's move, slackers!"

Max led the way with the group sprinting after her, weaving through the crowd.

El's pulse surged, the thrill of the hunt drowning out

the echo of her earlier vision. Mike's hand stayed in hers, his long strides matching her pace, while Lucas vaulted over a sleeping bag, whooping. Will trailed, his backpack bouncing on his narrow shoulders.

But they weren't alone.

Kyle and his crew lurched out of the shadows—they'd been spying on them.

"Scoops Ahoy, you heard the dweebs!" he called to Becks and Danny, who was slower on the uptake. "I knew they'd solve it fast," Kyle added.

"That's on the second floor, hurry," Becks added. They all gave chase.

"That's cheating!" Mike yelled behind him. "You're cheaters!"

"You can't prove it—we're going to beat you there," Kyle sneered. He shoved a younger kid aside, his crew cackling as they barreled after Max and El and their group, heading toward the escalators.

Max rolled her eyes, muttering, "Bring it, mullet!"

She skated ahead, weaving through the packed crowd. Her skateboard gave her an edge, her wheels humming, but Kyle's crew was gaining on them, their longer legs eating up the distance.

El's frustration bubbled up, a hot spark in her chest. Her powers hummed in her skull, but she clenched her fists against them, her knuckles white, remembering Mike's warning. She couldn't cause a scene—and let Kyle and his bullies ruin everything for her and her friends.

Max's shout snapped her back to attention. "Let's move! Hurry up!"

Max kicked off harder, her skateboard clacking as she aimed for the escalator. The group followed, their sneakers pounding. Above them, the mall's second-level food court loomed with Scoops Ahoy's nautical stripes visible. Steve's and Robin's sailor hats bobbed behind the counter as they scooped ice cream for customers.

But Kyle's crew pushed ahead, barreling through the crowd and shoving kids away without remorse.

"Oh no, watch out!" Max yelled, screeching to a halt as a kid darted in front of her with a goofy grin.

"Kid, get out of the way!" she barked, but it was too late.

Her board skittered out from under her. She managed to land on her feet, but her momentum was stalled.

Lucas, Mike, and Will plowed into her back, sending them all staggering forward and landing in a big heap on the floor. El avoided the collision, just barely—but Kyle and his crew reached the escalator first, blocking the narrow steps, their bodies a wall of menace.

Kyle spun, his sneer vicious.

"Going somewhere, freaks? Too bad—this ride's ours! You ain't getting past us."

Becks cackled, leaning against the railing, her frizzy bangs bouncing.

"Maybe try the stairs, nerds. Oh, wait—they're locked! Guess you're trapped."

Danny cracked his knuckles louder, his bulk filling the

escalator's width, daring them to push through.

Max recovered and grabbed her errant board, kicking it up to her hand.

"You're not winning this, Kyle," she spat, gripping her skateboard like a weapon. Lucas stepped beside her, his fists clenched, while Will hung back, his mind racing for a plan. Mike pulled El close, his jaw tight, scanning for a way around.

El's powers tingled, a spark flaring despite Mike's warning. The escalator's hum faltered, its steps jerking slightly, drawing a yelp from Becks. El's fingers twitched; the urge to fling Kyle's crew out of the way was overwhelming.

Just one push, and they'd crash into the fountain. But Mike's hand tightened, his eyes pleading, and she forced a breath, the escalator steadying.

The crowd behind them grew restless, kids shouting, "Move it!" and "What's the holdup?"

Mall cops circled closer, their walkie-talkies hissing as they eyed the bottleneck. Nancy's voice echoed from the atrium, sharp over the PA.

"Keep it moving, teams!" she barked. "No fighting, or you're disqualified!"

Kyle didn't flinch at the warning, but he did signal to his crew. They leapt over the safety railing and onto the escalator ahead of a bunch of kids, riding it to the top floor. They slowly ascended, clearly on pace to beat them to the next clue hidden at Scoops Ahoy.

Max leaned in, her voice a fierce whisper. "We're not

letting these burnouts win. Any ideas?"

Her eyes flicked to El, then Lucas, who squinted at the escalator's railing, muttering about angles. Will's mind turned to the mall's layout, his D&D instincts kicking in, while Mike scanned the crowd, searching for a gap.

El reached for her powers, not to obstruct the bullies, but to search for—*sense*—a solution. She locked on to it, a grin spreading over her face.

"Hurry, the elevator!"

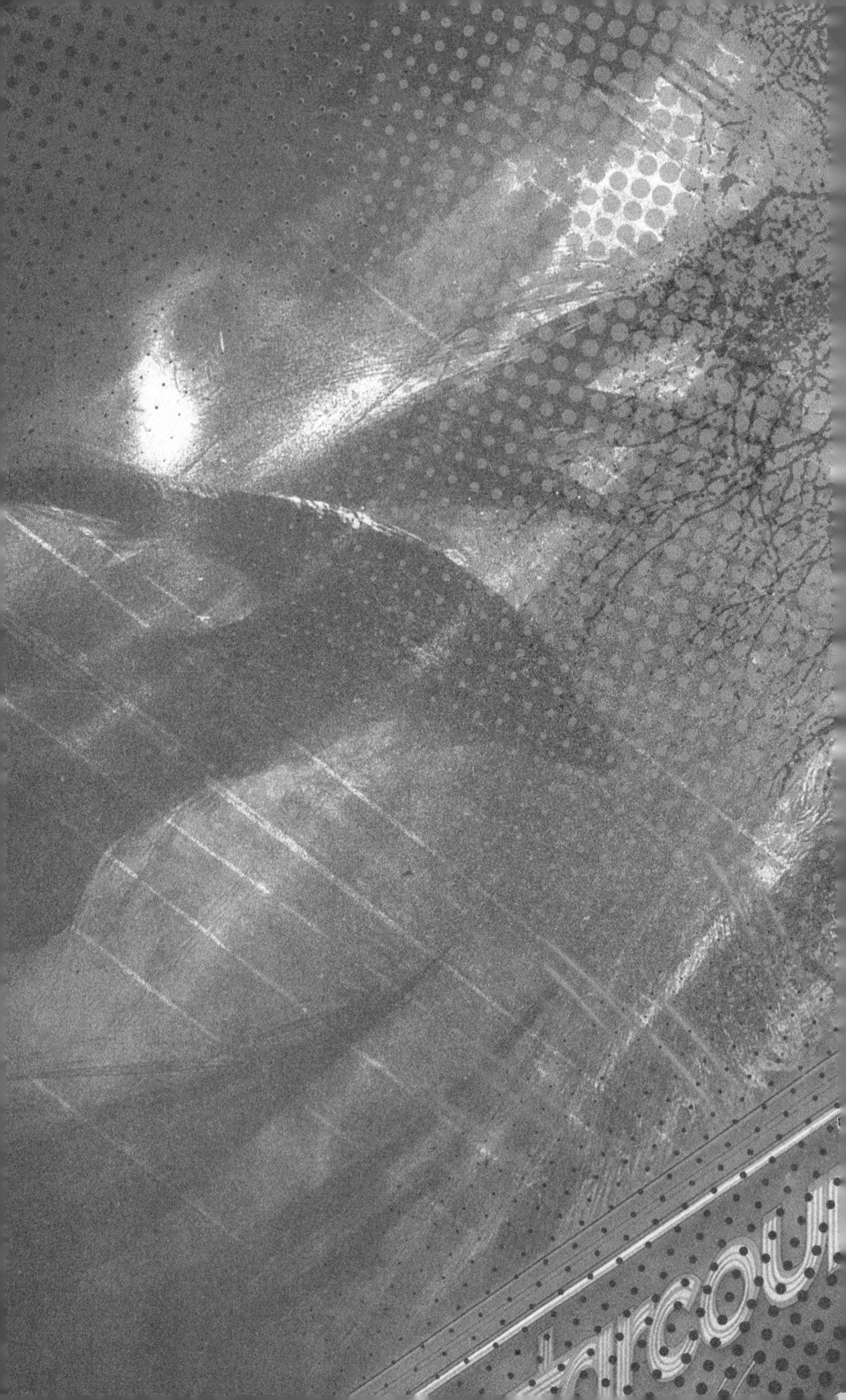

CHAPTER THIRTEEN

"Hurry, El's right!" Max pointed to the gleaming metal doors across the atrium, past Sam Goody's blaring pop music and Orange Julius's sticky counters. "The elevator—that's our only chance to beat them to the clue!"

She kicked off, her board's wheels humming, weaving through teens clutching glow-in-the-dark trinkets.

"Come on, slackers!" she added.

"Ahoy, matey!" Lucas joked. "Last one there swabs the poop deck!"

"What is a poop deck?" Will wondered aloud.

"What you'll be swabbing if you don't get going, landlubber!"

"Quit the nonsense," Max shouted over her shoulder, cutting through the atrium. "And get your butts in gear!"

The group bolted after her, abandoning the escalators for their alternate route. Mike reached for El's hand, pulling her along, the exhilaration of the hunt propelling them forward. Kyle and his crew rode up, slowly, about halfway to the second floor—and the food court where the next clue had to be hidden at the nautically themed ice cream shop.

They made it across the atrium, dodging sleeping bags and other detritus, and raced for the elevator.

Max reached it first and jammed the elevator button, her fist pounding the panel. "Come on . . . come on . . ."

It lit up, but the hum of the gears sounded distant and painfully slow. Upstairs, a crowd waited. Max groaned, "This is taking forever!"

Across the mall, Kyle and his crew were almost to the top floor. Luckily, the elevator intersected the food court, spitting them out closer than the escalators—if it ever came.

"Don't worry—I've got this," El said, stepping forward. A faint hum buzzed in her skull.

She focused, her powers expanding—gears grinding above, cables snapping taut, and the doors upstairs slammed shut, cutting off the waiting teens before they could board. They looked pissed.

"Hey, where's it going?" one yelled in confusion, jamming the button. "It's not supposed to do that . . ."

El flicked her wrist. The elevator lurched downward, moving faster than normal, summoned to their level.

DING! The doors slid open.

"El, you did it," Max said, rushing through the doors and holding them open for everyone. They piled in, Lucas elbowing for more space, Will squeezing back against the mirrored wall, and Mike and El clambering inside last.

"Hold on," El said.

She focused again, her fingers vibrating—the buttons glowed, the doors snapped shut, and the elevator surged upward, faster than it should.

Max grinned, pumping her fist. "Hell yeah, El! You're our secret weapon!"

But would it be fast enough?

The gears groaned and the car swayed on the cables, picking up speed.

Will held on to the railing, gasping against the flip in his stomach.

"Ugh, I might hurl," he hissed.

"Don't. You. Dare," Lucas hissed. "Swallow it back down . . . now!"

Will gulped, looking queasy. But mercifully, the elevator slammed to a halt, making them all stumble around.

DING! The doors burst open to the busy food court. Scoops Ahoy's blue-and-white stripes clashed with the flashing signs of Imperial Panda and Hot Dog on a Stick. Steve and Robin stood behind the counter, scooping ice cream.

Neither of them looked particularly thrilled to be working this late shift.

El and Max glanced around the food court, scoping

for competition, but their team had solved the clue the fastest. Other kids were still huddled in the atrium, trying to decipher the cryptic message—except for Kyle and his crew, who had cheated by eavesdropping on them.

And worse yet, they had reached the top floor, spilling from the escalator, their wristbands flashing.

"Max, watch out—" Lucas started, before Kyle shoved him hard, sending him crashing into a trash can.

Greasy takeout containers and empty soda cups scattered across the floor, drawing a yelp from a kid slurping an Orange Julius. Lucas groaned on the floor in pain. Meanwhile, Danny and Becks grabbed Mike and Will, restraining them and clearing the way for Kyle to reach Scoops Ahoy and beat them to the next clue.

He sneered and ran for it, but Max rocketed forward on her skateboard. She weaved through the busy food court, dodging kids carrying red plastic trays, then cut toward Kyle from the side.

She slammed the edge of her board against Kyle's shin, then flipped him off.

"Outta my way, creep!"

Kyle yelped, hopping back, his chipped tooth flashing in a snarl.

Max skated toward Scoops Ahoy, spotting the neon-green clue sticking out of a sailor's hat on the counter.

"The clue," she whispered, her eyes widening. "I see it! We were right . . ."

Max pumped her feet, speeding up on her board, but then—*WHAM!*

Kyle recovered and knocked her off, shoving her hard from behind.

She flew off and landed on the floor with a crash, her skateboard skittering away. Worse, she was helpless to stop Kyle. He loped toward the counter, limping slightly, and reached out to grab the clue from the hat—but then something unexpected happened.

"What the hell?" he hissed.

The sailor hat wobbled on the counter, then floated away into the air, unnoticed by the food court crowd, drifting into Max's outstretched hand.

Max snagged the hat out of the air, grabbing the clue with a fierce grin.

"Got it!" she said, pumping her fist. She hurried up and grabbed her board.

"But how is that possible?" Kyle said, eyes wide with shock and dismay.

He glared at Eleven, who was standing behind a column with a smirk. A trickle of blood dripped from her nose, but she quickly wiped it away.

"You'll pay for this!" Kyle yelled.

El giggled, then ran to Max. They both whipped around to flee the food court. Becks and Danny released Mike and Will, throwing them down and stomping on them, then turned to block the only escape route.

Kyle recovered, catching up to them and blocking their retreat, his sneer vicious. Max and El skidded to a halt, trapped between a rock and a hard place.

Danny and Becks closed in on them from one side and Kyle from the other.

"Hand it over, weirdos!" Kyle said. "The clue, dumbasses. Now!"

"What do we do now?" Max said, clutching the card tighter.

El felt a surge of adrenaline but pushed away the buzzing in her head. She'd already risked using her powers once to get the clue when only Kyle was looking—and got away with it.

But too many kids were watching their altercation now. The food court had fallen quiet. Almost *too* quiet.

Her eyes darted to the mall cops patrolling the corridors. She couldn't risk doing something stupid and getting caught. They could be kicked out of the scavenger hunt. Worse, the cops might summon Hopper to investigate.

"I . . . I don't know," El stammered, the bullies advancing on them.

But then a voice cut through.

"Psssst, over here . . . hurry!"

Steve gestured to them from behind the Scoops Ahoy counter. El and Max dashed toward him, slipping behind the counter and ducking down to hide.

Robin turned, gaping at them.

"Dingus, employees only!" she barked at them. "Pretty sure your kids aren't allowed back here."

Steve grimaced, waving her off. "Just cover for me, okay? Stall those jerks."

"Fine, but you owe me big," Robin shot back, crossing her arms, a sly smile tugging at her lips. She was enjoying their repartee, not to mention, holding something over his head for the future.

Steve led Max and El into the back of Scoops Ahoy, the door swinging shut behind them. The air shifted, turning cooler, tinged with the scents of vanilla and bleach, a strange chemical aroma.

Max spotted a whiteboard on the wall, two columns labeled "You Rule" and "You Suck," the latter packed with tally marks in the form of slashes.

She snorted, still clutching the clue and her board. "Wow, looks like somebody sure *sucks* a whole lot."

Steve flushed, scratching his neck. "Just so you know, that's not an accurate accounting of my interactions with eligible females. It's highly biased."

El and Max giggled, their laughter echoing in the tight space.

Robin poked her head in, her hat slipping. "Don't believe a word Steve says. Trust me, he gets shot down at least once a day. Somebody had to keep track of him bombing . . ." She formed her hands into a plane, crashing it with a—*BOOM!*—her grin wicked.

"Do not!" Steve said.

"Do too!" Robin countered.

A shout from the front cut them off.

"Hey, where did those losers go? And what's the next clue? Hello, is there anybody back there?"

Kyle's voice, sharp and pissed, carried through from the front counter.

Max and El backed away from the threatening voice. But Robin snapped into action, straightening her hat.

"Listen, I'll stall them—but don't forget you owe me an undetermined favor at a future date. Deal?"

"Deal," Steve muttered.

Robin slipped back out to the counter, but her voice could be heard through the open window to the front.

"Uh, what do you want, kid. Cone? Sundae? Banana split—"

"You can't hide them," Kyle hissed back. "That's cheating! I saw you—"

"So is pushing other kids into trash cans," Robin shot back in a low voice. "Should I summon the powers that be—and tell them what I saw?"

"Uh, that's okay, never mind," Kyle backpedaled. "But what's the next clue? You have to tell us. For the hunt?"

"Right, let's see," Robin said. "Was it something about unicorns? Oh wait, maybe dragons. Sorry, my memory sucks. Probably the fumes back here."

"What, how can you forget?" Kyle said in exasperation.

"Which is it? Unicorns or dragons? Come on, lady!"

Robin kept stalling them, but Max was worried. They had the next clue—and a head start on Kyle—but they were stuck. However, Steve was already moving farther back toward the massive walk-in freezers, where it grew colder.

"Uh, where are you taking us?" Max asked, shivering slightly. "Is this, like, where you keep the dead bodies?"

But Steve turned around, hissing, "Shhhh! Top secret. Employee perks. Don't ask questions . . . just follow me."

He unlocked a nondescript door in the back marked EMPLOYEES ONLY.

"For Dustin!" he said. "Just don't tell anyone—or I'll get canned. Got it?"

He cracked the door open, revealing the shadowy back corridors of the Starcourt Mall—dark and deserted, forbidden to patrons. The fluorescent lights flickered menacingly, barely fighting off the shadows threatening to creep in from the corners.

"Hurry, get lost!" Steve said, pushing them through the door, then shutting and locking it behind them.

THUD! Max and El stumbled forward, emerging into the forbidden corridors. El stared into the darkness, the air seeming to undulate like the Upside Down's vines. Her skin prickled, the rat's beady eyes from her vision flashing in her mind. She reached for Max, her fingers brushing Max's sleeve.

"Uh, is something wrong?" Max asked, her voice low,

her board tucked under her arm. She scanned the area, but it was empty, and nothing seemed amiss. Plus, it offered the perfect escape.

El shook her head, though her stomach twisted slowly. Something felt very, very wrong, but she couldn't name it.

Max hurried down the corridor, holding up the next clue. Her voice snapped El out of it. "Hurry up! We have to find the boys and decode this . . . and fast. Before they regroup!"

They proceeded deeper into the forbidden area. The farther they went, the darker it got. El felt another shudder ripple up her spine. Even Max looked a little freaked out by the deserted area.

Their sneakers slapped the concrete floors, their footsteps echoing, while the overhead lights flickered, snapping them in and out of darkness.

"Do you see that?" Max asked nervously, pointing to the lights.

"Don't look at me," El said defensively. "I'm not doing that . . ."

"Then who is?" Max asked.

The ominous question hung in the air. Suddenly—*squeak*—a rat shot out from a crack in the walls. The girls both screamed and backed away. The rat took one look at them, beady eyes glinting, then ran at them.

Fear jolted through El—it was like in her nightmarish vision with the rat exploding in a mass of bloody tissue that pulsed, almost like it was alive.

"Oh crap, run!" Max said, grabbing El. They bolted

through the shadowy corridors that were like a maze, turning in on each other. First, Max and El ran left; then they cut back right. They were breathing hard and, worse, they were completely turned around and lost.

"It's okay . . . it's gone . . ." El said, panting hard and scanning the corridor behind them and using her powers.

"Barf, they should call the health inspectors," Max said, still freaked out. She caught her breath a little and frowned. "But where . . . are we?"

"I don't know . . ." El said, feeling equally disoriented. There was more. These back corridors gave her the creeps and made gooseflesh stand up on her arms, but she couldn't explain why.

"Come on, let's try this way," Max said, throwing her board down and hopping on. She kicked forward. "There must be a way out of this maze."

They continued down the corridor with Max riding slowly so El could keep up, but the hallways all looked the same. All the doors were unmarked, too.

Suddenly, a door at the end of the corridor cracked open, and light spilled through. Three dark shadows stretched out toward them, their silhouettes backlit, their faces completely obscured.

Max and El froze in the cold corridor, the flickering fluorescents casting jagged shadows that twisted like the Upside Down. They looked like the void men from El's terrifying vision.

A stern voice barked out.

"What're you doing back here? This is a *restricted* area! You're trespassing. I'm going to have to call the cops!"

That meant . . . Hopper.

Max flinched back, while El felt a rush of adrenaline shoot through her.

But they were trapped.

CHAPTER FOURTEEN

El's fingers twitched, the air vibrating, while Max held her skateboard up like a club. Fear shot through them. The shadows elongated through the door, coming closer.

But then, laughter erupted—familiar, mischievous. Lucas stepped forward into the light, hands shaped like a gun.

"Put your hands up!" he barked in a stern voice, impersonating Hopper. "Or we'll have to arrest you."

"Yeah, this area is for . . . *employees only,*" Mike added, grinning. "What're you perps doing back here?"

Will trailed behind, sheepish, his grin barely contained. The tension drained from El's shoulders, her powers fizzling.

Max shoved Lucas hard, her board clacking.

"Not funny! You scared the hell outta us. El could've leveled you!"

"Well, it was a *little* funny," Lucas said, dodging another shove while Mike and Will stifled laughs.

"Worth it," Mike added. "You should've seen the looks on your faces."

"Yeah, you actually thought you got busted," Will said, shaking his head.

They all laughed at their successful prank, though Max still looked pissed.

"How'd you find us?" El asked, relaxing at the sight of their friends.

"Simple! Steve showed us where you went," Lucas explained, jerking a thumb back toward Scoops Ahoy's hidden door. "Let us back here to catch up with you."

"We're still by Scoops Ahoy?" Max said, glancing around the dim maze of corridors, crates, and pipes. "Wow, we really got turned around back here."

"Yeah, it's like a maze," El added, her unease lingering, the corridor's shadows too close to her visions.

Max's voice snapped her back as Max unfurled the clue, the edges damp from her sweaty grip. "Okay, focus, team! We don't have any time to lose. We gotta decode this sucker before Kyle's crew catches up."

They all shut up, excitement running through their group in anticipation. The overhead lights flickered, casting strange shadows over the corridor. But they were too focused to notice.

"Hurry up—what does it say?" Lucas said while Will pulled out his sketchbook ready to work on it. Mike and El huddled together.

Max read aloud from the clue card, her voice echoing down the corridor.

"'Want to claim the top score, player?'" Max said in a sharp voice. "'Only the bravest ones can become dragon slayers.'" Max snorted. "First sailors, now dragons? Who comes up with this wild scavenger hunt stuff?"

"Mr. Clarke," the boys said in unison, their voices proud.

"He's got a knack for this," Mike added. "Always makes science fun."

"You got that right," Lucas piled on, nodding with a grin.

Max nudged El, smirking. "Well, it's a good thing we brought our own brainy squad along. Otherwise, you and me would be totally lost, right?"

El giggled, her tension easing. She leaned into Mike, making him blush.

"Well, what does it mean?" Max asked. "You're the dragon experts."

The group huddled together and pulled out the Starcourt Mall map, their whispers echoing off the concrete as they batted different ideas around.

"I still say Waldenbooks," Will said to their collective groans. "What? Why are you complaining? It's a good guess."

"Nothing in this clue mentions books—or anything to do with them," Mike said pointedly. "It's gotta be something else. Everyone, think! Come on! We're running out of time to crack this code."

They all traded more ideas, still coming up short. Will fidgeted, pulling out a D&D die, its twenty sides glinting under the flickering lights.

Suddenly, El's eyes widened—she nudged Mike, pointing to the die.

"Look . . . the dice!"

Mike frowned, confused; then his eyes lit up. "El, you're a genius! Dragons are found in . . . games!"

"So, you're saying it is D&D?" Will said, brightening. He clutched the die. "I'm right. It's gotta be Waldenbooks—"

"No!" they all shouted back.

Mike signaled for quiet. They all clammed up; it wasn't easy.

"Like I was saying—dragons are found in games. And not just board games," he said, shooting Lucas a look. "Think about other games we like."

"Oh, you mean—*Dragon's Lair*!" Lucas said, snapping his fingers. "It's all about slaying dragons to win—and get the top score. 'Want to claim the top score, player?' " he quoted from the card. "The next clue's gotta be hidden there."

"Wait, the game you were playing at the Palace Arcade?" Max said with a frown. "But that's not at Starcourt."

Mike shook his head. "No, they've got their own arcade

here—Time-Out. That's why downtown has been so dead lately. The mall stole all their business."

"That's right," Lucas said, perking up. "I bet they've got a *Dragon's Lair* machine here, too. It's only, like, the most popular game."

"Exactly," Mike said. "But we have to hurry. Kyle doesn't have many brain cells left—but he loves that game. It's why those dicks pushed us off it."

"He's bound to figure it out," Max agreed, jumping up. "Come on—we have to get to the arcade before they do. And beat them to the next clue!"

"What's the best way out of here?" Mike asked. "We can't go back through Scoops Ahoy. Kyle and his crew are probably staking it out, waiting to pound on us if we go back that way."

"Yeah, I had enough of their *pounding on me* for one day," Lucas said, wincing and rubbing the painful bruise already forming on his upper arm.

"Right, this way," El said, narrowing her eyes and using her powers to focus.

With El leading the way, they ran down the corridor away from Scoops Ahoy. Her mind traveled through the corridors, snaking to the stairwell. She cut to the right, leading them that way.

"Where is she taking us?" Lucas asked, looking worried the deeper they went into the mall's secret corridors. El hurried ahead, moving faster and faster.

"Oh, I get it," Max said. "We can use the employee

passageways to get around the mall faster—and without being seen by Kyle and his crew. I just hope El knows where she's going."

"But you got lost earlier," Lucas pointed out, looking concerned.

"Uh, we got spooked by a rat . . . so we weren't thinking—more fleeing," Max said with a deep shudder, hoping no more popped out uninvited.

"Oh, gnarly," Lucas said. "But that's understandable. I hate rats . . ."

They ran side by side, and something sparked between them, partially from the adrenaline, but also from the camaraderie of being on the same team again.

Lucas sensed that his moment had come. He reached out—and latched on to Max's hand. She was shocked, but then she . . . squeezed his hand, a shared moment binding them back together.

Despite her protests that she'd never take him back, Max could feel that yearning creeping up on her again. His big brown eyes, soft lips, and goofy grins slowly melting her frigid heart.

How long could she hold out before taking him back? But then she remembered all the times he didn't take her feelings seriously, or chose impressing his friends over her. And she froze back up, jerking her hand away.

"This way . . ." El said, reaching what looked like a dead end. But there was a door. Mike shoved it open, revealing industrial metal stairs that cut through the concrete building.

They bolted down them, arriving back at the first level.

"Nice one, El," Mike said with a grin.

She gestured for them to follow her down another corridor, her mind locked in on the arcade. They came to a door and forced it open.

And burst into . . .

Time-Out Arcade.

Everyone cheered and whooped, feeling exhilarated after their adventure through the bowels of the mall, unaware of the greater dangers lurking down there if they'd taken one wrong turn.

They were immediately greeted by pulsing lights and electronic music.

Unlike the Palace Arcade's worn carpets and sticky joysticks, Time-Out resembled a flashy, futuristic cathedral, boasting brand-new machines, their screens pulsing with vibrant lights. Other rival teams were sure to swarm the arcade before long, searching for the next clue, but for now they had a head start.

"Spread out!" Max barked, skating through the maze of arcade cabinets. "Hurry, we've gotta find *Dragon's Lair*!"

El scanned the flashing screens, her heart racing. Kyle's crew would crash soon—Robin's stalling wouldn't hold them long. They'd figure out the clue and give up waiting in the food court.

Any second, they were sure to descend on the arcade, too.

Everyone ran in different directions, scoping for the prized machine.

Suddenly, Mike pointed to a corner, where the animated knight in *Dragon's Lair* glowed. "Over there—look!"

The coin slot was stuffed with what looked like a neon-pink clue card.

Max was the closest, plus she had wheels. She skated over, popping an ollie over a stray joystick cord, landing with a *clack!* that turned heads. She snagged the clue, smirking. "Too easy!"

She waved it overhead in triumph, a wide grin spreading over her face.

But Danny's bulk loomed from nowhere as he shoved her hard. She crashed to the carpet, her board skittering away. She landed on her back with a groan, still holding her arm up with the clue. Danny cackled, snatching it from her outstretched hand. "Here, boss!"

Kyle stepped over her, his chipped tooth flashing in a menacing grin. Becks followed after him, leaning over the *Dragon's Lair* machine. She kicked Max's skateboard for good measure. It rolled away, disappearing under the machine.

"Always trying to hog our game," he sneered at her. "Maybe this time you'll learn your lesson—and stay away."

"Yeah, that prize is ours, dorks," Becks added, her frizzy bangs bouncing.

Danny passed the new clue to Kyle, who stuffed it in his front pocket.

Max was helpless to stop them, her friends on the other side of the arcade.

El's eyes locked on to her.

The arcade lights strobed, machines whining as her powers flared. The *Dragon's Lair* screen stuttered, the knight glitching. She clenched her fists harder, fighting the urge to fling Kyle into a cabinet.

It was tempting—almost too tempting—but other teams were stampeding into the arcade now, having deciphered the second clue, and were beelining for the *Dragon's Lair* machine. All those eyes watching her. It was too risky.

Kyle saw her focused on them, and nudged Danny and Becks. His meaning was clear. *Let's get the hell out of here!*

The trio turned and sprinted off, their cackles echoing behind them.

"Freak!" Kyle yelled over his shoulder, the word slicing through the arcade. "You belong in a padded room!"

El flinched, the insult hitting harder than their fists. *Freak*. The lab's sterile walls flashed in her mind—Papa's voice, the hum of machines, her shaved head. Maybe she *was* a freak. Her shoulders slumped, doubt pooling in her heart. Meanwhile, Max was still sprawled on the carpet, looking equally forlorn, her board stuck under the *Dragon's Lair* cabinet.

The boys ran over, but the damage had already been done. They were too late. Lucas helped Max to her feet, while Mike and Will fished out her board from under the arcade cabinet.

"Those jerkfaces stole the clue," Max muttered. "All they do is cheat!"

Max stared after Kyle's crew, their wristbands vanishing

into the crowd. The fifty-dollar prize slipped further away. Other teams swarmed Time-Out, their shouts drowning out the beeps, but nobody had witnessed the theft of the clue.

"I guess we have to go back to Mr. Clarke and Nancy for the next clue," Mike said glumly. "There goes our head start."

"Damn it, you were so close," Lucas said, clenching his jaw in frustration. "It was right in your hand!"

Max shook her head. "Close isn't good enough. We're screwed."

El sighed, feeling defeated. Her voice was only a whisper. "What are we going to do now?"

CHAPTER FIFTEEN

The Time-Out Arcade thrummed with bright flashes and cheerful, electronic chirps that usually sparked joy in the group. But now they stood in a huddle, defeated, the sting of Kyle's crew stealing their clue burning fresh.

Max rubbed her elbow, wincing from her fall on the rough carpet, her reclaimed skateboard tucked under her arm like a shield. Lucas kicked at a stray prize ticket, his jaw tight, his earlier bravado replaced by frustration.

In desperation, Mike scanned the crowd, his dark hair falling into his eyes, looking for an employee who might've seen them shove Max, but the arcade was a sea of kids clamoring for the clue, their shouts drowning out any hope of finding help.

Will clutched his sketchbook, his pale face etched with worry. "Whoever finds the clue gets a head start," he said. "I bet we won't get a second chance fast."

El stood apart, studying the *Dragon's Lair* machine, its animated knight frozen mid-swing. Kyle's taunt—*freak*—echoed in her mind, slicing deeper than she wanted to admit, dragging her back to her past trauma.

"I can't believe they stole the clue," El whispered, her voice barely audible over the arcade's hum, her shoulders slumping as doubt pooled in her chest. "I should've stopped them . . ."

Her frustration surged, making the *Dragon's Lair* machine flicker and beep. GAME OVER flashed on the screen over a downbeat sound.

"No, you did the right thing," Mike cut in, draping his arm over her shoulders. "Anyone could've seen you use your powers on Kyle. And then we'd have to kiss our night goodbye."

"You're right, but I still don't like it," El said, frowning. The machine flickered one more time, then stabilized.

"But now what do we do?" Lucas said, echoing El's earlier question. "How can we ever catch up?"

His question hung in the air. But then Max grinned, a mischievous glint in her eyes.

"Uh, why are you smiling all psycho like that . . ." Lucas said suspiciously.

"Drumroll, please," Max said, thumping her hands over her board. "I happened to get a glimpse of the clue *before* that washout snatched it."

The group's heads whipped toward her, hope flickering. Mike's brows shot up, his voice cracking with urgency.

"You *what*? Do you remember it?"

"Sure do," Max said, tapping her temple with a smirk.

"Wait, are you some kind of super-genius?" Lucas said, blown away. "With a photographic memory?"

"I dunno," Max said, blushing. "It's kind of like remembering song lyrics. If you put words to music, you remember them. It's a little trick I learned a while back. I just have a knack for it, I guess."

"Lucas, Mike, stop interrogating her already," Will said. "We're against the clock here. Let me remind you, Kyle has a head start!" He turned to Max, pulling out his sketchbook and the mall map.

"You fools sure you're ready?" Max said, sweeping her gaze over them.

"Ugh, the suspense is killing me," Mike moaned. "Just spit it out already!"

"Shhhh!" Lucas hissed, shushing him. "You can't rush . . . genius!"

Max laughed at his outburst, then glanced around to make sure no other teams were eavesdropping on them.

"The coast is clear," El said, confirming they were safe.

"Clue number three." Max pursed her lips, summoning the riddle. Her voice came out in a singsong voice to the tune of a Kate Bush song. " 'Near the mall's glow, over the arcade's hum, find a spot where rhythm and sweat become one.' "

Lucas let out a low whistle, his mood lifting as he punched the air.

"Damn, Max, that's clutch! Okay, let's break this down. Rhythm and sweat? What's that supposed to mean? Some kind of . . . dance party?"

They huddled tighter in a corner by the front windows, not even tempted by their favorite games, their voices overlapping in a flurry of ideas, the arcade's chaos fading into the background. Will flipped open his sketchbook, marker poised over a blank page, his fingers trembling slightly.

"Maybe it's the music store," he suggested, his voice tentative. He pointed to it on the map. "Sam Goody! They're always playing tunes."

He started sketching the store with aisles of tapes and pricier compact discs, clamped in plastic antitheft devices.

Mike snorted. "Maybe, but doesn't that seem too easy? This is clue number three. I know how scavenger hunts work—and so does Mr. Clarke. The clues get harder as you go. The first two are really just warm-ups, partially so all the kids feel like they have a shot."

"Mike's right," Lucas said, frowning. "Sam Goody is the obvious choice. Too obvious. It's gotta be harder to solve."

"Yeah," Max agreed. "And what's with the *sweat* part? That's so random. Plus . . . look." She jabbed at the glossy map. "Sam Goody isn't *over* the arcade; it's on the other side of the mall."

"She's right," Mike said. "Over . . . it's got to be on the second level, right?"

Lucas perked up, pointing to another store. "What

about Spencer's? That's over the arcade, sort of. They've got all those black light posters and lava lamps. Glow, rhythm, sweat—kinda fits, right? Like, dancing under black lights?"

Max rolled her eyes, her board clacking as she shifted her weight.

"Lava lamps, really? You think it's about a rave party? Plus, it's not on the second floor either. And you're totally reaching with the *sweat* part."

They fell silent, stumped.

"Come on, Lucas, think harder!" Max said in frustration. "We're running out of time. Kyle and his goons have a jump on us. We can't lose that prize!"

"Well, you're the genius with the fancy memory tricks," Lucas grumbled. "Why don't *you* think harder?"

"Really, Lucas?" Max shot back, color reaching her face. "Oh, and we are so *never* getting back together."

She crossed her arms, irate. Lucas looked crestfallen at her low blow. They kept squabbling, hurling insults.

Will elbowed Mike and whispered in his ear, "Max is really serious about the breakup this time, isn't she?"

Mike shrugged. "I give it another week before they're back together. The bickering is just the preamble. Kind of like the warm-up with all that tension. Eventually, they'll have to kiss it out."

Will snickered. "A week? Wanna bet? A whole case of Twinkies?"

Mike grinned. "You're on."

While the lovers' quarrel played out, El stayed quiet.

She scanned the arcade, her eyes darting over kids shoving quarters into machines, their faces lit by glowing screens. Lines from the clue flashed through her head. *Past the arcade's hum.* What did that mean?

She looked to a nearby pillar just outside the arcade's entrance, where a glossy poster caught the light. It showed women in bright leotards, tights, and leg warmers, their white sneakers a blur as they struck poses under multicolored lights.

The text screamed in bold, bubbly letters:

Jazzercise at Starcourt!

Get Fit, Have Fun!

El's heart skipped, a spark of recognition cutting through her doubt.

She tugged Max's arm urgently, her curls bouncing as she pointed.

"Look . . . over there!"

Max pulled her attention away from Lucas, following El's gesture. She read the sign and scanned the pictures.

"Jazzercise studio?" Max said, frowning at the name. "What's that?"

But Lucas jumped in. "Wait, I think El's right! Jazzercise studio—it's upstairs! *Rhythm* and *sweat.* It's gotta be the aerobics place! That's where all those women dance their asses off!"

"All those housewives, you mean?" Mike said with a knowing wink. "Trying to stay in shape for summer?"

"Exactly," Lucas said, snapping his fingers excitedly. "That's the place—and the answer. Everything fits! It's on the second floor. *Over the arcade.* And trust me, they sure do *sweat* it out up there. You should see their killer dance moves. Those ladies have amazing *rhythm* . . . "

Max narrowed her eyes. "And *exactly* how do you know so much about an aerobics studio for women?"

"Right, just so you know . . . I have watched the classes before," Lucas confessed, but then backpedaled. "Observing them . . . only for research purposes! Gotta stay in shape, right?"

He demonstrated some of the Jazzercise aerobic dance moves, squatting down low and stepping up, but then he winced from a cramp.

Max rolled her eyes. "Of course you have." But then she got back to business. "I think El is right—it's gotta be Jazzercise. It checks all the boxes! Let's move before Kyle figures it out."

El's chest warmed, Max's fierce grin fueling her confidence. She wasn't alone—not with her friends, not with Max leading the charge. The weight of *freak* lifted slightly, replaced by the thrill of the hunt. They might still have a shot to win this thing if they hurried . . .

Max dropped her skateboard with a sharp clack, the wheels humming as she kicked off through the arcade and sped out into the mall's main corridors, bobbing and weaving, cutting toward the escalators to the second floor.

Mike pulled El along, his long strides matching hers, making her giggle in excitement, while Lucas and Will jogged behind them, Lucas wincing slightly from his earlier cramp but refusing to slow down. They had to win the hunt.

They weaved through the mall's crowded first floor, dodging teens clutching glow-in-the-dark trinkets and sleeping bags. The fountain burbled as they ran past it.

"Look, over there," Mike said with a grin. "They have the wrong idea."

Across the mall, he pointed to Sam Goody, the music store. Sure enough, Kyle and his crew charged inside looking for the next clue. They scoured the aisles, shoving kids out of the way.

But their search was futile.

"Looks like they fell for the *too easy* answer," Lucas agreed. "I just hope we're right about the aerobics spot."

"Ha, you're apparently the expert on Jazzercise," Mike joked back. "You and a bunch of bored housewives . . ."

Lucas play-punched Mike, sending him bumping into El, who pushed him right back. But they all laughed, enjoying the good-natured teasing and jokes that cemented their friendships.

"We got lucky," Max said, looking back breathlessly, her cheeks flushed. "That buys us time and erases their head start. Time to hit the gas . . ."

She kicked harder, propelling her board faster. The escalators loomed ahead, the metal steps gleaming, packed with kids hyped for the scavenger hunt. Max hit the escalator first, kicking up her board and tucking it under her arm, her ponytail bouncing as she vaulted over a kid's stray backpack.

"Move it, slackers!" she called, her voice cutting through the chatter.

They rode up the escalators that seemed to move painfully slow. El concentrated, subtly using her powers to turn the gears and speed it up.

"Nice one," Mike said, squeezing her hand.

El blushed, then let the gears slow back down before they reached the top and bounced off. The Jazzercise studio was just across from the food court. The kitschy, multicolored letters glowed faintly above a glass door.

They ran for it. The studio looked dark, the door propped open, but no music or voices spilled out—just an eerie silence that made El's skin prickle. The group slowed, their excitement tempered by the unsettling quiet. The air was cool, tinged with the faint scent of sweat, hairspray, and rubber mats, a stark contrast to the mall's kinetic buzz.

"This has to be it," Max said, her voice low, clutching her skateboard tighter. "But where's the next clue? This place looks creepy as hell."

They stepped inside, the polished floor reflecting the flickering sign outside. Mirrors lined the walls, doubling their shadows into distorted twins that danced across the room. Step aerobics platforms were stacked haphazardly in a corner, foam rollers and mats scattered like forgotten toys. The silence pressed in, broken only by the faint hum of the mall's ventilation system. El felt her senses go on full alert, ready for anything.

"Spread out," Mike whispered, his eyes darting to the

corners. "It's gotta be here somewhere. Check everywhere."

Max nodded, her face set in a determined expression. She met El's gaze, equally focused.

"We have to find the next clue if we want to win—and fast," Max said, leading them inside the studio. "Before Kyle figures out they got it wrong."

CHAPTER SIXTEEN

They fanned out, Lucas limping slightly from the cramp as he eyed the tall step platforms with a grimace. He checked behind a stack of mats, his fingers brushing the rubbery surface.

"Sheesh, I don't know how those ladies do it," he muttered under his breath, rubbing his sore thigh.

"Hot moms have aerobic superpowers," Mike said, keeping his voice low so the girls didn't overhear.

Meanwhile, Will flipped through a pile of fitness flyers on a table. Their glossy pages curled at the edges, advertising classes with names like "Power Pump" and "Sweat to the Beat." Max ducked behind the welcome counter, looking for any sign of the next neon card.

But . . . *nothing.*

"Where the hell is it?" Max said, straightening up too fast and bumping her head on the edge of the counter. She groaned, "Ugh, it's gotta be here somewhere."

El helped Max up, spying something tucked underneath the counter. A cardboard box marked *Lost & Found* with handwritten marker.

"I have an idea," El whispered. She poked around in the box, emerging with a black sweatband. She wrapped it around her eyes, blocking her vision completely.

Then she concentrated with her eyes shut, her senses sharpening, her powers unfurling like invisible tendrils, probing the room. Her face was set into a serious expression. The air felt heavy, charged with an unease she couldn't fully name, like the lab's sterile corridors or the Upside Down's suffocating vines.

She focused her powers, her mind stretching out farther, away from the studio, brushing against faint thoughts swirling downstairs.

Mr. Clarke's voice echoed in her head, his excitement about hiding clues in "unexpected places," and Nancy's frustration with the chaotic teams, her clipboard scribbled with their names.

A flash sparked from Mr. Clarke—*a rolled-up fitness mat, tucked in the corner, glowing faintly.*

"Got it—" El started, whipping off the headband. A trickle of blood dripped down from her nose.

But then suddenly, a shadow moved in the doorway. Before they could react, Kyle, Danny, and Becks burst from the darkness. It was an ambush.

"Gotcha, dorks!" Kyle said, his greasy mullet flipping in his eyes, his Van Halen tee stained with sweat.

Becks moved fast, sticking out her leg as Lucas stepped forward. He tripped, yelping sharply as his ankle twisted, and he hit the floor hard, wincing.

"Hang on!" Max yelled, skating back, her wheels screeching on the polished floor. But Kyle's crew closed in, Danny cracking his scarred knuckles with a grin, looming over her like a wall.

"Skater girl's done," Danny sneered, stepping closer. "Go home, loser."

Max didn't flinch. She kicked her board forward, wheels screaming, then jumped onto a step aerobics platform, launching at Danny with a fierce glare. He stumbled back, arms flailing to avoid her, his expression twisting into shock as he nearly toppled over a stack of mats.

Max landed with a smirk, flipping him off with both hands. "Try again, meathead!"

Lucas, limping, struggled to his feet, but he was clearly injured. Mike and Will rushed to his side. Mike clenched his fists, while Will tried to back him up, but with Lucas hurt, they were way outmatched. The bullies circled them like sharks smelling blood.

They started to close in.

Meanwhile, El stayed back, her heart pounding, her powers buzzing. The urge to fling Kyle's crew into the mirrors was overwhelming, but she hesitated—too much risk. She could damage the studio. The mall cops were nearby.

Instead, she focused on the mat in the corner, her earlier vision sharpening. She signaled Max, whispering urgently, "There! The mat! Grab it!"

Max nodded, her eyes fierce. El focused again, a trickle of blood threatening to spill. The top mat wobbled on the large pyramid, then rolled off the stack, landing near Max with a soft thud.

Max dove for it, unfurling the mat with a triumphant grin. Sure enough, a neon-yellow clue card fluttered out.

"We did it!" she shouted, grabbing the clue and stuffing it in her pocket, adrenaline pumping through her veins.

Kyle and his crew lunged for her, his chipped tooth flashing in a snarl.

"Give it here, freak!"

But Max was ready. She kicked her board hard, sending a stack of foam rollers and mats tumbling into his path.

Kyle tripped, cursing as he hit the floor. Becks tried to dodge them, but a roller caught her ankle, sending her sprawling with a yelp. She crashed into Kyle. Danny roared, charging forward, but slipped on a mat, stumbling with a loud thud.

Max swerved, dodging Kyle's hands, her ponytail whipping as she spun.

She reached the boys, high-fiving Lucas, breathless, her eyes blazing. "We're one step closer to the prize!"

Something passed between them . . . something fiery and smoldering.

Lucas grinned through the pain, his ankle throbbing but his spirit unbroken. "Hell yeah, we are! Keep it up, Max!"

But then she broke eye contact, blushing, the moment fractured.

"Time to bust a move!" She gestured for everyone to get the hell out of there.

Mike and Will braced Lucas, and they started shuffling forward, but the bullies were between them—and the front door.

"Stop," Lucas muttered. "We need another escape route."

"Over here!" El waved to them to follow her toward the back area, her senses sharp. She led them into the shadowy office where another door loomed—EMPLOYEES ONLY. From their earlier adventures, she knew that it led to the secret back corridors that connected everywhere in the mall.

She used her powers to bust open the lock. She held it open with her powers while they all limped through it, with Max skating through last.

The restricted door swung shut behind them with a heavy thud, the concrete walls closing in like a trap.

The corridors were a maze of shadows, lit by flickering fluorescents that buzzed and popped, casting jagged pools of light. Crates were stacked high, their splintered wood painted with strange, angular lettering. The air was cold, heavy with the scent of dust and something metallic, like blood or rust.

Suddenly, another door burst open farther down the dark corridor. Sharp voices echoed out in a strange language.

They sounded urgent and upset.

"Hide!" Mike hissed, yanking Lucas behind a crate, the rough edges scraping his arm. Will followed suit, his backpack bouncing as he ducked low. He rubbed his neck, getting that haunted look.

Max grabbed El, and they crouched beside the boys, their breaths shallow, their eyes scanning the darkness.

Two men in uniforms, clutching clipboards, burst into the corridor. Their silhouettes were cast in shadow, but they looked tall and imposing. They exchanged more heated words.

El stood guard, her senses heightened, her powers humming.

Suddenly, a rat scurried past them, emerging from a crack in the wall.

Max's eyes widened, but Lucas clamped his hand over her mouth.

"Don't scream," he hissed.

The rat stared at them with its beady eyes, cocking its head, seemingly wondering what they were doing there. Max squirmed in fear in Lucas's grip, but he held her tight.

El flicked her wrist, pushing the rat back. It squeaked, then fled, vanishing into another crack in the concrete wall.

Max calmed down, but then . . . the men craned their necks toward where they were hiding, hearing the squeak.

El's breath caught in her throat. The men stormed over toward the crates, pointing toward them and muttering.

They all froze, not daring to breathe, let alone move. The men leaned over where they were crouched down.

Any second, and they'd bust them. El closed her eyes, concentrating, summoning . . .

Another *squeak* echoed out, followed by rustling. Suddenly, rats burst from the crack in the wall, swarming out and crawling over their feet. Max almost screamed but controlled herself—*barely*—thanks to Lucas, who kept his hand clamped firmly over her mouth.

They all watched in horror as the rats rushed out from behind the crates and scampered down the corridor, drawing the men's attention away from them.

The men laughed in a disturbing way, pointing to the rats. Then they turned away from the crates, heading the other direction down the corridor.

A few minutes later, the men vanished into the dark stairwell, the door slamming shut behind them.

"El, you okay?" Mike whispered, his hand brushing hers, his eyes searching her face. She nodded slowly, exhaling. She wiped the blood from her face.

"Fine," she murmured, looking away from the crack in the wall.

"Did *you* do that?" Max hissed, thoroughly disgusted. "The rats?"

El shrugged. "It was all I could think of . . . I got them to leave, didn't I?"

"Dude, you weren't kidding!" Lucas said, also grossed out. "This mall does have a major infestation problem. They really need to do something about it."

They waited a few more seconds to make sure the men

didn't return before emerging from behind the crates.

"Hurry, the next clue," Will said, nudging Max, making her snap out of it.

She unfolded the card, her voice a fierce whisper, cutting through the tension. "Clue number four. 'Where celluloid adventures thrive, so big screen stories can come to life.' "

The group exchanged glances. Lucas rubbed his ankle, wincing but focused.

"This one is easy. Big screen, celluloid," he said with a grin. "Well, it's easy—if you're a film nerd like me."

"The theater, of course!" Mike said. "It's gotta be Starcourt Cinema. That all fits."

Will nodded, his sketchbook open, marker scratching as he jotted it down.

"You're right! The next clue's probably hidden in the lobby or near the projector. Or in one of the theaters."

Excitement rushed through their group. Max curled her hand around the clue, feeling her heart start to race. They were nearing the end of the hunt.

Mike squeezed El's hand, his excitement contagious. "We're back in this, all thanks to you, El! Hurry, let's go before Kyle's crew catches up."

"This way," El said, leading them in the direction of the stairwell that would carry them down to the first floor, where they could take the hidden route to the theater—that much closer to winning.

CHAPTER SEVENTEEN

The back corridors of Starcourt Mall were a labyrinth of flickering shadows and fluorescent lights buzzing like dying insects, casting jagged pools of illumination across the concrete.

El's sneakers slapped against the cold floor, her breath shallow as she ran alongside Max, who clutched the neon-yellow clue card from the Jazzercise studio.

Mike, Lucas, and Will followed close behind, Lucas limping slightly but fueled by adrenaline, his jaw set with determination. The air was heavy, thick with dust and a metallic tang that clung to El's throat, stirring memories of the lab—sterile, suffocating, wrong. The Russian lettering on the splintered crates loomed in her peripheral vision, their angular shapes pulsing faintly, like a heartbeat she couldn't ignore.

Max skated ahead, her board's wheels humming. "Come on, we've got this!" she called, glancing back, her voice sharp with urgency, snapping El from her thoughts. She unfolded the clue, reading it aloud again to keep the group focused.

"Yeah, it's gotta be Starcourt Cinema—downstairs!" Lucas shouted.

But El slowed, her steps faltering as she stared into the shadows at the corridor's end. Something felt *off,* a prickle of unease crawling up her spine, like the air itself was watching.

Nothing looked amiss. She sighed, worried that her imagination was running wild again, fueled by her nightmares and past trauma resurfacing, even though she'd closed the gate.

Will slowed beside her, his pale face taut, his sketchbook clutched tight. His eyes snapped to the same shadows, while he rubbed the back of his neck.

"El," he whispered, his voice barely audible. "You feel it, too, don't you?"

She nodded—*once, sharply*—her heart pounding. The Upside Down clung to them both like a shared scar that pulsed in moments like this, binding them in a way the others couldn't understand.

Abruptly, the air grew colder, the metallic scent sharper,

and for a moment, she swore she heard a low hum emanate from under their feet, like machinery waking in the mall's depths, buried under the metal and concrete.

"El, Will, come on! You're majorly lagging!" Max's shout cut through El's thoughts, her board clacking as she skidded to a halt. "We're in this together, and we have to get out of here!"

"Yeah, we need you, El," Mike added. "If we don't want to get lost. This place is like a total maze."

Lucas nodded, fiddling with the map. "This map is useless back here."

"I've got it," El said, hurrying to catch up. She sent her powers out, sizzling like electricity through the air, sensing the way to the movie theater.

"This way," she said, locking on to it.

Everyone followed her deeper into the corridors, then down the stairwell.

Victory seemed within reach.

▶

A few minutes later, they burst through an employee entrance that El unlocked for them, stumbling onto a dark red-carpeted hallway. Max looked around, confirming where they were.

"Look, we found it," she whispered, gesturing for everyone to follow her.

Starcourt Cinema glowed softly on the ground floor, its marquee lights casting a warm amber hue across the deserted lobby. Lit-up movie posters lined the walls within glass frames: *The Goonies,* with its treasure-hunting kids; *Rambo: First Blood Part II,* Sylvester Stallone's scowl glaring down; and *Back to the Future,* a DeLorean blazing through time. The air smelled of buttery popcorn and stale soda, a comforting contrast to the corridor's metallic chill.

"No one's here," Mike said, his voice low, scanning the empty ticket booth and concession stand. "Guess we're the first team to decipher the fourth clue."

"We've got a head start—but that's all it is." Max dropped her skateboard on the carpet with a muffled thud, her eyes darting across the lobby, searching for any sign of the final clue.

"Spread out," she continued. "The clue's gotta be here. Remember, it could be hidden anywhere in the theater. Let's find it before Kyle's crew crashes."

They fanned out, Lucas limping toward the velvet ropes, his fingers brushing the brass posts as he checked for hidden cards. Will flipped through a stack of movie schedules on the counter, their glossy pages curling, while Mike peered behind a large cardboard *Back to the Future* cutout display. He scratched his head, staring at the colorful display.

"I can't *wait* to see that one," Lucas said, pumped with excitement. "That's gonna be the movie of the summer!"

"Yeah, but how exactly do you go *back* to the future?" Mike said. "The title doesn't make any logical sense."

"Right, it's gotta be some kind of time paradox, I'm guessing," Will chimed in. "I bet Dustin could figure it out.

Too bad he's at science camp."

"Time-travel movies always mess up the science," Mike complained. "I bet this one is no different. It's probably pseudo-fantasy more than sci-fi."

"Well, think about it," Will said. "*Star Wars* takes place *a long time ago, in a galaxy far, far away.* Which also doesn't really make sense. Maybe it's something like that? To screw with your head?"

"Stop with spoilers!" Lucas said, plugging his ears. "We're all seeing it when Dustin gets back; then we can break down the logic. Deal? Now stop wasting time—we gotta find that clue."

Lucas dragged them away from the cutout to the ticket booth, where they started searching through the counter.

El moved toward the concession stand, her senses sharp as she scanned the shadows. The lobby felt safe, but the memory of those faceless men lingered, their strange words echoing in her mind. She shook her head to clear it.

"I think . . . it's over there," she said, pointing to the concession stand. "I got the *feeling* that Mr. Clarke was here."

Max vaulted over the counter, her sneakers thudding on the floor. She riffled through a pile of napkins and straws, coming up empty. Worse, something sticky stuck to her hand.

"Ugh, gross," she said, trying to wipe it off, but the napkins only stuck to it.

She held up her hand. It looked kind of like a mummy, covered in paper.

El giggled, but then they both turned more serious,

looking through the shelves, then the popcorn machine.

"Come on, where is it?" Max muttered, her frustration growing.

She kicked an empty popcorn bucket that was on the floor, and then froze. A faint glow peeked from inside, neon orange against the bucket's white rim.

Could that be it?

"Guys!" Max hissed, diving for it. She pulled out a clue card, its edges crisp, glowing under the lobby's lights. "Got it! This is it—the *final* clue!"

Sure enough, printed on the back was that message: "Final Clue."

The group rushed over, crowding around Max as she held the card high. Lucas pumped his fist, his pain forgotten.

"One more, and we win!"

Will's eyes flickered with rare excitement, his sketchbook open, marker poised. "Read it, Max!"

Max grinned, her voice clear and steady despite the adrenaline. "'Where signals hum inside this hut, victory awaits—if you use this device to call for backup, your chances inflate.'"

The words echoed out, then faded away. Silence rushed back in as the wheels turned in their heads. Everyone thought hard, batting around ideas.

"Signals hum?" Max asked with a frown. "What could that mean?"

"A hut?" Lucas said, frowning.

"What store looks like a hut?"

"Call . . . device," El said, her voice halting, thinking of the walkie-talkie and boom box in her room.

Then, all together, they hit on it.

"RadioShack!" they all yelled together.

"Only one of our favorite places," Lucas added. "Wow, Dustin is gonna be so pissed he wasn't here for this one."

"You can say that again," Mike added with a goofy grin. "*RadioShack* . . . more like *Radio Dustin*. It's practically his middle name. I can't wait to tell him."

A moment passed among them. Even though Dustin had only been gone a short time, it was clear they all missed their friend. His absence from their group was enormous and deeply felt.

"Jeez, this scavenger hunt really was designed by a nerdy science teacher," Max said with a grimace. "Good thing we've got you," she added, nudging Lucas. He lit up, smiling back at her.

Their hands snaked together, tentatively, affectionately.

"You see that? Here we go again," Mike whispered into El's ear, making her giggle. Then he elbowed Will. "You owe me for our bet. Twinkies, right?"

Will went into his backpack and started handing them over to Mike, who shoved them into his pockets.

Clearly, Max and Lucas's breakup wasn't going to last much longer.

But then Max snapped out of her moment with Lucas, jerking her hand away and picking up her board.

"Next stop, RadioShack—it's on the first floor, near the atrium! Back where we started. You ready for this?"

El reached out, and Max tossed the card to her, the paper sailing through the air. El caught it midflight with a flicker of her powers, the card hovering briefly before landing in her hand. She nodded, her curls bouncing, a fierce determination settling in her chest.

"We've got this!" Mike agreed, pulling El close. "Let's move . . ."

"But be ready for anything," Max cautioned them. "Usually, final clues aren't as straightforward as they seem. Plus, Kyle and his crew are still out there—probably waiting to ambush us. We have to hurry if want to win!"

Max dropped her board, the wheels humming as she kicked off toward the lobby's exit, her ponytail whipping behind her. El ran beside her, sneakers pounding, the thrill of the hunt drowning out the shadows in her mind.

The boys followed closely, Lucas wincing but keeping pace. They traversed the lobby, their sneakers padding over the brand-new carpet, so different from the trampled, dusty shag at the Hawk Theater in downtown Hawkins. Just like everything else at the mall, the theater had a fresh sheen that practically sparkled. But something still felt rotten underneath it all.

El shook her head, trying to brush off the unease that plagued her. She needed to focus if they were going to win this hunt. The prize—a fifty-dollar gift certificate, a summer of freedom—was within reach. They were so close, she could almost feel it. They just had to stick together.

CHAPTER EIGHTEEN

"We've almost got this locked up," Max whispered to herself.

Her skateboard wheels screeched across the polished marble, weaving through the busy mall, dodging other teams with their neon wristbands, all still working on prior clues. Many of the teens ran for Starcourt Cinema.

"*Celluloid* . . . it's gotta be the movie theater," she heard one girl tell her team as they rushed the opposite direction.

Max smiled in satisfaction, whipping past them, headed for the final location.

One more challenge left. Her heart raced in anticipation. They almost had the hunt in the bag. She wasn't going to let anything stop them now. The fountain burbled as she sped past, her red ponytail whipping.

El ran behind her, curls bouncing, her sneakers pounding in rhythm with Mike, Lucas, and Will bringing up the rear. Lucas limped, his ankle throbbing but his jaw set, fueled by the prize. They were all thinking the same thing.

Fifty dollars was a fortune.

It was easily more money than any of them had ever possessed at one time.

Max's eyes locked on RadioShack's glowing sign, its shelves of gadgets glinting across the atrium.

"Almost there!" she shouted behind her, kicking harder, her board a blur.

But a figure stepped out from behind a potted palm, right in her path.

"What the hell—" she yelped, pivoting at the last second, her board skidding sideways.

She stumbled forward, arms flailing, barely avoiding a bad collision.

Her deck clattered across the marble, spinning under a bench. A taunting voice cut through the mall's buzz.

"You should really watch where you're going. Speeding like that? You could seriously hurt someone."

A dark shadow fell over her. Max jerked her head up, her cheeks flushed with adrenaline, to find the reason for her fall.

Billy loomed over her, his mullet gleaming under the lights. He was throwing her insults from the car ride to the mall about his speeding right back at her—and he was enjoying it.

His breath reeked of stale booze, a sour tang that made her nose wrinkle. From experience, she knew it was never good when he got this drunk.

Worse, he was blocking their path to RadioShack, his smirk sharp as a blade. Behind him, the gaggle of high school girls in tight jeans and lip gloss giggled, their eyes flicking between Billy and Max, clearly enjoying the drama.

Why did her stepbrother always have to ruin everything? Fury surged through her.

"Outta my way, loser!" Max hissed, scrambling to her feet, her hands balled into fists. "Stop crashing my party!"

"Your party?" Billy smirked, stepping closer, his boots scuffing the floor. "Since when? Pretty sure it's a free country last time I checked."

"Just let us through . . ." Max groaned, her voice tight, her patience fraying. El and the boys skidded to a halt behind her, glancing between the siblings, unsure what to do about the family conflict. Billy continued to block them.

"Only if you say the magic word," he said, his grin widening, relishing torturing her. "Please."

The girls giggled at his antics. "Billy, you're so crazy," the blond one with crimped hair said. "Just let her go . . ."

"Tiffany, this is my *rude* little sister," Billy said, slurring slightly. "Max, meet my new friend Tiffany! And not until she learns some damn manners. Say it!"

He lurched forward, swaying on his feet. The smell of booze was stronger now. It made Max recoil in disgust.

"Really? You're the *rude* one," Max shot back, her cheeks burning.

She wanted to shove him and wipe that smug look off his face. Embarrass him in front of the girls. She squeezed her fists tighter. She was outmatched physically, but she didn't care. This wasn't the first time he got in her way, and it certainly wouldn't be the last.

But El's hand brushed her arm, her voice a soft whisper. "You always tell me . . . it's not worth it."

Max simmered, rage bubbling in her chest, but El broke through her anger. She was right. He wasn't worth it. Max wasn't going to let Billy ruin their night—not when they were this close.

It wasn't easy—*everything in her still wanted to fight him*—but she unclenched her fists and made herself back down.

"Fine," she grumbled, her voice dripping with disdain. "Pretty please. With a cherry on top. Let us go!"

"Well, that's all you had to say, little sister." Billy grinned, stepping aside with a mocking bow. He leaned toward the girls, wrapping his arms around their slim waists, their giggles shrill as they fawned over him. Across the atrium, something caught Max's attention.

A mall cop watched Billy closely, his eyes narrowing. A shudder rippled through Max. Billy was always trouble, and that was on a good day, but this felt different. That mall cop looked like he had some kind of grudge against Billy. However, El was right. There was nothing she could do about it. Her stepbrother was never going to change. The best thing was to let it go and try to avoid him for the rest of the night, not that it would be easy.

Max turned back toward her friends. El shot her a look of respect for backing off. El flicked her wrist, so that Max's board rolled out from under the bench.

"Come on, let's go!" Max said, snatching the board and hopping on.

She kicked faster to gain speed, weaving toward RadioShack. El and the boys followed. Their team pulled up in front of this 1980s bastion of electronic glory.

"We're the first ones here," Mike said, squeezing El's hand tighter.

Her heart raced, adrenaline shooting through her. They could all feel it.

RadioShack buzzed on the ground floor, the shelves stacked with walkie-talkies, boom boxes, and gadgets that blinked under flickering fluorescent lights, casting a sterile glow. The air smelled of plastic and metal, a tech whiz's paradise that would've made Dustin drool. Max skated in, her board clacking to a stop, her eyes scanning the store.

Nobody appeared to be working there. The electronics beeping and flashing without human attendants felt unnerving, almost like a sci-fi movie.

"'If you use this device to call for backup,'" Max muttered, repeating the clue under her breath.

Kyle's crew wasn't here—yet—but it was unlikely they had much time before they figured out the final location. El and her friends needed to work fast. They spread out through the store, running up and down the aisles, past the boom boxes and speakers, but nothing jumped out.

El froze and concentrated, thinking about the clue's wording. Suddenly, she flashed back to all those days locked up in her cabin when she used the walkie-talkie to call Mike.

"Look over there," El said, pointing to a display device on the counter, a small electronic gadget with a glowing dial.

Max followed her gaze and brightened. She skated over, snagging it off the glass counter with a grin. She held it up triumphantly. "This has to be it!"

Max turned the gadget over, but the buttons were unresponsive, the dial dim. She popped open the battery compartment, but nothing was hidden inside it.

A dead end. She frowned, her confidence faltering.

El ran over, breathless, her curls sticking to her forehead. Max thrust the gadget at her, repeating the clue. " 'Where signals hum inside this hut, victory awaits,' " she said in a low voice. " 'If you use this device to call for backup, your chances inflate.' "

Then she looked up in defeat. "But I don't understand . . . what else could it possibly be?"

El's brow furrowed, her fingers brushing the gadget's buttons. She thought hard, her eyes narrowing, then perked up. "Hurry. We need a battery."

Max jerked her head around, spotting the boys goofing off by a display of miniature disco balls. "Lucas, Mike, Will, we need a 9-volt battery! Hurry up."

"Roger that," Lucas yelled back, snapping a salute.

He bolted to the battery section, quickly snagging a 9-volt battery. He struggled to peel off the cardboard backing and rip it out of the plastic clamshell. "Jeez, this childproof packaging is impossible . . ." he groaned.

"Guess you must be a child, then," Mike joked, but then turned serious.

He joined in, trying to open it, but also failed. Will watched them in dismay. "Seriously, how many people does it take to open a box?"

He gave it a shot next, but the packaging was tricky.

Max felt impatience rush through her. "We don't have all day! Hurry up!"

Finally, the three of them got the battery out. They tossed it across the store, where El levitated it right into Max's hands, who shoved it onto the prongs.

She slid the plastic covering back on, then turned on the power and twisted the volume button higher. The red light came on, indicating it was working.

She handed the walkie-talkie to El. "There you go! What do we do now?"

" 'Call for backup,' " El repeated, pressing the talk button. Static hummed, a low crackle filling the air. She pointed at Max. "Say it . . ."

Max blinked, then leaned in, her voice hesitant. She felt silly for talking to nobody, but forced the words out.

"Um, I need backup, please . . ."

Static ripped back, sharp and grating, then silence. Max's shoulders slumped, but El held her gaze, unwavering. A beat passed, then Nancy's voice crackled through, loud and clear.

"Your prize awaits inside the tape deck."

Max's eyes widened. She threw the walkie-talkie down and lunged for a boom box on display, the silver casing gleaming. She rushed over, her heart leaping into her throat. Her fingers jammed the eject button, the cassette tray popping open with a click. There, folded neatly inside, was the fifty-dollar gift certificate, its paper crisp and the Starcourt logo shimmering.

"Look, we did it!" Max shouted, snatching it, her grin triumphant.

"You found it?" Lucas whooped, fist-pumping despite his injured ankle. He hobbled over, wincing but his grin breaking through the pain. "Did we actually win?"

Max high-fived Lucas, confirming their win. Meanwhile, Mike hugged El, his arms tight, while Will lingered back, his lopsided smile tinged with something quieter, sadder.

Suddenly, a sharp voice rang out.

"Thanks for solving it for us, losers!"

Three silhouettes darkened the storefront. Kyle, Danny, and Becks loomed in the entrance, their sneers vicious. Everything happened quickly. Danny and Becks boxed everyone out. Kyle shoved Max hard, his chipped tooth glinting. She crashed to the floor with a clatter, her skateboard flying away; then Kyle plucked the gift certificate from her hand, leering.

"Told you what would happen—once losers, always losers."

"Cheaters!" Max growled, tears pricking her eyes. "We

got here first! We already won! You can't just take it."

El surged forward, anger blazing in her chest. The store rattled, shelves trembling, the fluorescent lights strobing. The walkie-talkie on the counter popped with static.

A guttural voice barking in a strange language broke through.

The boom box blared to life, "The Power of Love" by Huey Lewis and the News screaming at full volume, the upbeat chords jarring against the chaos.

Other scavenger hunt teams crowded into RadioShack, younger kids staring at the commotion, their eyes wide with confusion. Was this part of the hunt?

Or was something . . . *wrong*?

A trickle of blood dripped from El's nose. Her powers hummed in her fingertips.

El wanted to fling Kyle's crew across the store and take the prize back. She could feel the power building in her veins.

But Max caught her attention and shook her head, her eyes fierce.

It was her turn to deliver a message.

They're not worth it, she mouthed.

El glanced at the younger kids with their worried faces. The store shook harder, electronics ricocheting off the shelves and hitting the floor. The boom box blared even louder, forcing kids to grab for their ears in pain.

Now they looked terrified.

El's breath caught in her throat. Kyle and his crew stood in front of her with the prize. The one they stole! A torrent of emotions surged through her. Shame, fear, regret—*but most of all* anger.

The store hummed louder, the static crackling, the foreign voices fading in and out. Max stepped closer, placing her hand on El's arm, her voice steady.

"El, it's okay. We can have fun without winning. We don't need that stupid prize. We've got each other."

Mike joined in, his hand brushing hers, trying to break through to her.

"Max is right. Don't you see? You can't let those mouth-breathers ruin our summer. We're together—*and we won this together*. That's what matters."

Those words hit El hard. She blinked hard, feeling tears prick her eyes.

"The Power of Love" swelled, the lyrics a cheesy but fitting anthem. El's breath hitched, her powers surging, but she focused on Max's fierce expression, Mike's steady gaze, Lucas's determined nod, Will's quiet support. Her friends were what mattered—not a stupid prize. Not even realizing it, she had already gotten the summer she dreamed of without needing to win the hunt.

With a shuddering exhale, she clamped down on her powers. The lights stabilized, the boom box cut off mid-chorus, the walkie-talkie fell silent. The store settled, the younger kids exhaling, their confusion easing.

But then, reality crashed back in. Kyle's crew had the certificate, their laughter sharp as they shoved through the crowd with their stolen prize.

Max's shoulders slumped, her board retrieved but her spirit bruised. Lucas rubbed his ankle, his frustration palpable. Mike squeezed El's hand, but his jaw was tight, while Will watched the scene unfold with a haunted look on his face. *Still, it just wasn't fair . . .*

The defeat stung not only because they lost—but because the other team had cheated their way to victory.

But then something unexpected happened. The walkie-talkie on the floor, all but forgotten in the chaos, abruptly came to life with a sharp burst of static. Then a familiar voice crackled over it, cutting through the defeat.

"Not so fast, Kyle."

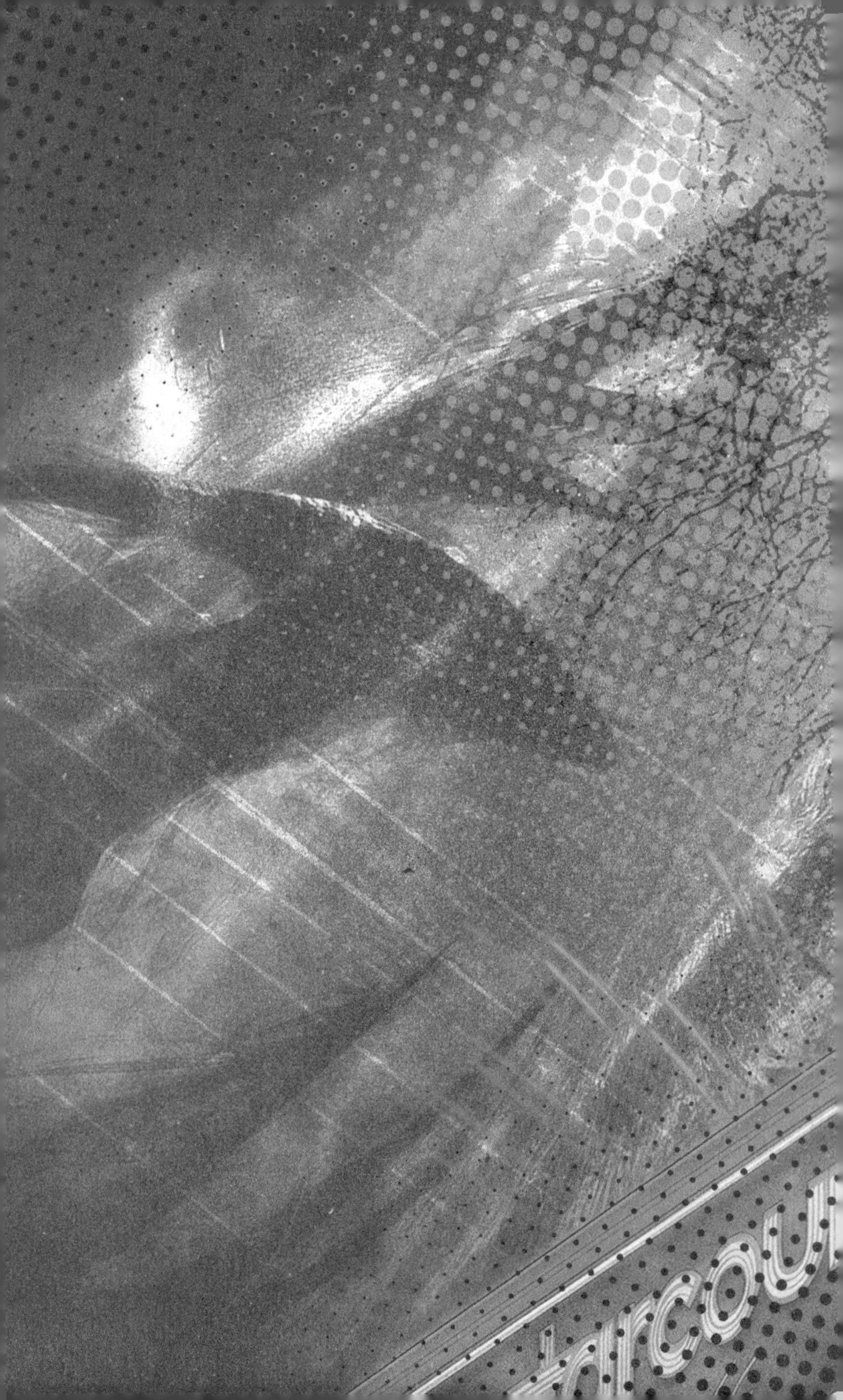

CHAPTER NINETEEN

"Hold on, we're coming in!" Nancy's voice boomed through the walkie-talkie, crisp and commanding, cutting the tension like a blade.

The store fell silent, the younger kids parting as Nancy Wheeler strode into RadioShack, her clipboard clutched like a shield, her ponytail swinging with purpose. The walkie-talkie peeked out of her over-the-shoulder purse.

Mr. Clarke followed, his tweed jacket rumpled and bow tie askew. His eyes looked friendly but stern behind his wire-rimmed glasses. The fluorescent lights steadied, the boom box silent, as if the store itself held its breath.

Nancy glared at Kyle, her lips a tight line. She flipped

through her clipboard, her pen tapping the paper where team names were scrawled.

"Mr. Clarke, Max's team got here first. They solved the clue by radioing me through the walkie-talkie and found the gift certificate in the boom box." She pointed at Kyle, her voice sharp. "Then *they* cheated and stole it from her."

Mr. Clarke's brow furrowed, his teacherly authority radiating. He adjusted his glasses, stepping toward Kyle, whose sneer faltered.

"Young man, is this true?"

Kyle's eyes darted to Danny and Becks, his confidence crumbling. He shoved the certificate behind his back, his voice a whiny snarl.

"No way! They can't prove anything! We found it fair and square! Possession is nine-tenths of the law, right?"

Nancy's eyes narrowed, undeterred. She raised her walkie-talkie, the red light glowing. "Oh, we've got proof."

She depressed the transmit button and spoke into the receiver, her voice calm but lethal.

"All clear! You can come out now."

A figure emerged from the back of RadioShack, his camera dangling around his neck, his shaggy hair falling into his eyes. Jonathan stepped into the light, a sly grin tugging at his lips. Will smiled at the sight of his older brother. He elbowed his friends.

"Look, he's got our back . . ."

Jonathan raised his camera, the lens glinting under the fluorescents. "Smile, losers. You're on *Candid Camera*."

The crowd gasped, kids whispering as Jonathan tapped his camera.

"No way," Kyle stammered, but he looked afraid. "You're both lying! I won the scavenger hunt fair and square."

"Got it all right here," he said, his voice dry. "I was back there to photograph the winners for the newspaper. Max grabbing the certificate, Kyle shoving her, the whole dirty play."

Max's jaw dropped, her eyes flicking to El, who grinned, her tension easing. They both couldn't believe this turn of events. Mike let out a low whistle, while Lucas pumped his fist, his ankle pain forgotten. Will's haunted expression lifted, a rare spark of joy in his eyes.

Nancy crossed her arms, her tone bossy but triumphant. "Kyle, hand it over. The gift certificate . . . now."

Kyle's face reddened, his sneer twisting into a scowl. He glanced at Danny and Becks, who shuffled awkwardly, their bravado gone.

"Yeah, and what if I don't?" he said in a haughty tone, his sweaty fist crumpling the gift certificate. "Until those pictures are developed, you've got no proof. It's just their word against ours. And my friends back me up."

"Yeah, we won," Becks said, but she looked away, not making eye contact.

"Uh, it's ours," Danny offered. But they both sounded like they were lying.

Mr. Clarke had heard plenty of kids try to lie their way out of trouble in his long career. His interior lie detector immediately clicked into high gear. "Then, young man, we'll be forced to call the authorities," Mr. Clarke said, stepping in. He nodded to the mall cops patrolling the corridors. "You clearly violated the scavenger hunt rules by committing *unsportsmanlike conduct.*"

He folded his arms, giving Kyle a disapproving look. "Not to mention, because that gift certificate has a sizable monetary denomination—fifty dollars, to be exact—this would be considered *larceny.* I think the cops might be interested to know about someone trying to commit theft at the new mall."

Nancy stepped away, whispering into her walkie-talkie for backup.

"Yeah, looks like we have a little situation . . . at RadioShack . . ."

Max reached over and squeezed El's hand, the tension thick. The last thing they needed was for Mr. Clarke to call the actual cops, and Hopper to come blazing in and play the hero, only to bust El for sneaking out with Max.

Meanwhile, Kyle's eyes jumped from Nancy to Mr. Clarke, then back to Jonathan and his big camera again.

"Kyle, you heard them," Max said, narrowing her eyes at him. "You stole that from us! Now give it back . . ."

Begrudgingly, Kyle thrust the certificate at Nancy, his hand shaking.

"This is garbage! I'll get you back . . ." he muttered, but his voice cracked.

Before he could say more, two mall cops appeared in

the entrance, their badges glinting. They zeroed in on Kyle.

Mr. Clarke waved them over. "Take them to the office. They violated the Slumber Fest rules. We'll call their parents to pick them up."

Just like that, Kyle's bravado shattered. His upper lip trembled, and tears spilled down his cheeks, his greasy mullet shaking as he started sobbing like a child. Becks rolled her eyes at him in disgust, while Danny stared at the floor, his scarred fists unclenching.

The mall cops flanked them, escorting the trio out, their sneakers scuffing the carpet. Mr. Clarke followed with his clipboard under his arm, muttering about "consequences."

"Ouch," Mike said, grinning as the crowd parted. "That's gotta sting."

"Sick burn," Lucas added, high-fiving Mike, his grin wide.

Will's smile widened. "Those mouth-breathers totally had it coming," he said softly but triumphantly.

Nancy turned to Max, her expression softening. She held out the fifty-dollar gift certificate with the Starcourt logo stamped onto the glossy paper.

"Congratulations, Max," Nancy said with a hint of pride coloring her voice. "Your team earned this."

Max took it, her eyes shining. She spun to El, pulling her into a tight hug, the certificate crinkling between them.

"Look—we did it!" she shouted, her voice muffled against El's shoulder.

El's eyes sparkled, a warmth spreading through her chest. Belonging sank in, deeper than ever before.

She hugged Max back, her curls bouncing, excitement bubbling up. "We won!" she said, her voice bright, the word *freak* fading like a bad dream.

Nancy leaned toward Jonathan, speaking out of the side of her mouth. *"Did you really get a picture?"*

Jonathan grinned, tapping his camera. "You'll never know." They both laughed, sharing a conspiratorial glance.

The other kids cheered, their neon wristbands flashing as they swarmed Max's team, asking questions about the hunt, and how they solved all the clues so fast. Lucas basked in the attention, retelling their escape from the Jazzercise studio, while Mike draped an arm around Eleven, his grin proud. Will sketched quietly, relishing the victory.

But victory came with a new problem—how to spend the gift certificate. The group huddled by the RadioShack counter, the certificate in Max's hand, their voices overlapping in a flurry of ideas.

"We should hit Waldenbooks," Will said, his voice tentative but firm. "They've got the new edition of the *D&D Monster Manual*—"

"No way," Lucas shot back, his hands on his hips. "The arcade's where it's at. Fifty bucks in quarters? We'd rule Time-Out for the next week! I can finally beat Dustin's score on *Dragon's Lair* and get my initials on the leaderboard."

Mike nodded, pointing at Lucas. "Or what about spending fifty bucks at the theater? *Back to the Future* is coming out soon. Remember the rad poster in the lobby? Oh, and I saw that *Dawn of the Dead* is getting rereleased.

We could catch all the big summer movies, get popcorn, candy, sodas—the works."

Max rolled her eyes, clutching her skateboard. "Ice cream at the food court. El still hasn't tried Scoops Ahoy. Or what about Spencer's? Band tees, lava lamps, blacklight posters! You know, we could get stuff that's actually *cool.*"

"What do you mean, *cool*?" Lucas shot back. "I'll have you know arcade games are cool. Mark my words, in the future, gamers will rule the world—"

"Yeah, right," Max said, rolling her eyes.

Lucas shrugged. "It's not my fault that you lack vision. Can't fight the future! *Dragon's Lair* awaits us—and our quarters! With any luck, I can best Dustin's top score before he gets back next week. He'll never believe it!"

"*Dragon's Lair* does sound tempting," Mike said, cracking a little.

"Well, at least it's a game with dragons," Will allowed glumly.

Max frowned in exasperation. Lucas was winning them over to his side, so she doubled down on a spending spree at Spencer's, partially fueled by the major breakup tension still crackling between her and Lucas like a live wire.

El watched them, feeling more and more upset. This was the *opposite* of what winning was supposed to feel like.

They kept arguing, bantering back and forth, and stomping on each other's ideas, and coming no closer to a decision about where to spend the prize.

El stayed quiet and studied Jonathan's camera, the lens

refracting the lights. She remembered the yearbook signing in Mike's basement, her face only a blurry smudge in the background, never part of the class pictures or group shots. She'd never had school pictures, her curls crimped and hair-sprayed into the stratosphere, her awkward smile captured forever.

Flash Studio resurfaced in her mind—a chance to have pictures with Max, Mike, Lucas, and Will, a tangible memory of this summer. But she didn't speak up, her voice caught in her throat, the idea feeling too big, too selfish.

The group's voices rose higher, their disagreement teetering on a real fight. Lucas crossed his arms, glaring at Will, while Max waved the certificate, her patience fraying. "We can't just stand here arguing! We'll never decide!"

Nancy, still nearby, overheard the squabble. She stepped in, tapping her clipboard, a smirk playing on her lips.

"Hey, don't spend it all in one place," she joked. "Well, you *have* to spend it all at Starcourt Mall, per the official rules. But you can spread it around different vendors. You don't have to just cash it in at one store. I bet if you're smart—and do the math—you can all get something you want."

The group froze, their eyes widening as the realization hit. Max grinned, holding the certificate like a trophy.

"She's right! We can split it up!"

Lucas pumped his fist. "Arcade *and* Spencer's! That sounds like a blast."

Will nodded, whipping out his sketchbook to write

down some calculations. "D&D stuff, too."

Mike squeezed El's shoulder. "And the movie theater. We're set!"

El's gaze flicked to Jonathan's camera again, her heart racing. She took a breath, her voice soft but steady.

"Flash Studio," she said, her cheeks flushing. "Pictures . . . with all of us."

The group turned to her, their faces softening. But then Mike frowned.

"El, that would be great and all . . . but we already have pictures. And well, remember the price tag?"

"Yeah, it was, like, almost fifty dollars just for one package," Lucas said. "That would mean—*poof!*—we can't get anything else."

His summer dream of beating Dustin's high score started to evaporate before his eyes. And so did everyone else's dreams. El could see the disappointment on their faces. "It's fine . . ."

But then another voice cut through.

"Maybe I can help."

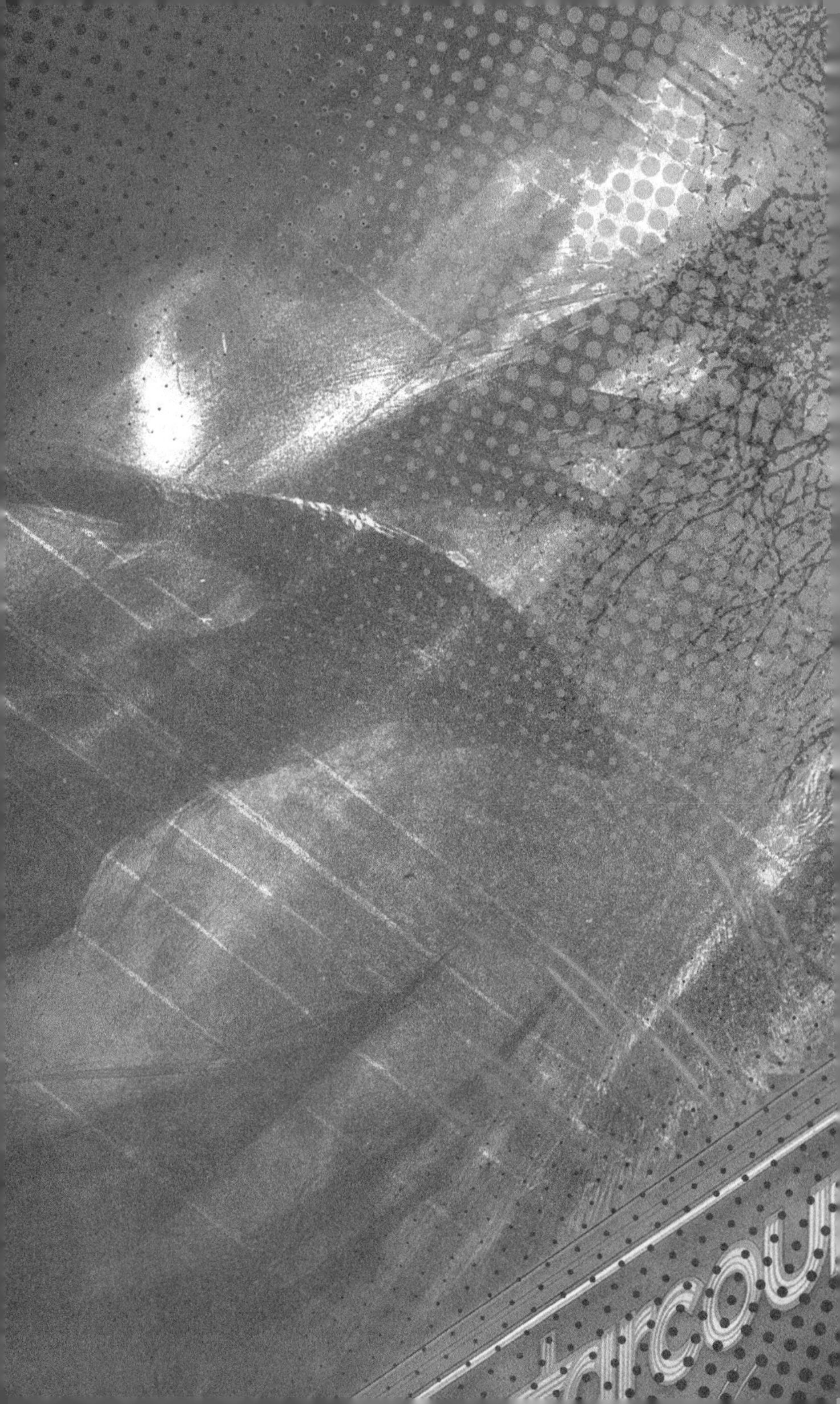

CHAPTER TWENTY

"Pardon the interruption," Jonathan said, leaning over them. "But I couldn't help but overhear your dilemma. And like I said, maybe I can help . . ."

The tension simmered within their group. They all turned.

El tried to put on a brave face, staving off her sadness. "What do you . . . mean?" she asked in a tentative voice, swallowing hard against her crushing disappointment.

Hope had always felt fickle—there sometimes, flickering just out of reach, but more often than not abandoning her when she needed it the most.

"Well, a bunch of my photography buds work at Flash

Studio. We all moonlight for the paper," Jonathan said, holding up his camera. "I could call in a favor. Maybe even shoot and develop the pictures myself to cover the costs."

"Really?" El said, clapping her hands together. "You mean it?"

Jonathan grinned. "Of course! I'm sure they can work something out. For special friends of my family, of course." He knew the role Eleven had played in helping his mother and saving his brother from the Upside Down.

"Without you . . ." Jonathan went on, glancing at Will, his voice faltering and swelling with emotion. "I'm not sure we would've found him . . . *alive.*"

Will shuddered and rubbed the back of his neck, jerking back to memories of that terrible time when he went missing in the other realm. But then he snapped out of it. "Thanks, bro. We owe you."

"No, I owe you," Jonathan said, his voice quiet but steady. "I'm happy to help with the photos, Will. Whatever you need."

That was settled. Flash Studio went on the list. Will jotted it down, along with all the other ideas, to run the calculations. Waldenbooks. Time-Out. Spencer's. A movie night. Last, next to Flash Studio, he wrote *FREE* with a goofy smiley face.

Will scribbled down the rough calculations, adding it all up. "Do we have enough?" Lucas said, on edge.

"Yeah, what's the tally?" Mike said, equally tense with anticipation.

"Come on . . ." Max said, crossing her fingers. Then double-crossing them.

"What, are you crazy?" Lucas said, grabbing her hand to uncross one set. "You're gonna jinx us with that!"

"Well, it's tight . . ." Will said, biting his lower lip and running the numbers one more time. "But I think if we stick to my budget, then we have just enough to do something for everyone . . ."

They all jumped up and down, cheering for the summer reward.

Max signaled for attention with a grin. "Then this summer, we've got a mall spending spree. Deal?"

"Deal," they all replied.

Nancy smiled warmly that all had ended well for their team. She wrapped her arm around Jonathan's shoulders, steering him away from RadioShack.

"You did good back there," she said. "We make a good team."

He blushed, clearly smitten with her. "This summer, the *Hawkins Post* won't know what hit them," he said, as they drifted away toward the atrium. "We'll be like Clark Kent and Lois Lane!"

"Did you seriously just compare yourself to Superman?" Nancy balked in a teasing voice. She squeezed his bicep, but it felt flirtatious. "I think you might need to pump some iron first."

Jonathan acted hurt, but then grinned. "Anything for you, Ms. Lane. You might just be my Kryptonite."

And with that, they exited RadioShack, leaving Max and El and their friends to finish their private deliberations on divvying up the prize.

Max's grin widened, her arm slinging around El's shoulders. "Hell yeah, El! Did you hear what Will's brother said? Flash Studio?"

Lucas nodded, his grin returning. "We'll look so rad. Like, movie-star rad. Get ready to glam up, squad!"

Will's smile was quiet but warm. "Yeah, my brother will make sure to get all the best shots. He's talented."

Mike kissed El's forehead, his voice low. "You're full of good ideas. That will make this a summer to remember. Maybe Jonathan can do some couples poses? You know, since we didn't get any shots together at the Snow Ball?"

El's chest warmed, the weight of her past—*freak*, the lab, the blurry yearbook photo—all lifting. They'd won, not just the hunt, but also a summer she'd never forget, captured forever in a photo.

But before they could plan further, a commotion erupted in the atrium.

Shouts echoed off the glass ceiling, the fountain's burble drowned out by a rising clamor. Max's head whipped toward the noise. She focused on the voice, her heart sinking.

The angry one shouting.

It sounded . . . *familiar.* Max looked up urgently, fear seizing a hold of her.

"What is that . . . Is it my stepbrother?"

El's senses sharpened, her powers unfurling like invisible

threads, probing the atrium. She zeroed in on the source—a flash of Billy's mullet, his leather jacket creaking, his voice slurred and angry as he shoved through a group of teens.

The mall cop from earlier that gave him a dark look loomed nearby, his eyes locked on Billy. They narrowed in hatred.

Another flash from the cop's mind—the blond girl, Tiffany—making out with him on his ratty sofa.

That was his girlfriend.

Heavy emphasis on the *was.* Until Billy intervened today and stole her away. And now, he wanted revenge.

"Get off my girl!" the mall cop yelled, charging at Billy and swinging wildly.

El snapped out of her vision. Her head swam with the vile energy. Her temples throbbed, making her wince.

Max started toward her and grabbed her shoulders, gripping them. "El, what is it? What did you see? Is it Billy?"

El nodded once, sharp, her meaning clear. "Yes . . . not good."

Max's face fell, her shoulders slumping in defeat. "Why is he always causing problems like this?" she muttered, her voice thick with frustration, her earlier triumph dimming. "Just when everything was going great, he has to ruin our night."

The group exchanged glances, the victory bittersweet.

El squeezed Max's arm, a silent promise—they'd face this together, just like the hunt.

Max grabbed her skateboard, and they rushed out of RadioShack and back toward the atrium to get a better look at the commotion. Noises echoed through the mall—

rowdy shouts of teens, the splash of the water fountain, and the sharp crackle of mall cop walkie-talkies.

"Look . . . over there," Lucas said, pointing to the fountain where two men were brawling. "Is that Billy?"

"Unfortunately . . ." Max muttered, immediately recognizing him.

Billy's leather jacket was soaked from his tumble into the fountain, his mullet dripping into his eyes and blinding him as he grappled with the mall cop.

The cop—his face twisted with jealousy-fueled rage—threw a clumsy punch, grazing Billy's shoulder.

Billy stumbled back, his whiskey-soaked smirk unwavering, and then returned the swing, his fist badly missing as he slipped on the slick marble.

They were both hot messes.

"Keep your hands off my girl, you creep!" the cop bellowed. He tackled Billy, both of them ending up splashing around in the fountain again.

Meanwhile, Tiffany shrieked from the sidelines as she clung to her friends, her eyes wide with a mix of fear and exhilaration, clearly enjoying the attention of them fighting over her.

Max stood rooted in place, filled with both fury and embarrassment.

"Goddamn it, Billy," she hissed, her voice lost in the crowd's gasps. "Why do you *always* have to ruin everything?"

Billy swung again—a wild punch—that clocked the cop in the jaw. Blood seeped out of his mouth from where he bit down on his tongue, staining the water.

El fixated on the blood, feeling a flashback to the lab rush through her. But she forced it back and concentrated on the scene, hovering with her friends in the periphery, craning for a closer look. Violence always drew a crowd.

Everything was getting out of control. Now Mr. Clarke rushed onto the scene, looking disheveled, followed by Nancy in a panic. Water splashed everywhere. The crowd grew rowdier, egging them on. Shoving broke out.

The remaining mall cops not involved in the altercation surrounded the area and, at Mr. Clarke's direction, used their walkie-talkies to radio for backup.

A few minutes later, sirens blared in the distance. They grew louder.

Whispers shot through the crowd. "Watch out—cops are coming!"

It was only a matter of minutes before the cops stormed inside to break it up. Mike heard them, too, his eyes widening. "Oh no, anything but that!"

He grabbed El's arm, his grip tight, his dark eyes wide with panic.

"Hopper's on duty tonight, right?" he whispered. "You and Max have to hide! If he catches you here, with me, after you lied about staying with Max? You're back in that cabin till Christmas!"

"More like until I'm eighteen," El said, remembering Hopper's threat.

"Ha, make that thirty," Lucas added, looking worried.

“This *is* Hopper we’re talking about! He tends to . . .”

“Overreact?” Will supplied. “Yeah, kind of like my mother.”

“Yeah, that.” Lucas nodded. “Especially when it comes to Mike.”

He jerked his thumb toward the unhappy couple. El’s heart pounded, her breath shallow. The thought of being on lockdown again—those wood-paneled walls closing in on her—twisted her stomach. She’d fought too hard for this night, this freedom, these friends.

She couldn’t lose it all now.

Lucas nudged Max, who was rooted in place watching her stepbrother, his voice sharp. “Max, move! We’ve gotta get you out of sight before Hopper rolls in!”

Max’s jaw clenched, her eyes locked on Billy, now wrestling the jealous mall cop in the fountain’s shallow pool, water splashing everywhere. The strong scent of chlorine soaked the air.

The crowd chanted “Fight! Fight! Fight!” while others backed away, sensing the party had turned sour.

Max’s gaze hardened, her jaw set.

“He’s gonna get arrested,” she whispered, her voice hot with resentment. “Again.”

Lucas nudged her, his pleading eyes finding hers. “Max, please! Hopper’s coming any minute. We’ve gotta get El out of here.”

Max snapped to attention, her eyes blazing. “You’re right—Billy can rot.” Her voice was fierce, unyielding. “We have to protect El. Come on, we have to hide her. Now!”

She grabbed El's hand, yanking her away from the fountain, weaving through the riled up crowd. But there were people crowded everywhere.

"Where do we hide?" El asked.

"Hurry, behind the planter!" Max hissed, pointing to a massive ceramic planter filled with fake palms, its wide base offering a shadowed hiding spot.

They dove behind it, crouching low, the cool marble pressing against their knees. Max tucked her skateboard close, her breath ragged. Mike squeezed in beside El, his hand brushing hers. Lucas, wincing from his ankle, slid in next, while Will crouched at the edge, his eyes darting to the mall's glass doors.

They were hidden—for now.

But one wrong move, and their summer was over.

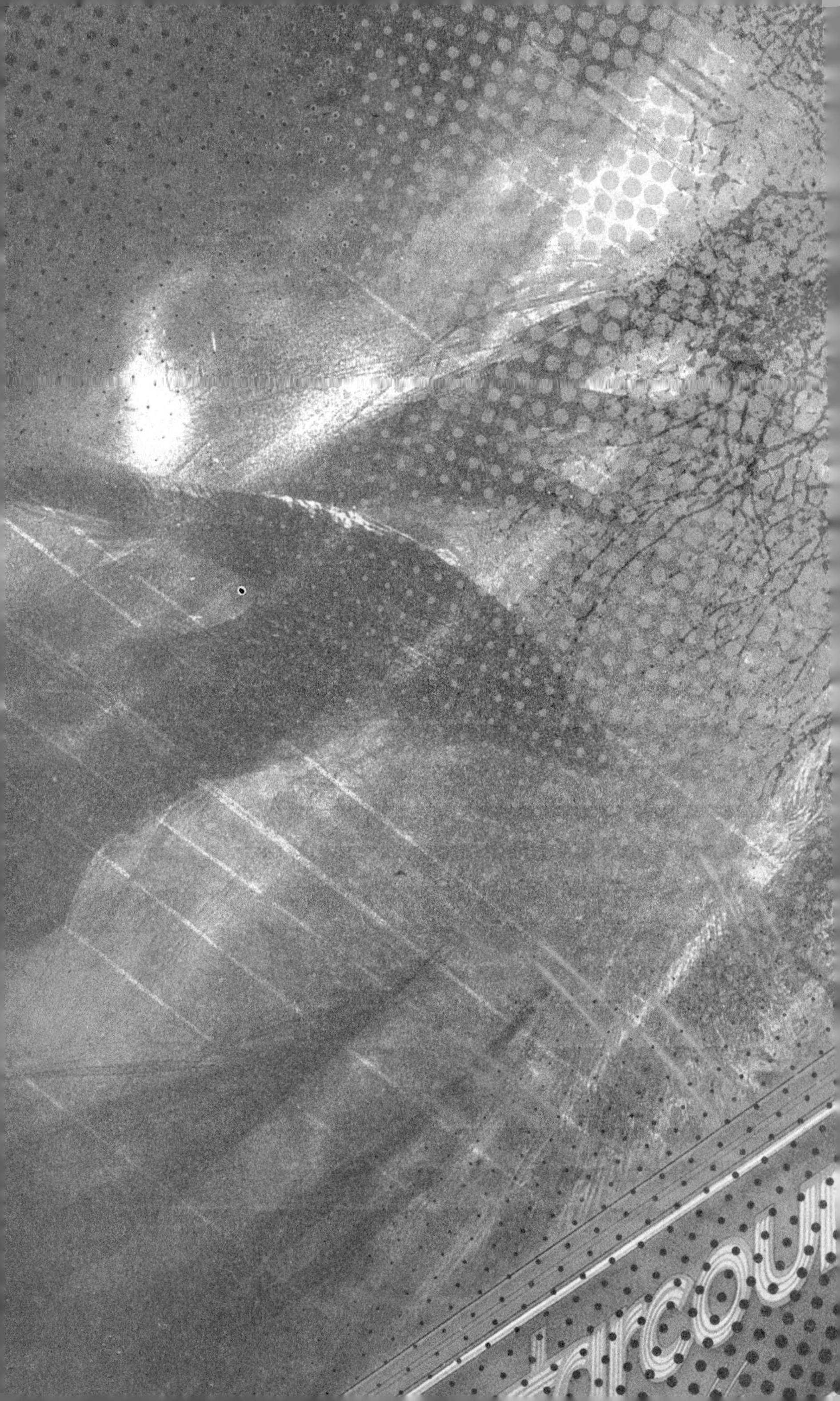

CHAPTER TWENTY-ONE

Mike's whisper was hot against El's ear.

"Whatever happens—stay down. We can't let Hopper see you."

El nodded, her throat tight. They were all crouched behind the planter, but it was a flimsy protection. Sirens echoed in the distance, growing louder. If Hopper caught her here, after she'd lied about staying over with Max, it was back to the cabin . . . maybe forever.

Her freedom hung by a thread.

She pulled her hoodie up, cinching the drawstrings, and peered through the planter's fronds, her heart hammering.

Billy and the jealous mall cop were still brawling in the

fountain, the crowd surging around them. Billy shoved the cop back, his laugh wild and slurred.

Meanwhile, Mr. Clarke continued to yell over the PA system. "Please, back away—and stop the fighting at once!"

But everyone ignored him. The other mall cops stood around helplessly, unsure what to do since the altercation involved one of their own coworkers.

Tiffany screamed, "Stop it, Billy! You're gonna hurt someone . . ."

But he ignored her.

Drunkenly, his fist swung wide, aiming for the cop, but he accidentally shoved Tiffany into the water instead.

She yelped in surprise, her bleached, permed hair turning soggy and limp.

"You asshole!" she screamed, climbing to her feet, then slogging through the water to shove Billy back.

He went down with a ginormous splash that soaked the nearest onlookers, who shrieked with delight and yelled for more. This was almost better than the official entertainment.

Now it was two-on-one—with Tiffany and the mall cop versus Billy—and the crowd was loving it, going crazier and cheering them on. "Slug him, girl!"

Behind the planter, Max's shoulders slumped in defeat, her skateboard tucked close, her eyes locked on Billy.

"He's such an idiot," she muttered, her voice barely audible over the crowd's roar, heavy with shame.

Lucas snorted, watching Billy take a clumsy punch from the cop, staggering.

"Dumbass move!" he whispered, smirking. "Gotta Karate Kid that shit!"

Lucas's amusement evaporated as he watched Max's posture go rigid. He knew she was simultaneously exhausted and furious. Will, quiet beside them, rubbed his neck.

The crowd's noise dipped suddenly, a heavy hush settling over them as the sirens grew louder. Max bit her lower lip, her gaze flicking between Billy and the glass doors. Something shifted in her expression—resolve, mixed with dread.

"Damn it, we have to warn him," she said in frustration. She started to get up from behind the planter, but Lucas grabbed her arm, yanking her back with a firm tug.

"Are you crazy?" he yelped, his voice a harsh whisper. "You *hate* him!"

"Yeah, and Billy is kinda terrifying," Will added, his eyes wide. "Worse than *Gremlins*. More like, *Nightmare on Elm Street* terrifying."

"Look, this isn't about helping Billy." Max looked back in exasperation. "Think about it! If Hopper arrests Billy for the fight, then he might snitch to cut a deal and get out of it. If he talks, then El's busted. Hopper will lock her up—permanently."

"Yeah, but Hopper will be here any minute!" Lucas tried again. "What if he sees you helping Billy? It's too risky . . ."

Max's jaw tightened. "I don't care about Billy," she said, her voice cold. "He's nothing to me. But El's not losing everything because of his mess."

El glanced at Mike, his arm still around her, his nod

subtle but fierce. Max reached back and squeezed El's hand, a silent promise.

They were in this together—and they'd get out of it together, too.

"Okay," Mike said, his voice low, his brain already spinning. "We warn Billy, get him out before Hopper shows. Fast."

Lucas groaned but nodded, his ankle twinging as he shifted. "Fine, I'm in on this crazy plan. But it better work."

"Yeah, or Hopper might arrest all of us at this point," Will said. "My mom will *freak* out, too."

Max's eyes blazed with determination. "It will work. It has to . . . just follow my lead. Okay?"

The group snapped into action, their movements quick and quiet. Mike slid out from behind the planter, his face crumpling into a dramatic, fake sob.

"My sister!" he wailed, snotty and loud, stumbling toward a mall cop near the periphery of the crowd. "I lost my baby sister! Help me!" The cop turned, distracted, his radio crackling as Mike's performance drew more eyes.

Seizing on the distraction, Max grabbed her skateboard, crouching low, and glided silently behind the fountain, her wheels humming against the marble. The crowd was still thick, buzzing with excitement as Billy grappled with the cop, wrestling in the shallow water. Tiffany was now cheering on the cop from the sidelines.

"Jeez, girls are *so* weird," Max muttered under her breath, dodging a kid with a melting ice cream cone.

She reached the fountain's edge, her heart pounding.

Billy was a mess—his mullet dripping, his jacket soaked, his fists swinging wildly. The cop had him pinned down now, but Billy's laugh was defiant, slurred with whiskey.

Max scooped a coin from the fountain's shallow water, its copper glinting, and chucked it hard.

It pinged off Billy's shoulder.

He whipped around, his eyes flashing with anger. "Who the—"

"Psst, sheriff's coming!" Max hissed, her voice sharp but low. "Split . . . *now*!"

Billy's face shifted, understanding washing over it, softening his snarl.

For a split second, their eyes locked—sibling to sibling, a rare flicker of gratitude. *Thank you,* he mouthed, the words unspoken but clear.

Then, with a surge of strength, he shoved the cop hard, sending him splashing into the water. The crowd gasped, some cheering, others scattering out of the way of the sloshing fountain.

Billy didn't hesitate. He vaulted out of the water, his boots slipping, then steadying. Tiffany, still dripping, reached for him, her voice high.

"Billy, wait! Where are you going?"

Billy grinned and grabbed her, pulling her close for a long, deep kiss, her friends giggling and swooning nearby. He dipped her back, then broke away with lipstick all over his face.

"Later, ladies," he quipped, flashing a cocky grin before

bolting toward the glass doors, his jacket flapping.

The crowd broke out in raucous cheers as he bolted away after that dramatic goodbye. Max rolled her eyes, but she was unsurprised by his antics.

What was new?

Billy ran for the emergency exit at the back of the atrium and vanished through the swinging doors.

A whiny alarm sounded, then shut off as the doors slammed shut.

A minute later, his blue Camaro flashed by the front glass doors, speeding out of the parking lot, the tires emitting a high-pitched squeal.

Relieved he made his escape, Max slid back behind the planter, her breath ragged as the group huddled together.

"He's gone," she whispered, her eyes scanning the crowd. "And trust me, nobody's gonna catch him now."

Meanwhile, across the atrium, Mike saw Billy make his great escape and stopped crying. "Uh, never mind. I just remembered! We left my kid sister at home. What was I thinking? My bad!"

The mall cops looked confused, scratching their heads as Mike backed away. He rejoined them, his fake tears gone, his face flushed with adrenaline.

"Nice one, Max," he said, nodding. El squeezed his hand in appreciation.

"You should try out for drama club with that little performance," Max said, impressed. "You've got hidden talents."

That prompted El, still hiding under her hoodie, to peck Mike's cheek.

Lucas smirked. "That guy may be a total jerk, but damn, he's fast."

The crowd began to thin out, the mall cops regaining control. Tiffany and her girlfriends huddled by the fountain, whispering excitedly over the dramatic turn of events, while the cop Billy had fought climbed out, cursing and soaked.

Will stayed quiet, his eyes fixed on the doors. "I hate to break up the celebration, but we're not out of the woods yet," he murmured, rubbing his neck, that haunted look creeping in.

El nodded, her senses prickling. Billy's escape had bought them a moment, but the danger wasn't over.

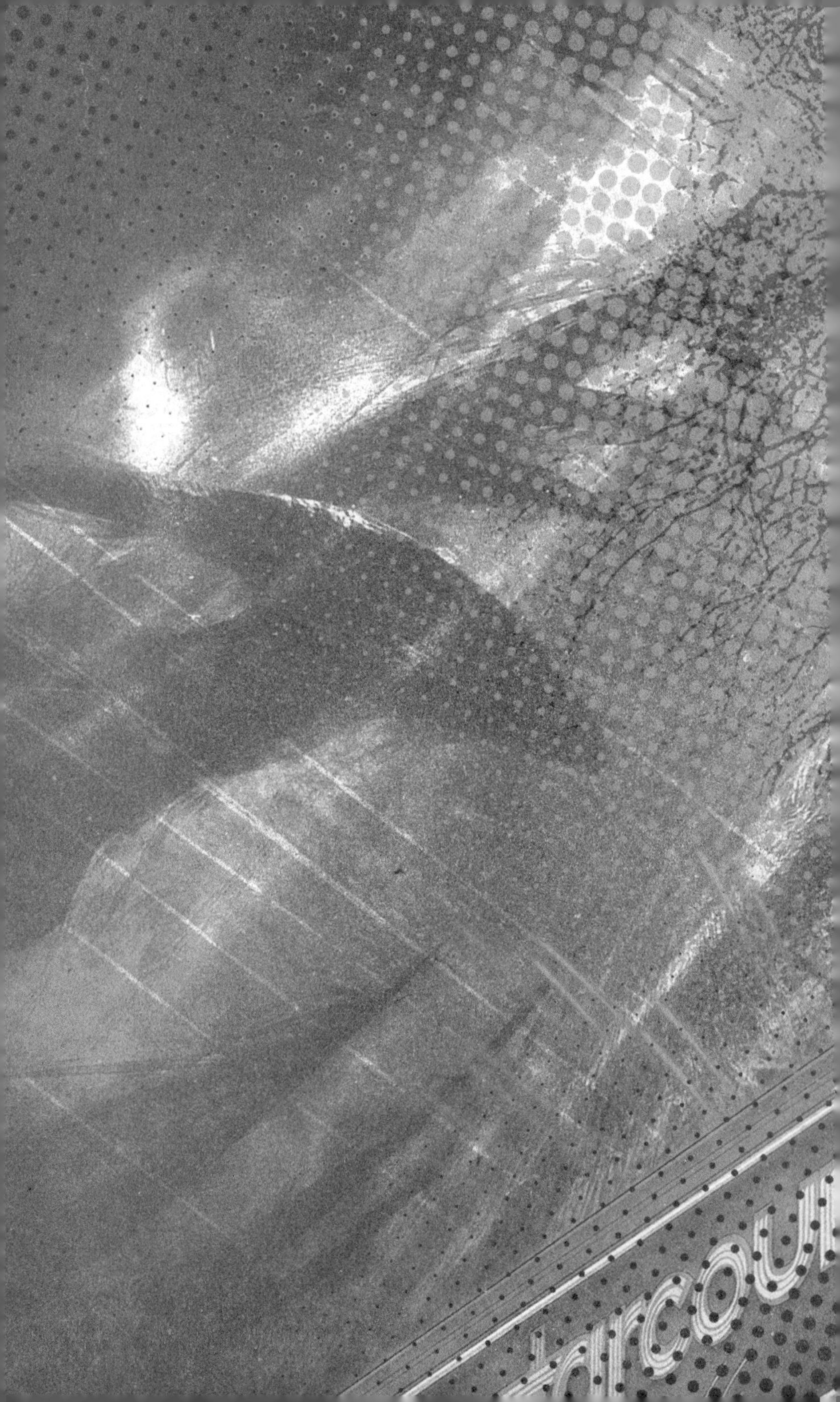

CHAPTER TWENTY-TWO

"Hopper . . . close," El whispered, her voice halting, eyes closed as she reached out with her powers, sensing him coming. Her heart pounded, heavy with fear.

"You sure . . . Hopper?" Max asked, her voice low. "Not . . . other cops?"

"Hopper," El said, opening her eyes. Fear sparked in them.

"Oh God," Mike said, starting to panic. "We're done if he spots us with El."

"Why did Billy have to make a scene?" Max groaned. "It's bad luck."

"Yeah, and why is Hopper on duty tonight of all nights?" Mike added, sounding equally upset.

"Ugh, and why are we hiding behind a planter?" Lucas added, yanking off a frond and throwing it down.

They turned to glare at him.

"The planter? Really?" Mike said with a scowl. "Lucas, focus! We've got bigger problems than plants right now."

"Sorry," Lucas said. "I was just trying to be part of the misery list."

Will just shook his head, watching them with a worried expression.

Before they could complain more, the sirens grew deafening, red-and-blue lights flashing through the entrance.

El's senses sharpened, reaching out again. Her stomach twisted. Abruptly, the sirens cut off, a heavy silence settling over the mall. El jerked her gaze to the glass doors.

That's when it happened.

Hopper's shadow loomed closer, his boots thudding with purpose. He paused in front of the doors. He looked ready for trouble. Worse, he seemed to be in a bad mood.

El shrank back, her breath catching. She reached for Max's hand, clutching it tight, while Mike held her other one. They all crouched lower.

"He's . . . scary," Mike whispered, his eyes darting to Hopper's imposing figure—bushy mustache, wide-brimmed hat, beige uniform with a gold badge over his heart. "Why does your dad have to be the chief of police?"

El gripped Mike's hand tighter, her voice a halting whisper. "If Hopper finds me . . . no more friends."

The words stumbled out, raw and jagged. Her thoughts surged, vivid with dread: No Max. No Mike. No summer. Stuck in the cabin. Alone. Fear choked her, her heart racing at the thought of being locked up in the cabin again for the rest of summer and losing her friends.

Mike's arm slid around her protectively, his dark eyes steady.

"Not if we stick together," he said softly, trying to comfort her. But his voice cracked, his words sounding hollow, even to him.

They watched the mall cops, including the one who got into the fight with Billy, hurry to the front entrance. He had a black eye and a bloody lip.

A heavy *clank* echoed out as the mall cops unlocked the atrium's glass doors, the sound slicing through the chatter like a knife. Hopper strode in, his sheriff's badge catching the light, glinting like a warning flare.

His scowl carved deep lines into his weathered face and his hat tipped low, casting shadows over his eyes as he clocked the remnants of Slumber Fest—the sea of sleeping bags, many now soaked with water from the fountain, chip bags and other trash scattered around, the crowd looking away and dispersing in the wake of the fight.

Each step of his heavy boots thudded against the marble, a slow, deliberate drumbeat that reverberated in El's chest, syncing with her racing pulse. His presence was a force, a storm cloud rolling through the mall, and the kids knew what it meant: trouble.

"Stay down," Max hissed, her voice a frantic whisper as she shoved her skateboard under the wide base of the ceramic planter.

They ducked lower, their bodies pressed tight against the cool marble, the planter's fake palm fronds trembling slightly above them. El's heart hammered. She gripped Mike's hand, her knuckles white, her hoodie pulled tight over her curls to hide her face.

The coarse fabric scratched her cheeks, but she didn't care—anything to stay invisible. Her breath came in shallow bursts, each one a battle against the panic clawing at her throat.

Her eyes darted to Hopper's looming figure, his broad shoulders cutting through the crowd as kids parted instinctively, deferring to his authority.

His radio crackled at his hip, a low buzz that set her nerves on edge.

The planter offered flimsy cover, the wide base barely shielding them.

Hopper's boots stomped even closer, each step a slow, deliberate *thump* that echoed in El's skull. She squeezed Mike's hand harder, her nails digging into his palm.

Hopper's nose twitched, scenting the air, his eyes scanning for something amiss. It was like his sixth sense kicked in—and that was locating his daughter.

"He's right there," Will whispered, his voice trembling as he clutched his backpack to his chest. "If he looks down . . ."

El's breath caught, her vision focusing on anything that might give them away. That's when she noticed it.

The skateboard's edge stuck out slightly from under the planter, the wheels glinting under the fluorescent lights, a dead giveaway if Hopper's sharp eyes caught them. Her mind raced. What if he saw it?

She nudged Max urgently—and pointed to the deck sticking out. Max's eyes widened. She slowly reached out, gently rolling it back toward them.

Squeak.

The wheels emitted a faint noise.

Hopper paused, his boots scuffing the marble just beyond the planter, his eyes cutting their way suspiciously.

The kids froze, holding their breath, their bodies rigid.

The air felt charged, heavy with the weight of his presence, like he could *sense* her. His shadow loomed, stretching across the floor, the brim of his hat casting a jagged outline that seemed to swallow the light. She could smell him now—coffee, cigarettes, the faint musk of his aftershave. He was so close she could've reached out and touched the hem of his uniform.

The seconds stretched, each one an eternity, the silence deafening as Hopper's radio crackled again, a low murmur of static and dispatcher chatter.

"Any update, Chief?" asked the voice from dispatch. "You at Starcourt?"

"Roger that," Hopper replied. "I'm on scene. The disturbance seems to have passed. Conducting reconnaissance."

Suddenly, there was movement across the atrium. Tiffany and her gaggle of high school girls, their permed hair bouncing like a flock of colorful birds, slipped through the crowd with practiced ease. Their heels clicked softly as they wove through the sleeping bags, heading for the emergency exit.

Tiffany's lip gloss gleamed under the lights as she stage-whispered to her friends. "Time to split! Party's over. Smells like bacon." Her voice carried, sharp and defiant, a smirk playing on her lips. "I'm finding Billy. No way I'm snitching to *that* guy."

She jerked her head toward Hopper, her friends giggling as they slipped through the exit, vanishing outside into the warm air like ghosts. The crowd barely noticed, their attention still fixed on the aftermath of the fountain brawl.

"Good riddance to rubbish," Max muttered, rolling her eyes. "Let her chase that dumbass." But her voice sounded tight, filled with worry for her stepbrother, despite everything.

Then something else drew Hopper's attention away from them.

Mr. Clarke rushed over, looking disheveled, his bow tie askew.

"Hopper! Thank God . . ."

"Scott! What the hell happened here? Who was the troublemaker?" His tone was all business, sharp and demanding.

Mr. Clarke clutched his clipboard like a lifeline, his voice steady but tinged with exasperation.

"Billy Hargrove," he said, adjusting his glasses. "Crashed Slumber Fest. Nancy confirmed—he didn't have a ticket. Got into a brawl with security."

Hopper frowned. "What kind of operation are you running here?"

"Everything was going great," Mr. Clarke backpedaled defensively. "Until that hooligan decided to cause a scene."

Hopper grunted, his radio hissing as he scribbled something in his notebook. "Billy Hargrove, huh? Figures. Kid's a walking disaster. Just yesterday, I caught him speeding, but before I could pop him, he got away."

"Guy's an escape artist. He did the same thing tonight. Looks like he slipped away."

"Figures." Hopper nodded, scanning the crowd again. "You're sure? He's gone? Did you check everywhere?"

Hopper gestured around, coming perilously close to the planter where El and Max and the boys were hiding. His stare lingered for a heartbeat too long.

"He's gonna see us," Will whispered, his voice barely a breath, his hands shaking so hard his backpack slipped, hitting the marble with a soft *thump.*

Max's hand shot out, grabbing it before it slid into view, her eyes fierce with warning. Lucas's breath was ragged as he pressed closer to Max, his hand gripping hers protectively.

El thought hard, panic rushing through her. She had to do something—*anything.* If Hopper decided to search the mall rather than chase Billy, even just the atrium, then he'd be sure to find them. The planter barely hid them.

Her eyes narrowed, her focus sharpening despite the fear. She reached out with her mind, probing the atrium, searching for a distraction. The projector booth by the theater entrance caught her attention, its wiring a tangle of possibility. She focused harder, her temples throbbing, her nose bleeding.

Just one spark.

A sharp *POP!* erupted from the projector at the back of the atrium, followed by a shower of sparks that lit up the ceiling like a Fourth of July firework. The crowd gasped, heads turning, kids pointing as the overhead lights flickered wildly, casting jagged shadows across the atrium. The smell of burned wiring cut through the popcorn and chlorine stench, sharp and acrid.

Hopper spun, cursing under his breath. "Goddamn it, what now?"

He stomped toward the booth, his boots pounding, as he barked orders to the mall cops.

"Check the wiring! Nobody move!" His voice was a growl, his attention yanked away from the planter. "Scott, is this damn thing even up to code?"

He pointed to the plugs shoved into power strips stretching across the floor.

"Oh God, it must be water that spilled on the wiring from the fight," Mr. Clarke said, frantically hurrying over to check out the problem.

Max exhaled, her breath ragged, her eyes dancing as her grin broke through. "Nice work, El," she whispered, her voice fierce with admiration. "You're a freaking genius."

El wiped her nose, the blood smearing across her sleeve, but she managed a shaky smile. Her head throbbed, her powers settling like smoldering embers, but she'd done it.

They were safe—for now.

Suddenly, Hopper's radio crackled louder, a dispatcher's

voice cutting through the chaos.

"Suspect Billy Hargrove, blue Chevy Camaro, reported speeding on Main Street. Last seen heading west."

Hopper's jaw tightened, his eyes flashing with purpose. "Roger that. I'm on it. He's not pulling a fast one this time. That kid's got it coming!"

Max's stomach dropped at that, despite her annoyance at Billy for causing . . . well . . . all of this—the brawl, Hopper crashing their night. But they weren't in the clear yet. She held her breath.

Hopper turned on his heel, his boots pounding as he stormed toward the glass doors. But then he stopped by the planter, giving them another scare. El flattened herself, pressing into Mike.

"Oh, and get those wires cleaned up—and we'll let that little violation slide. Got it?" Hopper barked to Mr. Clarke. "Can't let one jerk and a little water ruin the kiddos' summer fun, now, can we?" he added, his expression softening.

Despite his hard-ass attitude, Hopper really was a softie on the inside, especially when it came to the local kids.

"Aye, aye, Chief!" Mr. Clarke said, sounding relieved. "We'll get it fixed and back up and running in no time. Can't have them miss *Ghostbusters*!"

"Who you gonna call?" Hopper joked, his eyes twinkling. "But seriously, call us back if Billy shows up again—or any other troublemakers. Okay?"

"Of course, thank you!" Mr. Clarke said with a relieved smile.

Hopper nodded one last time, then jerked back around. The mall cops let him out, then locked up behind him, the doors slamming shut and clicking into place. A moment later, his Chevy Blazer roared to life outside, red and blue lights slashing through the parking lot as the sirens wailed, and he screeched away, fading into the humid night.

They waited until the sirens faded away completely before letting their guard down. They slumped against the planter with their breaths coming in shaky bursts, their bodies trembling with the aftershock of adrenaline.

Max clutched her skateboard, her grin returning, fierce and triumphant.

"We're in the clear."

Lucas let out a low whistle, rubbing his ankle, his face pale but relieved.

"That was *way* too close. I thought we were done for. But then El did some ghost stuff—*pop*—and distracted him!"

"Yeah, and Billy being spotted downtown," Will added. "That was clutch timing! He caused the trouble—but then he saved our asses, too."

"Yeah, hopefully Billy can keep Hopper on a wild-goose chase the rest of the night," Mike agreed. "So we can enjoy the rest of Slumber Fest in peace."

Mike squeezed El's hand, his fingers warm and steady, his face flushed with adrenaline. He brushed his lips against her forehead, sending a jolt of warmth through her chest. El's cheeks flushed, the fear receding like a tide, replaced by the glow of his words and kisses.

Max jumped up, her energy infectious as she pumped her fist. "It's almost *Ghostbusters* time! We earned this, people."

They slipped out from behind the planter, blending into the crowd as the atrium buzzed back to life. The projector booth's sparks were forgotten, the mall cops distracted, the sleeping bags rustling as teens settled in for the second flick of the double feature—*Ghostbusters.*

El grinned at her friends, her heart lighter than it had been all night. Her ruse was safe—for now. The Slumber Fest stretched before them with the promise of another movie, laughter, and friends. She thought of the gift certificate with the Starcourt logo glinting like a trophy, a reminder of their hard-won victory. The shadows that lingered—the bullies, the lab's echoes, the Upside Down's pull—could wait. Tonight, they'd won, not just the hunt but a summer she'd never forget.

And no one—not even Billy or Hopper—could take it away.

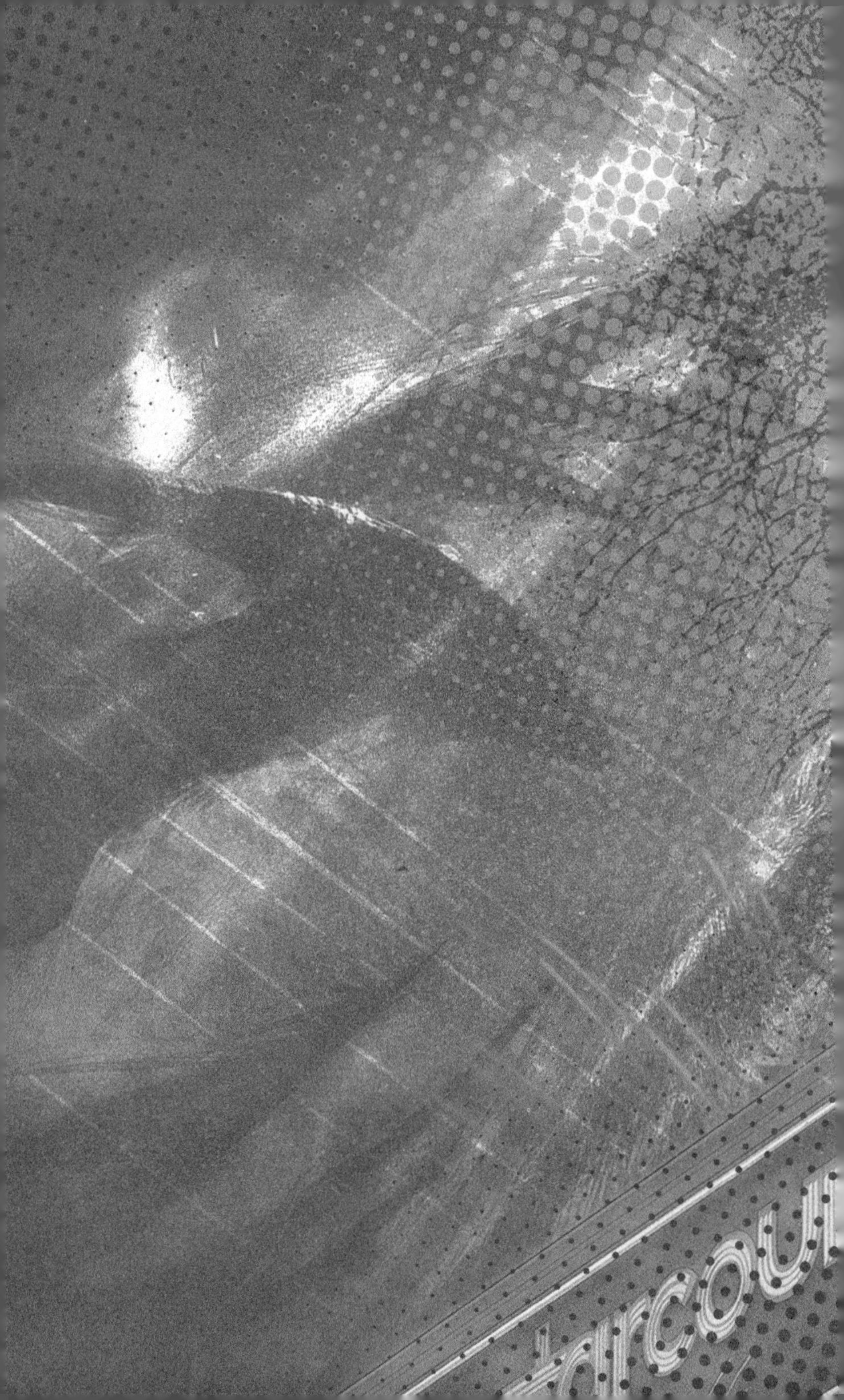

CHAPTER TWENTY-THREE

"Slumber Fest attendees—who you gonna call?" Mr. Clarke announced in a dramatic voice over the PA system, having fixed the wiring issue.

"Ghostbusters!" the kids chanted back, their voices filling the atrium.

Cheers erupted as the lights turned off, casting the mall into darkness. The movie flickered to life on the massive screen rigged above the fountain. The projector's beam cut through the dim light, throwing a glow over the sea of sleeping bags sprawled across the marble floor—neon pinks, blues, and yellows clashing like a multicolored quilt.

Popcorn crunched underfoot, the buttery scent mingling with the fading tang of chlorine from the fountain.

Kids lounged in clusters as they whispered and laughed, quoting lines before the characters could deliver them. "He *slimed* me!" a group chanted as Slimer appeared onscreen for the first time in all his neon-green glory, drawing giggles from the crowd.

"Back off, man. I'm a scientist!" Lucas joked, making everyone laugh, except El, who didn't get the joke yet.

"Don't worry, it's coming up," Mike said, snuggling into her arms.

Max plopped down beside Lucas on his sleeping bag, tossing a handful of popcorn into her mouth.

"Scared of ghosts, Lucas?" she teased, smirking as she nudged his shoulder, her skateboard clattering against the marble as she shifted.

Lucas scoffed, shoving her back playfully, his grin wide. "Please, Slimer isn't even scary. He's adorable! Look at the little guy! And that goofy grin?"

She rolled her eyes. "You act like he'd make a great pet. No thanks! He *slimes* everything. Gimme Gizmo any day of the week over that snot-fest."

"Gizmo?" He gaped. "Are you crazy? He makes like *actual* monsters. Lots of them. And they're slimy little critters. I'll take my chances with Slimer."

El snuggled into Mike on their shared sleeping bag, her hoodie bunched under her head like a pillow. His arm draped around her, warm and steady, and she giggled as

Slimer's gooey green face filled the screen, slurping hot dogs with gleeful chaos.

The movie was a revelation—wild, funny, nothing like the lab's sterile walls or the cabin's grainy TV. It brought a whole world to life. She tilted her head to Mike, her curls brushing his cheek.

"This is . . . fun," she whispered, the word feeling new, like a gift she was still unwrapping. "I like movies."

Mike grinned, his dark eyes soft in the flickering light. "Told you. *Ghostbusters* is the best. Wait till the Stay Puft Marshmallow Man shows up."

"The *what* Marshmallow Man?" she asked, raising her eyebrows.

"*Stay Puft* . . . you'll see," he laughed, and squeezed her shoulder.

Her heart fluttered, the fear of Hopper's close call fading under the warmth of his touch.

Will sat cross-legged on his sleeping bag, his sketchbook open in his lap, his pencil dancing across the page as he captured Slimer's goofy grin. For once, his shoulders relaxed in the thrall of creating. His pencil scratched softly, a quiet rhythm against the movie's proton pack zaps and the crowd's laughter.

He glanced at his friends, a faint smile tugging at his lips. Dustin's absence still hung over them—they'd promised to recap every detail for him—but Will felt lighter, the night a rare escape from the weight he carried.

Lucas leaned over, peering at Will's sketch. "Dude,

that's awesome. We gotta show Dustin when he gets back, right? He'll be so jealous when he hears about all our crazy adventures!"

The movie rolled on, the crowd roaring as the Ghostbusters battled the Stay Puft Marshmallow Man, his sugary rampage crumbling under proton streams. El's eyes widened, enraptured by the chaos, her hand tightening in Mike's. She'd never seen anything like it—heroes who joked, who fought, who stuck together no matter what.

It felt like her friends, their own little team against the world.

Max whooped as marshmallow goo rained down onscreen and the Ghostbusters saved the city from Gozer, tossing more popcorn into the air, some landing in Lucas's curls. He swatted at her, laughing, and the sleeping bag rustled as they wrestled playfully.

And that's the moment it happened—their lips met—and they kissed, camouflaged by the flickering movie. And once they started, they didn't want to stop. This was how it always happened after they broke up. Eventually, they found their way back together again. Their make-out session was interrupted by raucous cheers. They broke apart, blushing.

"Told you it was only a matter of time," Mike said with a big grin. "Looks like I won our little bet . . ." Meanwhile, El nudged Max's shoulder, and they both giggled. Sometimes movie magic led to real-life magic that was impossible to resist.

▶

The credits finally rolled, and the atrium erupted in cheers and clapping. "Ghost-bust-ers! Ghost-bust-ers!" the chants rang out. Nobody was ready for the movie doubleheader to end.

Max stretched her arms high, her voice ringing out. "Best night ever!"

Not only did they win the scavenger hunt, but she got something else, too. She flopped back and leaned against Lucas, her grin wide and triumphant.

The mall's lights remained dimmed—this was supposed to be their bedtime—but nobody was about to sleep. The night stretched ahead, a canvas of possibility, and the group buzzed with energy, not ready to let the magic fade.

Will closed his sketchbook, his eyes bright. "Now can we play D&D?" he asked, pulling out his battered *Player's Handbook* and a velvet pouch of dice. His voice was tentative, but there was a spark there, a hope that tonight, they'd dive into the fantasy world he loved.

Max groaned dramatically, rolling her eyes, but her smile betrayed her.

"Fine. You win. But only because you're so pathetic when you beg." She nudged him, and Will laughed, a rare, unguarded sound that made El's heart lift. Even Max, for all her teasing, couldn't say no to Will's quiet enthusiasm.

They huddled in a circle on the sleeping bags, the atrium's noise fading to a low hum as the boys set up a quick campaign. Dice clattered across the marble, their colors glinting—red, blue, green, like tiny jewels. "You ready?" Mike asked before launching in.

His voice took on a storyteller's cadence, weaving a tale of a haunted keep and a cursed amulet.

Lucas leaned in, strategizing, while Will hung on every word. El listened, her brow furrowed, still learning the rules, but loving the way her friends lit up, their voices overlapping in a chaotic symphony.

Max, restless, tossed a die in the air, catching it with a smirk.

"This is cool, but enough of this nerd stuff. Let's spice it up. Truth or Dare. Who's first?" Max's eyes gleamed with mischief, and the group groaned, knowing her dares were legendary.

Lucas pointed at her, matching her mischievous grin. "You're on. Dare."

Max focused, scanning the atrium for something good. "Drink a sip of fountain water. I dare you! Right now."

The group erupted in disgust, Mike gagging dramatically. "That's nasty! Billy was just wrestling in there!"

Lucas paled but stood, limping slightly on his sore ankle. "That's pretty foul, but fine! No way I'm losing."

He scooped a handful of water from the fountain, screwed up his expression, then slurped it down, grimacing.

"Tastes like . . . chlorine and regret."

The group howled, Max clapping like a proud coach. "That's my man! Who's next?"

Will raised his hand, his voice soft. "Dare," he said to everyone's surprise.

Max pointed to someone's discarded Scoops Ahoy container filled with melted ice cream, a crumpled bag of Doritos, and the remnants of a chili dog left on the lid of the trash can. "Mix melted ice cream, crushed Doritos, and the rest of that hot dog. Eat a bite. I dare you."

Will's eyes widened in disgust, but he nodded, not daring to back out. He grabbed the ice cream cup, shook in the Doritos crumbs, and added the chili dog, stirring it into a lumpy mess.

He grimaced and took a cautious bite. The group stifled their laughter, tears streaming as Will chewed, his face twisting, then brightening with surprise.

"Tastes . . . surprisingly good," Will said, grinning. "You should try it!"

"No way!" Lucas said, miming barfing. They all laughed again.

Once they recovered, Mike was next, and Max's grin turned wicked. "Dare. Kiss El. Right here, right now."

Mike's face turned beet red, and the group catcalled, Lucas whistling. El's cheeks flushed, but she leaned in, her heart racing. Mike's lips met hers, soft and quick, a spark that sent warmth through her veins. The group groaned, Max fake-gagging, but El smiled, her fingers brushing Mike's hand, the moment perfect despite the teasing.

Max's turn came. She knew if she picked dare, then Mike would make her kiss Lucas as payback, but their reconciliation still felt too fresh to have the additional scrutiny right now.

"Truth," Max said, her voice bold. She glanced at Lucas, and he looked relieved. *Thank you,* he mouthed.

El hesitated, her question soft but heavy. "Are you *really* my friend?"

The group fell silent, the atrium's noise fading. Max's grin softened. "Like, obviously," she said, her tone light but her eyes serious. "You're stuck with me, whether you like it or not."

They all laughed. Max pulled El into a tight hug, and El's throat tightened, the acceptance washing over her.

The game continued, dares growing sillier—Max skated down the atrium stairs, her board clattering as she landed with a whoop, drawing glares from mall cops. Lucas had to sing "Never Gonna Give You Up" at full volume, his voice cracking as kids nearby laughed.

The night grew later and blurred into a montage of giggles, dares, and a few deeper truths, the group's bond tightening with every shared moment.

Dawn peeked through the glass dome, a soft pink glow filtering through the atrium. The kids were exhausted, their eyes heavy, but their smiles lingered. Mr. Clarke clapped his hands, his voice cheerful despite the long night. "All right, Slumber Fest! Time to roll up those sleeping bags and pack up. Our night is officially over!"

Kids groaned, yawning as they folded their gear, the atrium buzzing with sleepy chatter.

Jonathan snapped a few last pictures, then joined Nancy while she packed up the registration table. They both yawned, but looked happy. Robin and Steve rode the escalator down, having finally locked up Scoops Ahoy.

"Dingus, don't forget to say goodbye to your kids," Robin joked, shoving him their way. He stumbled over, looking disheveled. His iconic hair stuck up at least two inches and had what looked like chocolate ice cream caked into it.

"Uh, bye . . . let me know when Dustin gets back, okay?" he said, sounding bleary and exhausted.

El helped Mike roll up his sleeping bag, her heart full. The night had been everything she'd dreamed—movies, friends, a taste of normalcy. She glanced at Max, who collected her skateboard and her backpack. Lucas and Will argued over who'd carry the D&D gear, their voices warm with familiarity.

As the mall's glass doors unlocked with a heavy *clank*, the crowd shuffled toward the exit, the morning light harsh after the dim light of the mall. They were headed toward the doors when a figure darted through the crowd, her permed hair and chunky earrings bouncing.

Tiffany, Billy's crush from the night before, rushed up to them, her lip gloss smudged, her eyes wide with nerves.

"Max!" she hissed, grabbing Max's arm, her voice low. "There you are!"

Shock ripped through Max, chased by a healthy dose of suspicion. "What are *you* doing back here? Didn't you run off with my meathead stepbrother?"

Tiffany glanced nervously at the mall cops standing by the doors. "Listen, Billy's out back with a message. You have to get out of here . . . now!"

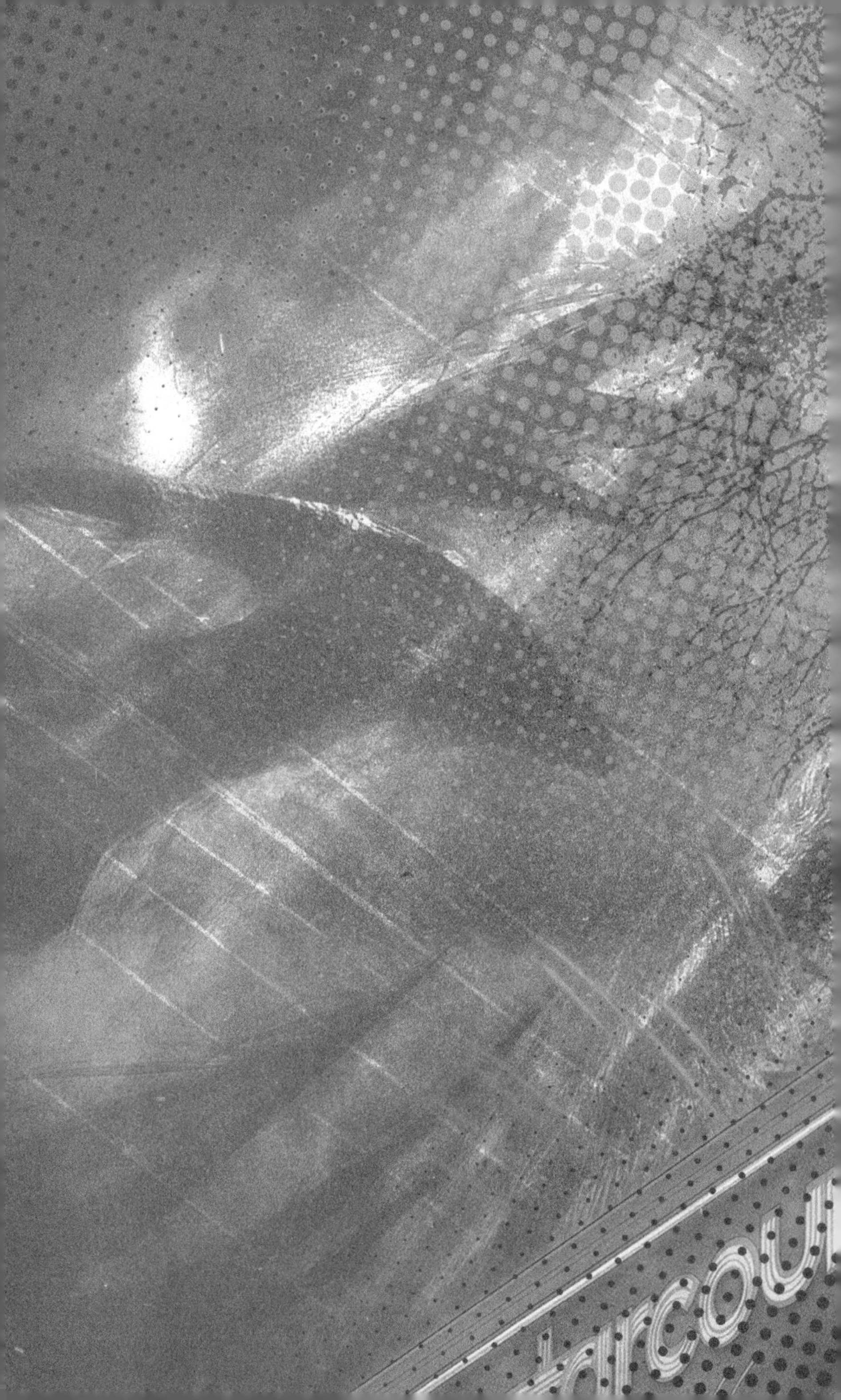

CHAPTER TWENTY-FOUR

Tiffany grabbed Max's arm, her voice a sharp hiss. "Max, listen! Billy sent me to warn you. Hopper's been sniffing around your trailer—came by looking for you. *And* his daughter."

Max's face paled, fear erupting. "What do you mean? What did he say?"

Tiffany shrugged, her permed hair bouncing. "Well, he was chasing Billy but put it together. Something about you two not being where you're supposed to be. He's pissed. Billy bought you some time—sent him on a wild-goose chase to that sketchy skate park in the woods—but Hopper's not dumb. He'll figure it out soon."

El's face drained of color, her breath catching. "Oh no . . . that's bad."

The word *lockdown* echoed in her mind, a prison door slamming shut. She'd fought too hard for a normal summer to lose it now. Meanwhile, Max cursed under her breath, her eyes blazing.

"She's right. That idiot bought us time, but not much! Not to mention, he caused this whole mess." She spun to the group, her voice urgent. "We gotta move—*now*!"

Lucas's eyes widened, panic flashing across his face. "You're right—it's only a matter of time before he circles back to check the mall. We're so dead!"

Mike grabbed El's hand, his grip tight, his voice cracking. "We can't let him find you here!"

Will rubbed the back of his neck, his haunted look returning. "Another chase? Seriously?" His eyes darted to the glass doors, scanning for Hopper's Chevy Blazer roaring up.

El closed her eyes, her powers unfurling like invisible threads, probing the world beyond the mall. A familiar pressure swelled behind her eyes. She felt it—the low, predatory hum of Hopper's Blazer engine, heading back toward Starcourt Mall, the headlights slicing through the dawn's pink haze. Her stomach twisted, dread spiking like a knife.

"He's already on his way!" she whispered, her voice raw. "He's close."

Max's jaw tightened, her decision made. She clutched her skateboard, her red ponytail swinging as she turned to El. "We're getting you home like we promised before he can bust us."

"But how do we get back to the cabin?" El asked, feeling panicked.

Tiffany cut in, twirling her hair around her fingers. "Bill's out back waiting. Can't he take you?"

They all perked up.

Max nodded. "You're right. Billy's our ride—he owes me that much. I never thought I'd say this, but we're in luck. He drives really fast. If anyone can evade your scary cop dad and get you back home, it's Billy."

El remembered their stomach-churning trip to the mall but forced herself to embrace the need for speed. Billy was definitely their best—and really, only—option at this point.

But then another obstacle occurred to her. El looked to the mall's front entrance, where Hopper's truck would appear any second. The emergency exit at the back was no good—Mr. Clarke and a cluster of mall cops lingered there, chatting and sipping coffee. The atrium was a trap, the open area offering no cover.

"I hate to be a bummer," Mike said, "but how do we sneak you out of here?"

Max's eyes lit up, a spark of rebellion flaring. "I've got it—Steve! He can get us into the employees' area. We'll sneak out through Scoops Ahoy and find Billy in the parking lot!"

"Steve?" Lucas asked, his brow furrowing. "You sure he's still here? I just saw him leaving. Guy looked like he was about to pass out."

"He's our best shot," Max said, already moving. "Come on! We have to catch him before he dips."

Mike and Lucas sprang into action, weaving through the crowd of yawning teens rolling up sleeping bags. They spotted Steve near the fountain, his Scoops Ahoy uniform rumpled, his iconic hair a chaotic mess of chocolate-streaked curls. Robin stood beside him, her arms crossed, smirking.

"Uh, don't look now, dingus, but your kids are back," she quipped, nudging him. "You're *so* popular."

Steve blinked, bleary-eyed, his voice groggy. "What now? I just locked up. You guys need *more* ice cream?"

"I never thought I'd say this—but there's no time for ice cream!" Mike whispered, his voice urgent. "We need your help to get into the employees only area again. Hopper's coming back, and well . . . El *can't* be here."

Steve's eyes widened, the exhaustion fading as he clocked their panic. He put together that Mike *plus* Hopper's daughter meant major trouble.

"Hopper? Say no more." He glanced at Robin, who was already grabbing her backpack. "You in?"

Robin sighed dramatically but nodded. "Fine, but only because this sounds like a way better story than crashing out at home." She smirked at Steve. "Guess we're back on babysitting duty. Let's move, superfreaks."

"You're not leaving without me," Tiffany said. "Your brother might be a mess—but he's a mess I can't resist."

Max gaped at her, then hissed to El. "What is wrong with . . . *girls*? Plus he's my *step*brother."

But there was no point ditching her. Plus, she'd come to warn them.

Lucas nodded to Mr. Clarke and Nancy, who were still hanging around, overseeing the Slumber Fest cleanup.

"We'll distract them, buy you more time," Lucas whispered. "Just hurry!"

Mike nodded. "Don't get caught, El. We'll meet you back at the cabin later."

He gave her a quick kiss—his soft lips lingering on hers for a moment longer—then reluctantly broke away.

"Get a room already!" Lucas groaned, pulling him away. Watching Lucas, Will, and Mike leave, El's heart raced, both from the kiss and Hopper's imminent return.

She and Max followed Steve and Robin, with Tiffany tagging along, toward the escalator. They clambered onto it, but the metal steps were still, the mall powering down for the morning, but El focused, her powers humming.

With a flick of her wrist, the escalator groaned to life, jerking upward. Max yelped, grabbing the railing, while Steve muttered, "Jesus, warn a guy!"

"Uh, how'd she do that?" Tiffany said, clutching the railing in fear. "Is this some kind of magic trick?"

"Don't ask—just hold on," Max shot back, already scrambling toward the top. "It's gonna be a wild ride."

They reached the food court, the Scoops Ahoy sign glowing faintly in the dim light. Steve fumbled with his keys, his hands shaking from exhaustion or nerves—or both.

"Come on, come on," he muttered, the key scraping the lock.

El's senses sharpened, her powers probing outward. A

jolt hit her—Hopper's truck screeched into the parking lot, its headlights flooding the glass doors below. "Hurry!" she gasped, her voice tight. "He's here!"

"Dingus, let me try," Robin snapped, snatching the keys. Her fingers were steadier, and the lock clicked open with a satisfying *thunk*. She pushed the door wide open, and they bolted into the back of Scoops Ahoy, the smell of waffle cones and melted ice cream thick in the air.

Below, Hopper strode into the atrium, his boots thudding on the marble, his badge glinting under the fluorescent lights. El's powers zeroed in on him, her vision tunneling as she sensed the exchange unfolding. Mike stood near the fountain, his face pale but composed, Lucas and Will flanking him.

Hopper's unmistakable voice boomed, cutting through the chatter.

"Mike Wheeler, where's my daughter?" His tone was pure dad-cop, sharp and unyielding. "Don't lie to me, kid. I know she's not at Max's house."

Mike swallowed hard, his voice steady despite the sweat beading on his forehead. "I don't know, sir. Just us boys here!" His voice cracked badly. "Except Dustin—he's at summer sleepaway camp."

Hopper's eyes narrowed as he sized Mike up.

"Checked Max's place, like I said, chasing her no-good stepbrother Billy. *Empty.* Checked that damn skate park in the woods, too—nothing but punks causing trouble. You telling me you don't know where she is? And that she wasn't at Slumber Fest last night?"

His voice was sharp; his steely gaze bored into Mike, making him squirm.

Lucas jumped in to save him, his voice smooth. "Did you try downtown? Max likes to skate there. They might be waiting for Palace Arcade to open?"

"Oh yeah, that's right!" Mike face-palmed himself. "We had tentative plans to meet up later today."

"Yeah, you know, to do *innocent* kid stuff . . . like play video games," Lucas provided with a big, forced grin. "Maybe they're killing time nearby?"

Hopper grunted, his suspicion lingering, but he took the bait.

"Downtown Hawkins, huh? Better not be wasting my time, Sinclair." He pivoted to Mike, glaring at him. "And I'll deal with you later. Got it?"

"Yes, sir." Mike gulped, not liking the sound of that.

Hopper turned, his boots stomping toward the exit, his radio crackling as he barked orders to check downtown and the arcade. Back upstairs in Scoops Ahoy, El exhaled, her nose bleeding slightly from the effort of her powers.

"Hopper's leaving . . . he bought it," she whispered, wiping the blood with her sleeve. "But not for long. I have to get back to the cabin . . . and fast."

"Then we move *now*," Max said. She led the way through the back of Scoops Ahoy, past the industrial freezers and stacks of waffle cone boxes toward the door marked EMPLOYEES ONLY.

Using his keys, Steve unlocked it. The door swung

open with a reluctant groan. They stepped into the dimly lit corridor. The walls beyond were cinder block, the air cool and musty, a stark contrast to the chaos of the mall. Steve and Robin followed, their sneakers squeaking on the linoleum. Tiffany wandered behind them, looking more than a little freaked out.

"This way," Steve said, pointing to a freight elevator at the corridor's end. "This will take you down to the loading dock out back where Billy's waiting."

Max nodded, her grip tight on her skateboard. "He better be. I'm not in the mood for his games."

"You're telling me," Tiffany said, rolling her eyes. "He better not have ditched me after I stuck my neck out."

They reached the elevator, but the control panel needed a key to summon it. Steve cursed, patting his pockets. "Damn, I don't have the key for this one."

El stepped forward, her eyes narrowing. "I do." She focused, her powers surging, a trickle of blood dripping from her nose. The lock turned slowly, then the down button lit up. The elevator groaned to life, and a few seconds later, the large door retracted.

Steve gaped, but Robin just grinned.

"Remind me not to piss you off," she quipped, holding the door open.

Max, El, and Tiffany boarded the elevator. Max jammed the button. The door slid shut, and the elevator carried them down to the first floor, making their stomachs flip. A few seconds later, it spit them out into a large loading dock filled with wooden crates, all marked with strange letters.

Dark shadows stretched out, grabbing for them. A rat scampered away—*squeak*—as if offended they invaded its territory. "What is all this . . . stuff?" Tiffany asked. "Is this like mall merch?"

"Probably," Max said, but she frowned. Something about the shipments felt . . . off. But she couldn't explain it. El looked equally concerned.

A quick flash hit her—a gash in the concrete spilling out fiery light, a tentacle ripping through the gate into their world, wrenching it open—but then she blinked, her breath hitching in her throat. And it was . . . gone.

"El, you okay?" Max said, jerking her back. "Hurry, we have to find Billy."

The garage door to the loading dock was half raised, letting morning light spill in, breaking up the shadows.

"Over there!" Max said, throwing her skateboard down and kicking forward. El and Tiffany followed her.

Suddenly, two men in dark coveralls marked with *Lynx Transportation* spotted them. They looked up from their clipboards, shouting at them in a strange language. The words were foreign—but the threat was clear.

"Oh no," Max said. "Run!"

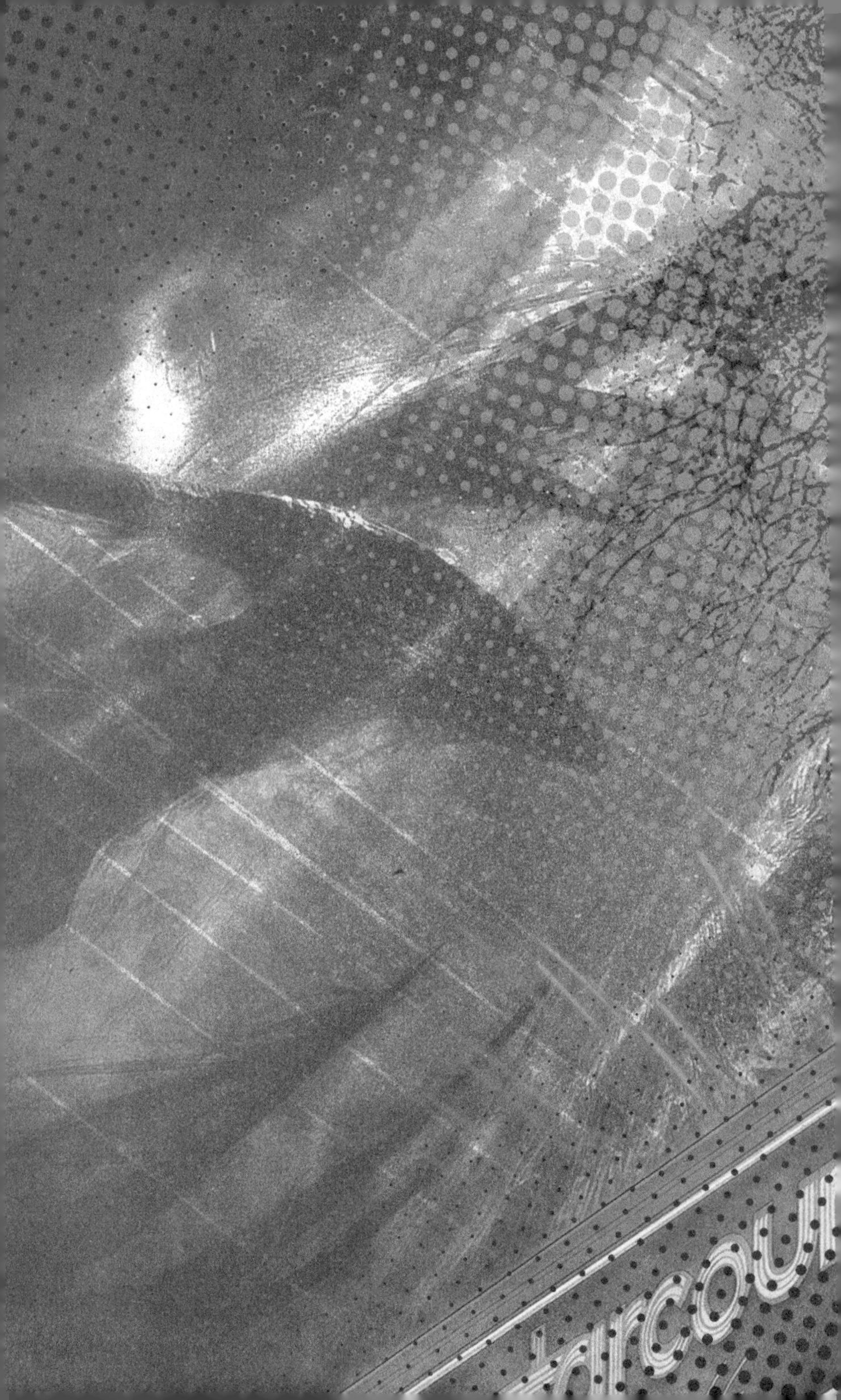

CHAPTER TWENTY-FIVE

"This way!" Max said, her skateboard clattering as she kicked forward through the cavernous loading dock with El and Tiffany sprinting behind her, their breathing ragged.

Max leaned low and pivoted toward the crates, skating between them. The men in dark Lynx Transportation uniforms shouted and chased after them, their voices sharp and guttural, spitting words in an unknown language—harsh, clipped, not English. El glanced behind her. Their faces were obscured, not quite right, like masks of shadow under their caps.

"Let's Houdini!" Max hissed as she dodged a stack of crates marked with strange, angular symbols. El's heart pounded, her powers buzzing, sensing the men's boots pounding closer, their shouts echoing off the cinder-block walls.

"They're just mall security, right?" Tiffany panted, her voice high with panic.

"I dunno," Max said uncertainly, kicking faster. "But pretty sure we're not supposed to be back here!"

El's gut twisted. Something about the men felt *wrong*—too menacing for mall cops chasing stray kids. Her mind flashed to the lab, to Papa's cold orders, to faceless figures in sterile halls. She shook it off, focusing on Max's back as they sprinted toward the garage door, the sliver of sunlight a beacon.

"That's our ticket out!" Max pointed, her board skidding as she swerved around a forklift. "Follow me!"

The door loomed ahead, half raised, the gap just wide enough to slip through. El's powers hummed, itching to lash out, but she held back—too risky, too many eyes. She had to trust Max.

The men's shouts grew louder, boots slamming closer. One grabbed a walkie-talkie and barked into it. El glanced back, her vision sharpening—their faces were still blurred, like a photo out of focus, sending a chill down her spine.

"Faster!" she urged, her voice tight. She nudged Max's board with a flicker of thought and the wheels spun faster, propelling Max toward the exit. Tiffany yelped, stumbling but keeping pace.

They dove under the garage door, ducking and rolling into the service lot, the morning sun blinding after the loading dock's gloom. The air hit them all at once—hot, thick with asphalt and diesel fumes. The day promised to be an early summer scorcher.

"Where's the dumbass?" Max muttered, clutching her board and scanning the seemingly empty lot.

"That *moron* better not have ditched me!" Tiffany whined, jerking her head around. But then El shut her eyes.

"Back there—behind the dumpster!" she whispered, pointing.

They bolted that way, cutting around the rusty metal dumpster. Sure enough, Billy's blue Camaro idled at the lot's edge, the engine growling like a caged beast, heavy metal blaring from the open windows. Billy sat behind the wheel, his mullet sweaty and slick, a half-burned cigarette dangling from his lips. His leather jacket creaked as he straightened, spotting them, his smirk whiskey-soaked but sharp.

"Nice of you to show up, Mad Max," he drawled, his eyes flicking to El. "You and your weird friend in trouble?"

"Shut up and drive," Max snapped, yanking open the back door.

El slid in beside her, the leather seats hot against her skin, the car reeking of cigarettes and booze. Tiffany hopped into the front, her lip gloss smudged, her grin defiant. He popped a kiss onto her lips. "You miss me?"

She slugged him. "You better have missed me! I did you a solid with your brat sister. Now you owe me one."

"Does this help?" he asked, passing her the flask. She sipped at it, appeased.

Max's heart hammered faster. They got away—*for now*—

but it was only a matter of time before those men came looking for them. They were bound to get spotted. Not to mention, Hopper was on the prowl, looking for El.

"Hey, Bonnie and Clyde," Max snapped. "What part of shut up and drive did you *not* understand?"

Billy raised his hands in surrender. "Don't have to tell me twice, little sis!"

With another smirk and drag on his cigarette, he floored the gas, the Camaro's tires screeching as it peeled out of the lot. Tiffany squealed, then took another swig, while Max and El gripped the seat, their stomachs lurching as the car swerved into a narrow alley, churning loose gravel. A minute later, it spit them out onto a back road, the mall shrinking in the rearview mirror.

El's powers buzzed, tracking Hopper's Blazer—it was heading toward the arcade, but he'd realize soon enough that it was a dead end.

"So, where to?" Billy asked. His voice sounded sarcastic, but something else animated it. He knew Max saved his ass from the cops earlier that night. He owed her.

Max leaned forward, her voice urgent. "Right, we need to get El back to the cabin before Hopper figures out that she didn't sleep over at our place."

"Ha, you pulled a fast one on her cop dad?" Billy snorted, his eyes on the road. "Wow, you're crazier than I thought, Mad Max," he quipped.

"Please, I don't need a lecture," Max said with a scowl. "Can you get us back to the cabin before he busts us?"

"Can I? How dare you insult me!" Billy smirked, the cigarette bobbing. "Do I have a need for speed or what?"

He gunned the accelerator to emphasize his point, then whipped the car into a 180-degree turn, cutting the other way toward the cabin. Gravel spewed, chased by bitter exhaust. El reached for Max's hand, gripping it.

"Hopper's obsessed with catching me, but I'm faster." Billy glanced at El in the mirror, his smirk softening. "Don't worry, kid. I'll get you home."

El nodded, her throat tight. The Camaro roared through Hawkins's back roads, weaving past cornfields and dense pines, the morning sun glinting off the hood. They were moving fast, but so was Hopper in his truck.

El closed her eyes, her powers unfurling like invisible threads, probing for Hopper's location. A quick flash hit her—his brown Chevy Blazer slicing through the pink haze, engine growling as it barreled down a parallel road.

Too close.

A fork was coming up—they were going to intersect. A trickle of blood tickled her upper lip.

"No, Hopper's coming that way! Hurry, turn left!" she gasped, her eyes snapping open. "Now!"

Billy shot her a look in the mirror, his brow furrowing. "How the hell does she—"

"Don't ask questions—just do it!" Max cut him off, her voice fierce, covering for El's secret powers.

"You're both crazier than I thought," Billy said, but he yanked the wheel hard in the direction El pointed.

The Camaro swerved onto a narrow dirt road, gravel spraying, the tires skidding as they ducked under a canopy of pines and into a field.

A minute later, Hopper's Blazer roared past on the main road, missing them by seconds. She and Max ducked low in the back seat, their heads below the windows, hearts pounding. The trees hid Billy's car, offering protection.

Tiffany twisted around in the front seat, her eyes wide. "Seriously, how did your little friend know that?"

"Mind your business," Max snapped, her tone final. Tiffany shrank back.

Max watched El closely, waiting for her direction. El finally nodded.

"Okay, coast is clear," Max said, turning around. "Let's do this . . ."

Billy revved the engine, taking off in the opposite direction, following the route that Hopper just left. A few minutes later, they blew through downtown Hawkins, the closed Palace Arcade a blur on their left, the sign dark. The streets were empty, except for a lone jogger who dove out of the way, cursing as the Camaro screamed past.

Max rolled her eyes at Billy's driving, making El giggle despite her nerves. They relaxed slightly, the danger behind them, blowing down Main Street.

When suddenly—

A sharp siren wailed behind them, red and blue lights flashing in the rearview mirror. El's heart stopped.

Hopper.

She dove down, pulling Max with her, their breath caught in their throats.

But Billy's laugh was maniacal, his foot slamming the gas. "Hold on, girls!" he declared, the Camaro surging forward, the speedometer climbing.

Hopper gave chase, almost closing the distance, but Billy pulled a few crazy moves, cutting down an alleyway, blowing onto more side roads.

"Come on, baby," he purred, patting the dashboard. "Gimme just a little more sugar. You can do it . . ."

He jammed the accelerator, and the car responded. The tires screeched as he abruptly drove down a hill and swerved under a low bridge, the concrete looming inches above the roof.

Billy cut the engine, the car plunging into silence, hiding in the shadows under the bridge as Hopper's Blazer roared past overhead, sirens blaring.

Max's eyes widened, a grudging respect flashing across her face. "Holy shit, Billy," she said, almost impressed. "You're actually good for something."

"Don't get used to it, sis." He smirked, restarting the engine with a low rumble. He caught her eyes in the rearview mirror. "Also, don't you dare spoil my little secret—or I'll kill you!"

He dragged his finger across his throat, tapping the gas and gunning out of their hiding spot. "This bridge move has saved my ass more than once."

That explained how he evaded the cops and got away with speeding.

A few minutes later, the Camaro snaked through the woods, then cut onto the dirt road to Hopper's cabin, the ruts jostling them as Billy slowed.

The cabin loomed ahead, the sagging porch and wood-paneled walls a welcome sight after the night away. El's chest relaxed—home. It felt good after having time away on her own terms.

Billy skidded to a halt just short of the driveway, the engine idling.

"End of the line," he announced, his voice gruff but not unkind.

Max rolled her eyes but nodded. "Thanks, jerko!"

He grinned, revving the engine. "Anytime, Mad Max." Then he turned back, softening. "And well, thanks for saving my ass tonight . . ."

He mumbled the last part, feeling awkward expressing the sentiment.

"Did you actually say . . . *thanks*?" Max gaped, feigning shock. "Wow, going soft in your old age, Billy Boy."

That drew out his scowl. "Soft? Not even close!" He jerked his finger at her. "And consider my debt paid. Got it?"

"Yup, got it," Max said, smiling.

"Good—because you're on your own from here," he said, his voice gruff. "Don't expect me to play hero again."

Max rolled her eyes but nodded. She and El slipped out

from the back seat, crouching low as they darted toward the cabin. Behind them, Billy sped off down the dirt road, vanishing in the distance before Hopper got home.

Max and El clambered up the creaky porch. The front door was locked, but El pulled Max around to the back by her bedroom. She glanced at the window, the latch glinting in the dawn light. She focused, her powers surging, a trickle of blood dripping from her nose.

The window flew open with a soft *creak,* the curtains fluttering.

"Go!" Max whispered, boosting El through. El tumbled inside, her sneakers hitting the creaky floorboards. Max clambered in behind her.

They froze, listening, the cabin silent except for the hum of the fridge and the faint chirp of morning birds. El's powers probed outward—Hopper's Blazer was closer now, the engine growling as it turned onto the dirt road.

"He's coming," she whispered, her voice tight, wiping the blood from her nose. "We have to act . . . normal!"

Max moved fast, shoving her skateboard into the closet, erasing their tracks. El dove onto her bed, her heart hammering as Max settled next to her. "Wait, the wristbands!" Max hissed, and snatched them off their wrists before cramming them in her pocket.

They grabbed the big stack of teen magazines, flipping them open and trying to steady their breathing.

But something was missing. Max elbowed El, pointing across the room. El used her powers to flip on her pink boom box, a tinny song echoing out—"Everybody Wants to Rule the World."

They waited in tense silence. They beat Hopper back to the cabin, but they weren't out of the woods yet. They still had to calm Hopper and his suspicions.

It wouldn't be easy.

Suddenly, outside the cabin, sirens wailed, red and blue lights sweeping the yard as Hopper's Blazer roared up the driveway. The engine cut off, and then his boots were crunching gravel, his shadow looming through the front window.

El closed her eyes, her powers quieting, and tried to act like nothing was awry—like she hadn't snuck out and had the time of her life last night.

But her heart still pounded fiercely, thumping in her chest, as the lock rattled, then twisted, and the door creaked open.

He's here.

CHAPTER TWENTY-SIX

"El, are you here?" Hopper's booming voice, sharp and laced with suspicion, sliced through the faint echo of "Everybody Wants to Rule the World" fading from the pink boom box.

His boots tramped into the cabin, each step shaking the creaky floorboards.

El's heart lurched at the sound of his arrival. She and Max were sprawled across her bed, surrounded by a mess of teen magazines. Max fished a few discarded Eggo boxes from under the bed, scattering them around to create the impression they'd been there longer.

El's eyes darted to Max, wide with panic. "He cannot

know," she hissed, feeling her heart pulse with adrenaline.

She'd faced a lot of scary things in her short life so far—but her adoptive father was easily at the top of the list.

Max nodded, flipping a page with forced nonchalance. "Just act normal," she whispered. "Well, *normal* for you, which is probably a little weird. Got it?"

El swallowed hard, unsure what that meant exactly. But she had to do her best. Her fingers gripped the glossy pages of *Seventeen,* the cover quivering in her hands. She forced her breathing to regulate, like when she needed to control her powers. *In. Out. In. Out.*

"El, are you in here?" Hopper's voice grew louder, his boots stomping closer.

The bedroom door was ajar. El used her powers to nudge it wider with a soft *whoosh.* Light flooded in, casting Hopper's shadow across the wood-paneled walls, long and imposing, his sheriff's hat tilted low over his brow.

He looked . . . suspicious.

"Hey there, Chief," Max called out, her tone breezy, as if they hadn't just outrun him with her psychotic stepbrother in a heart-pounding escape through Hawkins. She leaned back, propping herself on an elbow, the magazine open to a quiz on "Summerizing Your Style."

Hopper loomed in the doorway, his uniform rumpled. He scanned the room—the scattered magazines, the empty Eggo boxes, the boom box playing "Shock the Monkey."

"You okay?" he asked, his voice low and probing, like he could sniff out their lie. "What're you two doing back here?"

El forced a smile, her heart hammering. Max side-eyed her.

"Fine," El said, her voice clipped but steady, though her fingers twisted the quilt's edge. "Just . . . hanging."

Max held up the magazine, her grin disarming. "Learning how to make our summer *fabulous.* You should try some neon, Chief. Spice up that uniform."

They both giggled at that suggestion. Hopper grunted, unamused, searching for cracks in their unified front. He stepped inside, the floorboards creaking, then knelt down to check under the bed, as if expecting Mike's lanky form to be hiding there.

"Uh, what are you doing?" El asked, watching him fish under the bed. But all he came up with was another Eggo box and some impressive dust bunnies.

"No Mike?" he asked, still suspicious. "He's not in here?"

"Nope," Max said, popping the *p* with exaggerated innocence. "Just us girls."

He straightened, his eyes lingering on El, then moved to the closet next, yanking it open. "Gotcha—" he started, but then his face fell.

The door rattled, revealing only flannel shirts and a lone sneaker.

"What's going on?" Max asked, exchanging a look with El.

"Well, I went by your house looking for your stepbrother," Hopper said. "But you two weren't there. He had some story about a skate park in the woods. But you weren't there either . . ."

He took another step toward them, looming over them.

"So, then I got this crazy idea that you snuck out and went to the Starcourt Slumber Fest. I stopped by the mall and found Mike and your friends . . . but no sign of you . . ."

"Uh, exactly!" Max said, a little too quickly. "Because we weren't there!"

She elbowed El to chime in. "Right, because we did sleep over at Max's. But then . . ." El started, trailing off.

"My idiot stepbrother came home," Max provided. "And crashed our slumber party. Billy was a total buzzkill. Stumbled in drunk, trashed the place. So, we bailed and hiked back here."

Hopper's mustache twitched as he sniffed for deception, looking for holes in their story. He paced around, hands on hips, his badge glinting in the dim light.

"Well, you should know—that's not all Billy *crashed* last night," he grunted. "Your stepbrother is currently suspect number one in a big fight at the mall."

El paled, remembering the brawl in the fountain, but Max saved her.

"Figures," Max said, her face falling. "He had some bruises when he came home. Wouldn't be the first time."

She put on a brave face, but Hopper knew about the problems she faced at home. He softened his tone.

"You sure that's it? You two didn't . . . go *anywhere* else last night?"

El's throat tightened, but Max jumped in, her voice smooth.

"Nope, *straight* back here. We had to cut through the

woods. That's probably why Billy thought we went to that skate park. But I don't like those punks."

"Good, punks is right! Stay away from them," Hopper said. "They're bad apples. What they're doing out there is illegal—not to mention dangerous."

"Exactly, sir! Those ramps are an accident waiting to happen! So yeah, we decided to come back here, where it's safe and quiet." Max waved the magazine, her grin daring him to call her bluff.

"El's been teaching me how to . . . *summerize* my wardrobe," she added, making them both giggle again.

Hopper scanned the room one last time, but it offered no further clues to their adventures last night—no trace of Starcourt Mall or the Slumber Fest. And most importantly, no sign of the boys. Just two teen girls doing teen girl things. Hopper pointed at El.

"Next time, tell me where you go," he said, patting the walkie-talkie strapped to his belt. "Always call me. No exceptions. Got it?"

El nodded, her voice small but firm. "Okay." Her thoughts swirled with relief.

He rubbed his temples, still decompressing from all the chaos last night, mostly caused by Max's brother.

"All right, you girls, keep doing . . . whatever that is," he said awkwardly. He turned, his boots thudding toward the door, but then paused and looked back.

"El. No trouble."

"Yes . . . Dad," El said, her lips twitching into a faint smile. "Sorry."

"It's okay, kiddo," he said, smiling at her affectionately. "Live and learn."

Somewhat satisfied, Hopper stomped off muttering about *mall chaos* and *damn teens.* Her bedroom door squeaked closed behind him. The latch caught, clicking into place, and only then did they breathe a sigh of relief.

Max exhaled, flopping back on the bed, her ponytail fanning across the pillow. "Holy crap, that was close! Too close. He's like a human lie detector."

"I know," El said. "Do you think he . . . believed us?"

Max shrugged. "Well, he's probably still suspicious. But he doesn't have proof. We just need to keep it that way."

El laughed, shaky but real, relief flooding her. "We did it," she whispered, her heart still racing.

They collapsed into giggles, the tension unraveling. Max grabbed *Seventeen* again, flipping to a page about "Summer Bucket Lists," jabbing at the article. "That sure was one hell of a way to kick off our summer, right?" Max said. "So, what do you want to do next? We have the whole summer ahead of us!"

El grinned, the idea sparking warmth. "Spend it with . . . friends," she said softly, the word precious.

Max reached over, squeezing her hand. "Well, then I've got an idea for tomorrow," she said, raising her eyebrows. "And it's pretty rad!"

"What . . . is it?" El asked, the anticipation tensing her body.

Max's grin returned, mischievous. She glanced at the door, aware of Hopper's proximity in the small cabin.

Assured that it remained shut, Max reached into her backpack, pulling out the Starcourt gift certificate. She held it up, catching the morning sunlight. The glossy logo looked especially shiny.

El's eyes widened. With the chase home and everything, she'd almost forgotten about their fifty-dollar prize.

Max lowered her voice. "How does a shopping spree at Starcourt sound? Wow, that's a total mouthful," she added, stifling a laugh. "Scoops Ahoy ice cream, arcade fun, Spencer's swag, a glam photo shoot!"

El's lips twitched. "*Shopping,*" she said, testing the word, picturing the mall's glowing wonderland. "Yes."

Max laughed. "That's my girl. Early tomorrow morning, we hit the mall. You, me . . . the boys. No drama. No psycho older stepbrothers. Just fun."

The way she said *boys* made El smile. It didn't escape anyone's notice that Max and Lucas had rekindled their rocky relationship at Slumber Fest.

"Should we tell them?" Max said. "But we have to make sure Hopper can't hear us . . ." she said, leaping off the bed.

She grabbed the boom box and cranked it up, setting it by the door to block out any sound of their activities. The catchy chorus from Prince's "Raspberry Beret" blared out, providing camouflage. El grabbed the ginormous walkie-talkie from under her pillow.

She depressed the talk button, emitting a bunch of static, then spoke into it.

"Mike, do you copy?"

Static. Then . . . nothing.

"Mike, it's important," she tried again. "I need to talk to you . . ."

Still nothing. Just static.

El frowned. "Where could they be?" she asked in frustration, worried that Mike was ignoring her . . . again.

Max looked upset on her behalf. She grabbed the walkie-talkie and jammed down the receiver. She hissed into it.

"You'd better stop goofing off and answer your girlfriend! Or she's dumping your ass—"

"Max, calm down." Mike's voice cut through the static, warm and teasing. "I'm here—loud and clear! So nobody's getting dumped today. Okay? Over."

"Okay," Max said with a stiff nod. "But do better. Got it? Over." She handed the walkie-talkie back to El.

"Better! Roger that," Mike said. They could hear the smile in his voice.

Then other voices crowded in. "He almost got his ass dumped," Lucas whispered, the receiver picking him up in the background. "Man, that sucks . . ."

"You should know!" Mike shot back. "Seeing as you've been dumped like a million gazillion times . . ."

"Hey, it's not getting dumped that matters. It's how you

bounce back!" Then Lucas spoke into the walkie-talkie. "And we're so back! We can't be stopped. Max, do you hear me? Roger?"

Static erupted. Max tried to look annoyed, making him wait longer, but a sheepish grin crept over her face.

"Wait, did you change your mind?" Lucas said, suddenly worried. "We are back on . . . aren't we? Damn it, don't tell me you decided to dump me again! It's only been like two *freaking* hours. Over."

"No, dumbass," Max said, taking the walkie-talkie. "We're back on. Your dumb ass is mine. Roger that?"

She released the button.

The response was immediate. The boys all whooped into the walkie-talkie.

"Damn," Max said, glancing at the door. El acted fast and used her powers quickly, cranking up the volume even louder to block Hopper's sharp ears.

Now Will picked up the walkie-talkie. "You know, for the record . . . I've never been dumped. Not once—"

"That's because you've never had a girlfriend," Mike cut him off. "Talk to us once you've got experience—" The sound of shoving erupted, then static.

Max rolled her eyes, then depressed the button, taking over the call.

"Okay, listen up. And stop being dense. We have a plan. Code name: *Starcourt Shopping Spree.* Tomorrow. Ten a.m. sharp. At the mall. Roger that?"

This time, they didn't have to wait. Mike confirmed

their plans immediately. Their excited banter vaulted back and forth, filling El's room with the best sound in the world.

The sound of her friends. She couldn't ask for anything better. Her heart raced, imagining all the fun tomorrow. Then Max perked up.

She depressed the transmit button. "Will, don't forget to tell your brother to meet us there. For the photo shoot."

"Roger that," Will said. "I'll make sure he doesn't space. I've got you!"

"Okay, losers," Max said. "See you tomorrow. Don't be late. Over and out."

▶

Max stayed the afternoon, goofing off with El and dissecting the whole Slumber Fest adventure in vivid detail, their hushed whispers filling the room—from the scavenger hunt and besting Kyle and his friends, to Billy's brawl, to Lucas winning her back—then as the sun dipped, she took off with her skateboard tucked under her arm.

"See you later, El," she called out with a wink, signaling that *later* meant tomorrow morning. Even if El had to sneak out again, she wasn't missing it.

Hopper felt bad for his earlier interrogation, so he made waffles for dinner, her favorite. He brought a plate into her bedroom, depositing it on her bed. He backed away, but stopped in the door, lingering awkwardly.

"Uh, nice friend you got there," Hopper was forced

to admit. "You should have her over again. I like her way better than her stepbrother. Or Mike—"

El raised her hand, slamming her bedroom door shut before he could rant.

"Really?" Hopper grunted at the door. "We're doing that again?"

Then he stormed off. Some things changed, but others stayed the same.

El devoured her waffles, savoring the buttery soft pillows drenched in syrup, then climbed under her covers. She expected to pass out right away. But she lay there awake, strangely exhilarated even though she'd had almost no sleep.

The magazines lay scattered around her bed, but as she glanced at them, she realized that something had changed.

Something important.

Her heart didn't lurch with envy at the sight of those glamorous photo spreads—because she had her own perfect summer now. It might not look like the same kind of perfect as those glossy pictures, but that didn't matter.

It was *perfect* for her.

She sighed contentedly and shoved them under her bed, then fell asleep with a smile on her face, knowing that the amazing fun wasn't ending.

Not even close.

It was only just beginning.

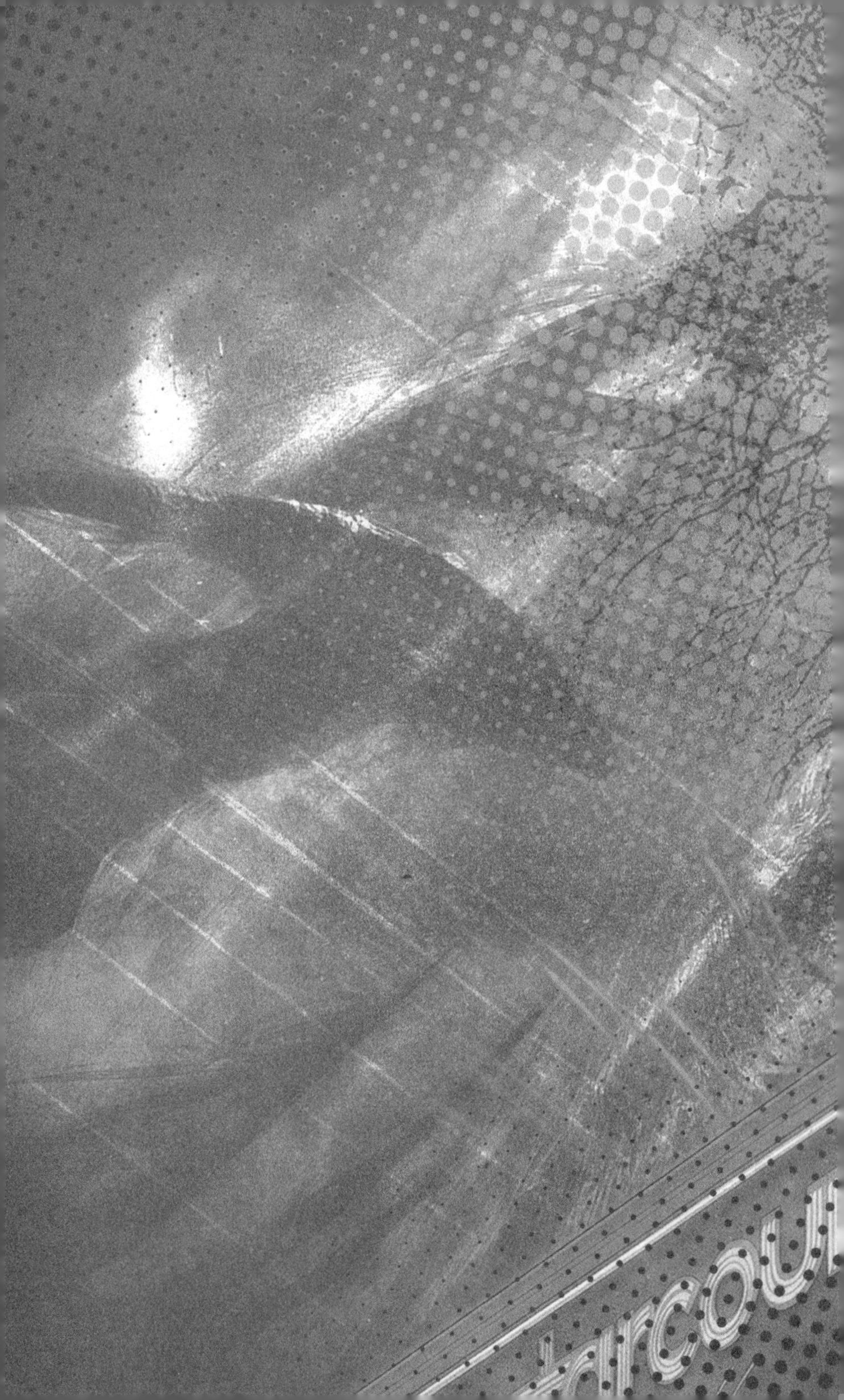

CHAPTER TWENTY-SEVEN

The Starcourt Mall was packed with Monday-morning traffic, a kinetic mix of suburban moms and kids, along with tweens and teens roaming the marble corridors, in stark contrast to Slumber Fest and its after-dark adventures. The whole place looked different in the light.

"We're loaded!" Max announced, her red ponytail bouncing with every word. She clutched the gift certificate like a precious gift. "Fifty bucks. One mall. What's the plan?"

El's white sneakers squeaked on the polished marble as she stepped off the escalator, her heart pounding with anticipation. The air was thick with the scent of waffle cones, fryer grease, and teenage dreams—a perfect summer cocktail. They met up with the boys, huddling by the gurgling fountain, the water shimmering under the glass dome's morning light and washing away any memory of Billy's brawl.

"Remember what Nancy said," Max added, plopping down on the edge. A light spray of water dusted her skin. "We don't have to spend it all in one place. We can spread it around the stores."

Lucas pulled out a calculator, while Will produced his sketchbook with Saturday night's rough draft budget.

"We have to be scientific about this," Lucas said. "If we all want in on the spending spree . . ."

Max rolled her eyes. "Lucas, where's the fun in that? The way you're doing it—it's not much of a *spree.* Can't we just, like, buy stuff as we go? Maybe a one item limit per person until we run out?"

Lucas shook his head dramatically. "No way. You risk stiffing one of us! Trust me. I'm not letting you near Spencer's until we have a solid budget."

Max threw her hands up in surrender, the good vibes between them having softened their banter. But only a little. Annoyance still simmered under the surface.

"Well, in my defense," Max said, "Spencer's does have super-rad gear. Lava lamps. Black light posters. Band shirts. You name it, they've got it."

"You've got ten bucks to spend—anything you want," Lucas said, tapping it into his calculator. He elbowed Will. "Write that down . . ."

Mike grinned, his dark hair flopping into his eyes. "Put

me down for the arcade! I say we blow my share on quarters. Try to beat Dustin's top score."

Lucas grinned, tapping on his calculator while Will scrawled it down.

He looked up. "Ten bucks in quarters buys a lot of games. Think you can do it? Dustin always dominates . . ."

"Can't win if you don't play," Mike quipped with a goofy grin. "I'll even share some turns with you fools."

They all laughed, the fun infectious. This was more money than they'd ever had to spend in one day.

"Okay, if he's got the arcade covered," Lucas said, scratching his head and thinking, "and Max has fun swag, then I think we need some *serious* eats. Sundaes, hot dogs on a stick, you name it. Just please, not that weird Chinese place. It gives me the creeps!"

He shuddered in emphasis.

"Serious?" Max snorted, elbowing him. "You drank Billy's *fountain* water runoff on a dare, Lucas. We might be back together, but you're still gross."

Lucas flashed a grin, slinging an arm around her. "And you're totally into it."

Max groaned, her eyes sparkling. He pecked her cheek.

Will perked up. "Okay, then I want to spend my share at Waldenbooks—"

"For D&D books," they all said, finishing the sentence for him.

"Trust me, we *know,*" Lucas added, tapping the figure in his calculator. "Well, write it down already . . . ten-dollar budget. That should get you a whole lot of dungeons *and* dragons. And maybe even some mages and fey, too."

Will grinned, for once not complaining, his pen moving across the page, adding the entry.

El smiled, their easy banter warming her chest. She glanced at Mike, catching his shy smile, their fingers brushing, sparking memories of their Slumber Fest kiss under the atrium's flickering films.

"What are we missing?" Lucas said. "We've got ten bucks left to spend."

"El's photo shoot," Will chimed in. But then he wrote "$0" next to the entry. "My bro got it covered! It's a freebie."

El blushed, feeling awkward. "Pictures? With . . . everyone?"

"Right, I *hate* taking pictures," Will said. "School picture day is the bane of my existence. But I'll do it for you, El."

"It's just cuz you're not as photogenic as me," Lucas said, grinning and adjusting his collared shirt printed with colorful geometric shapes.

"You wish!" Max said, rolling her eyes. "I'm the photogenic one. Got it?"

"And what about couple shots?" Mike said hopefully, raising his eyebrows. "You know, me and El?"

Will nodded. "I'm sure we can work that out. Flash Studio also has all these fun backdrops and accessories."

"So, what do we do with the remaining cash?" Max asked, scanning Will's sketchbook. "Who knew it could be this hard to spend money? Talk about having high-class problems."

She gave Lucas a mischievous look. "You want to try a Jazzercise class? With all those suburban moms?"

Lucas blushed and feigned innocence. "Who . . . me? I only have eyes for you, my love." He blinked his long lashes at her, drawing a playful jab.

"Plus, in my defense," Lucas added. "You *dumped* my ass. So technically, we were on a break. I was a single man."

"Yeah, but you were trying to win me back," she pointed out. "So, technically . . . it was cheating."

"Cheating? In what universe?" Lucas sighed in exasperation. "That's not how a *breakup* works, Max. You said you meant it. How was I supposed to know that my wooing would work?"

Max glared at him.

Mike nudged him, then zipped his lips. "Shut up. You can't win," he whispered, drawing a scowl from Max. "Or you're gonna get dumped again faster than you can say . . . *Jazzercise.*"

"Good point," Lucas said, then pivoted. "I'm sorry—I was heartbroken. But you're the only girl for me . . ."

Max rolled her eyes, then turned back to the group. "But seriously, what do we do with the last ten bucks?"

Everyone thought for a moment, the fountain burbling up coins like wishes.

"Dustin needs a new hat," Mike said firmly. "Max, think you can find one for him at Spencer's?"

"Oh, you don't need to tell me twice," Max replied. "Talk about a fashion disaster. I'll hook him up . . ."

That settled it. Will made the last note, tallying it all up. Then they set out into the mall to execute their plan.

▶

The mall unfolded around them like a vibrant playground, the escalators whirring, speakers blasting Cyndi Lauper and Madonna, the patrons packing the corridors with foot traffic.

The group wound their way through the crowd to hit up Spencer's first, goofing off with the lava lamps. El had never seen anything like this store before and watched them, mesmerized. The goo floated to the top then flip-flopped and sank back to the bottom, lit up from beneath in different colors.

She reached out to touch the lamp, but Mike grabbed her hand. "Hot! Be careful . . . that's how it works. The water heats the lava up. It's thermodynamics."

"Hot," El repeated in awe.

They circled through the tight aisles together, holding hands and pointing out different quirky finds.

But this shop was Max's domain, the walls a tapestry of band tees, kitschy trinkets, and glow-in-the-dark posters. She snatched a Metallica *Ride the Lightning* shirt off a mannequin. She held it up to her chest. "This is so metal! Billy's gonna choke with jealousy."

Next, she riffled through a display of baseball hats, grabbing a NASA logo trucker cap for Dustin off the wall.

"Perfect—it's nerdy, but way cooler than whatever he's been sporting."

"Plus, it'll soften the blow when I beat his top score later," Mike said with a wink, making them all laugh.

Lucas high-fived him. "You're on—"

"Dude, you wish," Will cut in. "I'm telling you—Dustin's unbeatable. Nobody can top his score! But you can waste quarters trying if you want."

"Come on, Will," Lucas said. "Lighten up for once. You can play a few turns. You never know. You might get lucky!"

Meanwhile, El eyed a pair of chunky neon-pink clip-on earrings, hesitant, her fingers hovering. They looked like the pictures in her teen magazines.

Max grinned, tossing them into the cart. "Get 'em. Rock 'em for our glam photo shoot!" El beamed, imagining the earrings catching the flash's light.

Their cart hit ten bucks exactly—Lucas's math was spot-on. They all whooped as Max passed the gift certificate over to the cashier and got a receipt back stapled to it. It showed how much money they had left to spend.

The next stop—Waldenbooks, the shelves a labyrinth of paperbacks and comics. Will led the charge, his fingers trailing spines, eyes wide as he hunted D&D treasures. "This one!" he yelped, pulling out a new edition of *Deities & Demigods.* "It's got Cthulhu stats!"

Lucas flipped through it, whistling. "Eight bucks? Steep, but your next campaign's gonna kill it. Literally."

El wandered nearby, her fingers grazing a *Sweet Valley*

High cover, the smiling twins so foreign yet magnetic. She flipped it over, reading the back.

She pictured herself in their world—school, dances, babysitting, boyfriends, no powers, no monsters. Her heart tugged, a mix of longing and doubt. Could she ever be like those girls?

Max nudged her, grinning. "You into that? Grab it. It looks like a fun read!"

Lucas shot them a look, but Max waved him off. "Okay, budget police! Move along! Mind your own business."

El smiled, tucking the book under her arm. "Maybe," she said, her voice soft but curious. "Okay . . ."

They checked out, the cashier sliding their swag into a Waldenbooks bag.

Next up, the Time-Out Arcade throbbed with electronic beeps and flashing lights. "Is it me—or does something feel off about this place?" Lucas asked, scanning the floor.

Mike sniffed. "Right, that's because it doesn't smell like used diapers and decay."

They all laughed. But he had a point. The arcade was brand-new compared to the vintage vibes of the Palace Arcade.

"We can level up for a day," Lucas said, clapping his arm around Mike. "Before we slum it in downtown."

They beelined for *Dragon's Lair,* quarters clinking into the slots.

"This is for Dustin!" Mike declared, jamming the joystick as the animated knight dodged obstacles. Lucas leaned in, barking tips, but the screen flashed GAME OVER in a matter of seconds.

"Ugh, this game's rigged!" Mike groaned, kicking the cabinet.

"You suck—let the professional take over." Lucas smirked, shoving him off.

But Lucas didn't fare much better, nor did Will. GAME OVER flashed again.

Lucas checked the leaderboard—Dustin's name still blazed at the top.

"He's untouchable. *Dig Dug* next?" He darted to the machine, his competitive streak flaring as he popped and crushed enemies, muttering strategies.

Max owned the game as usual, her fingers a blur, El cheering as the score climbed. Lucas watched in frustration.

"I don't get it—how do you always dominate this game?" he marveled, running his hand over his hair.

"Oh, are you jealous?" Using the joystick, Max entered her name onto the leaderboard top spot—MADMAX.

"More like hungry," Lucas said, patting his belly in an exaggerated gesture. "I'm famished! Food court?"

He got no arguments there. They bolted out of the arcade and ran for the escalators, riding them to the top floor.

At Scoops Ahoy, the air was sweet with waffle cones. They headed for the counter, where Steve greeted them. His sailor hat was askew. He looked tired.

"Pulling a double, can you believe it. I *have* to be here. Working for the man. But seriously, what's your excuse?"

Max slapped the gift certificate down on the counter. But he waved them off.

"Save the big bucks for something epic," he said, winking. "On the house, but don't tell the boss man."

Sundaes piled up on the counter with the works. El's eyes widened. Robin smirked, tossing napkins at them. "He's soft for all of you. Don't abuse it."

El savored her chocolate fudge sundae, the cold sweetness melting on her tongue. Mike fed her a spoonful, his grin shy, and Max gagged dramatically.

"Really? Get a room, you two." Lucas laughed, ice cream smudged on his chin, while they all dug in.

"Take the rest to go!" Max said, reaching the bottom of her sundae. "Time to get our supermodel on!"

Leaving the food court, they headed across the way to Flash Studio.

But then a jeering voice echoed out.

"Well," Kyle drawled, tossing a soda can. "Freaks from the Slumber Fest. Got that prize money?"

Becks cackled, her voice cutting. "Greedy nerds, can't wait to spend it. We figured you'd be here today."

Danny cracked his knuckles, stepping closer. "Hand it over, or we'll make you."

El felt her powers beginning to vibrate. She stepped forward, eyes narrowing, her presence heavy.

Mike grabbed her arm, whispering, "Easy, El." The Party closed ranks—Lucas glaring, Max gripping her skateboard like a weapon, Will clutching his backpack but standing tall.

"Back off, Kyle," Max snapped, her voice fire. "Or you'll

eat pavement again. Remember last time?"

El stared, unblinking, her voice low and steady. "Leave. Now."

The fountain's water rippled without wind, and the atrium's lights flickered.

Kyle smirked, but his eyes flicked to El, unease creeping in. "What's with her? She gonna pull that dumb trash can trick again?"

Max folded her arms. "No, something worse. Remember what happened at RadioShack?"

She nodded to a mall security guard, badge glinting, watching from across the corridor. Danny flinched, his bravado cracking. Becks tugged Kyle's sleeve, her voice low. "Kyle, security's right there. They'll call our *parents* again."

Kyle's smirk faded, his face paling at the memory of his dad's punishment.

He glanced at El, her unblinking stare chilling, her reputation looming.

"Yeah, they'll call your parents," Max repeated, folding her arms. "Remember how you turned into a giant wuss? And started crying like a baby? If you don't *apologize,* then I'm going to spread that story all over Hawkins."

Kyle swallowed hard, raising his hands. "All right, chill. You're right!" He backpedaled. "I . . . I'm sorry, okay? For Slumber Fest, for this. We were jerks. Didn't mean to go that far."

Danny's jaw dropped. "You serious, man? You're actually apologizing—"

"Shut up," Kyle hissed, elbowing him. Becks nodded, her sneer gone, her voice softer. "Yeah, sorry. We're done bothering you. No more crap, promise."

They all stared, stunned. Max crossed her arms, skeptical. "Wow, you're pathetic when you're scared. But an apology? That's new. I'll take it."

Lucas grinned, relaxing. "Smart move. Mall cops don't mess around. And neither does my girlfriend. If that story gets out, it'll ruin your reps."

Will's eyes softened, catching Kyle's hunched shoulders. "We accept your apology," he said quietly, his empathy shining. "Everyone screws up sometimes. Let's put it behind us."

El wiped a trickle of blood from her nose. "Okay," she said, her tone firm yet forgiving.

Max hesitated, then nodded stiffly, her voice sharp but even. "Fine. No more trouble. Let's call it even."

Mike raised an eyebrow, but Kyle shrugged, smirking. "Even? I can live with that." Even Becks and Danny relaxed, their tension easing at the truce.

"You got it," Max said, her eyes still wary but firm. It was a truce settled with a nod—a fragile peace that just might hold for the summer.

▶

After burying the hatchet with the bullies, they pushed on to Flash Studio, their bags heavy with loot. "You ready to strike a pose?" Max asked El, fishing the neon-pink earrings out of her bag. El giggled in response but then frowned as they reached the studio.

The storefront was dark, the CLOSED sign swaying on the door. The curtains were pulled over the front windows, concealing the interior. El's heart sank—she'd pictured glamorous photos, like *Seventeen*'s glossy spreads.

"Closed?" she asked, her voice small. She wanted pictures with her friends more than anything in the world.

Max banged on the door, undeterred. "No way Jonathan flakes on us."

Nothing happened, but then something rustled inside the studio. A minute later, the door unlocked and Jonathan stepped out, his camera slung around his neck, hair mussed.

"Who's here for a private photo shoot?"

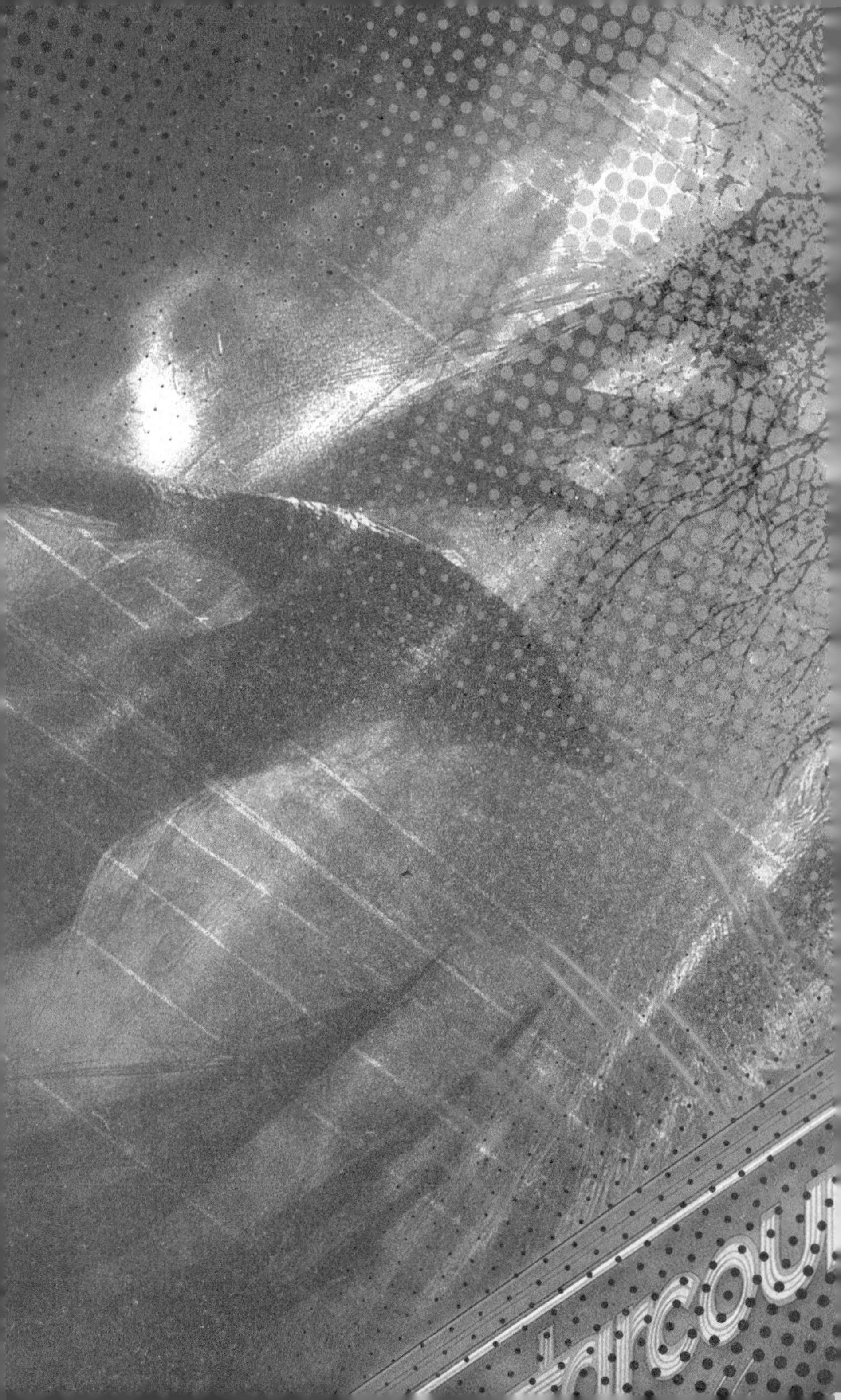

CHAPTER TWENTY-EIGHT

"Right this way," Jonathan said, holding the glass door open. "Today Flash Studio is closed for your private photo shoot. VIPs, follow me . . ."

"VIPs?" El asked, glancing at Max.

"*Very important persons,*" Max whispered. "That's us today. Looks like we're getting the glam treatment."

El stepped inside Flash Studio, padding over the concrete floors, her breath hitching at the colorful space. She'd never been inside a professional photo studio, or even posed for pictures. The center of the unfinished space, with exposed ceilings and brushed concrete floors, was filled with lights, tripods, backdrop stands, and more.

Everyone trailed behind Jonathan, their bags stuffed with swag from their shopping spree crinkling, eyes wide at the professional setup. A massive backdrop of starbursts and lightning bolts glowed under silver umbrellas, hung behind a raised, carpeted stage, while a makeup station brimmed with glittery compacts and fake eyelashes, hair products, and roller brushes.

"Holy crap," Max whistled. "This is, like, Madonna's dressing room or something." She propped her skateboard against a wall, feeling awkward and unsure if she belonged.

Lucas strutted in. "Nah, this is where *Prince* gets ready. We're about to be legends." He struck a pose in his geometric shirt and acid-washed, cuffed jeans. Max rolled her eyes.

Across the room, Nancy wrestled a glittery purple backdrop into place.

"Jonathan, help me with this thing! It keeps falling," she called, her voice sharp but playful. "It's gonna crash and burn before we even get started!"

Jonathan grinned, clutching his camera, his hair flopping into his eyes. He rushed over to catch it before it fell on their heads, then carefully clipped it into place.

"Patience, Nance. Genius takes time," he said with a shy smile, then looked through his camera lens.

Satisfied, he stepped back and turned to El and her friends, slinging his camera strap over his shoulder.

"You guys ready to steal the show? We're going full glam today."

El's fingers grazed her neon-pink Spencer's earrings, her

heart pounding. She felt a stab of insecurity, feeling suddenly out of place. Her fingers tugged at her curls. They'd grown in a lot since she had her head shaved back in the lab.

But she questioned herself and whether she could be glamorous.

As if sensing her doubt, one of the studio employees bounced over, her leg warmers flashing. She wore a flouncy neon-green shirt paired with a tight jean skirt. Her hair was teased high, adding a few inches to her petite frame, while her face was slathered with brightly colored makeup—teals, purples, bright pink lipstick. Her name tag read *Shelly*.

"Oh, pretty!" she said, spotting El clutching the earrings that Max had fished out of the Spencer's bag.

El smiled tentatively, holding them up. "I want to wear them . . . for the pictures."

"Well, I think they'll go perfectly!" Shelly said, helping El into a makeup chair aimed at a big mirror with raw bulbs framing it. Shelly pulled the earrings from the cardboard backing and gently clipped them to El's ears, then spun her back around to face everyone.

Max and the boys cheered. "Those look pretty," Mike said, blushing.

Shelly clapped her hands together, bouncing on the balls of her feet. "Big news, kids! Flash Studio is throwing in free hair, makeup, *and* costumes! Let's make you rock stars for a day!"

She herded them to the styling station, where another employee—Lori, according to her name tag—brandished a curling iron and a mega-sized can of hair spray, ready to deploy them.

Max hopped into the chair next to El, smirking. "Gimme the Cyndi Lauper treatment. I want to be punk rock."

Shelly and Lori tag-teamed and got started on Max, piling on green eyeshadow and rouge, teasing Max's ponytail into a wild cascade. Lori doused it with spray, making Max cough. "I'm a freakin' rock goddess!" she said, sitting up straighter and admiring her reflection.

Lucas plopped down next, puffing his chest. "Make me Eddie Murphy cool. *Beverly Hills Cop* vibes. You feel me?"

Lori trimmed his hair with a buzzer, then lined his eyes with black. When she smeared gold glitter to highlight his high cheekbones and tone his skin for the finishing touch, Max laughed, nearly dropping her skateboard.

"Glitter, really?" Max teased in a good-natured way. "You look like a human Christmas ornament."

Lucas was undeterred. "Well, I gotta keep up with you!" he shot back, winking. "Cyndi Lauper needs a worthy suitor. Admit it, you're obsessed."

"You wish," Max snorted. But then he hopped up, pulled her close, and mugged for the mirror. Even Max had to admit they looked good together.

"Fine, I never thought I'd say this," Max said, "but I like the eyeliner."

"You two are camera ready," Shelly said, shoving them toward the stage, where Jonathan was setting up with Nancy's help and adjusting the lights.

“Okay, who’s my next victim?” Lori called out, holding the hairspray and spinning the faux leather chair around.

“Don’t look at me!” Will yelped, hiding behind a rack of feathered boas, clutching his new D&D book.

But Mike grabbed a curly red wig, plopping it on Will’s head.

“If you won’t let them style you, then allow me.” Mike laughed, dodging Will’s swat. “Come on, join the fun!”

Will yanked the wig off, his cheeks pink, but a grin broke through. He pushed Mike over to the chair, where Lori attacked his floppy head of curls, trying to coax them into submission.

“That’s one impressive head of hair you got there, young man,” she quipped, making Mike blush. But he was enjoying her ministrations.

Finally, it was El’s turn to slide into the styling chair. She stood rigidly as Shelly approached, her pulse racing.

“Your turn, hon,” Shelly said, her smile warm, helping her into the chair. Then she got to work, coaxing El’s curls into a towering blowout, each strand sculpted with spray until it stiffened into crimps and defied gravity.

Next, it was Lori’s turn to tackle the blank canvas of her face. She painted El’s eyelids turquoise, then dusted her cheeks with pink blush and her lips with glossy lipstick. El stared at her reflection, her breath catching. She touched a curl, her eyes sparkling. She’d never looked like this before. She was bold, vibrant—like the girls in *Seventeen* magazine.

Mike leaned in, amazed. “You look . . . wow, El. Total

rock star." His voice was earnest, warming her cheeks.

"Really?" she asked.

Mike nodded, and their hands brushed. Impulse took over—she leaned in, and their lips met, a quick, tender kiss that lit up the studio. Max whooped, and Lucas clapped loudly.

"Save it for the camera!" Lucas hollered, grinning as Max elbowed him.

Jonathan chuckled, adjusting his lens. "All right, Romeo and Juliet, let's capture that magic. Couple shots first?"

He pointed to a sequined silver backdrop, tossing Mike a studded vest and El a fringed jacket. They donned the costumes and posed, Mike's arms wrapped around her, holding her from behind, their smiles shy but radiant.

Jonathan started by using a Polaroid to take a few test shots; then once he was happy with the lighting scheme, he picked up his bigger rig with the longer lens. The camera flashed, freezing their moment, El's heart soaring.

Jonathan directed them through a series of classic couples poses, finishing with a tasteful kissing picture.

Mike pulled away, flushing. "We're gonna have to hide that one from Hopper," he whispered into her ear, making El giggle, her cheeks flaming.

"Gorgeous!" Jonathan said. "That's a wrap. Where's my other couple?"

Lucas beamed while Max blushed. They bounded onto the stage. Max sported a lace mini dress like Cyndi Lauper, while Lucas had pulled on a purple tuxedo jacket and glitter bow tie.

They looked positively dashing.

Jonathan worked quickly, directing Nancy to change the backdrop to the starry night and pushing them through a series of poses, capturing the magic of their newly reignited relationship.

Finally, he checked his camera, loaded another roll of film, and turned to them. "Now, group poses. Go nuts."

They all dove into the costume rack, chaos erupting. Max snagged a leather skirt and shades, leaping onto her skateboard for an ollie mid-shot, her hair whipping.

"Top *that*!" she shouted, landing with a clack as the camera snapped. Lucas grabbed a zebra-print jacket, flexing like a bodybuilder, his glitter catching the light. "King of the mall!" he declared, winking at Max.

"Jeez, you're such a clown," Max fired back, but their chemistry was crackling. "Always goofing off."

"Takes one to know one!" Lucas shot back, gesturing to her skateboard.

Will draped a gold mesh scarf over his shoulders, waving his D&D dice. "For the dungeon master!" he said, tossing them as Jonathan clicked. Then he hopped down. Next, Mike slipped into platform boots and a feathered wig, wobbling comically onto the stage, making El giggle as he nearly crashed into a light stand.

"Careful, Cher!" Lucas laughed, steadying him. Their friendly, teasing banter filled the studio, a vibrant pulse that gave life to the austere space.

"All together!" Jonathan called out as they piled onto the stage with their props and goofy costumes. The backdrop he chose featured a microcosm of the universe—a ball of light pulsing with planets rotating around the sun. And this group of friends was like a whole universe, spinning around each other, orbiting the sun, and that sun was Eleven.

She beamed brighter than the backdrop, while Jonathan snapped, capturing them in perfect vivid detail.

El's powers stayed quiet, the studio a safe haven. She glanced at her reflection in the mirrors across the studio—blowout high, makeup bold. She wasn't the girl from the lab nightmares.

She was El, and she belonged.

Jonathan waved them over, his camera resting, having captured them.

"El, this one's for you." He handed her a Polaroid, the image sharpening in her hands—a group shot, with Max mid-ollie, Lucas flexing, Will's dice soaring, Mike's arm around El, all laughing.

El's throat tightened, tears welling. This was her first real photo—not a lab record, but proof of her found family.

"It is . . . perfect," she whispered, her voice trembling. "Because . . . us."

Max slung an arm around her, glitter smudging, while Mike squeezed her hand. "For you, El! You're one of us."

Lucas nodded, grinning. "Hang it up on your wall. That's our masterpiece."

El clutched the photo like a treasure. She'd never had a yearbook, never signed a memory for her friends.

"Wait," she said, sparking with an idea. She grabbed a

marker from Lori's table, holding out the Polaroid. "Will you sign it for me? Like . . . friends do?"

Max's eyes lit up. "Rad idea!"

She grabbed the marker and scribbled *MadMax—Ride or Die!* across the edge. Lucas added *Lucas the Legend!* with a flourish. Will's was careful: *Will the Wise!* Mike's was last, his handwriting neat: *Mike & El—Always,* beside her face. El's chest warmed, each signature a promise.

She held the Polaroid close, ink smearing her fingers, a smile breaking through her tears.

"Thank you," she said, her voice fierce. This was her crew, her home.

Jonathan clapped. "One more for the road!" They piled together, clad in ridiculous costumes and giddy, Max's skateboard underfoot, Lucas's arm around her, Will's scarf fluttering, El and Mike in the center. The flash popped, sealing their summer.

Shelly handed them each extra Polaroids from the day, grinning. "You kids are wild. Come back soon!"

They strutted out, their laughter echoing. El gripped her signed Polaroid, her blowout bouncing, her heart full. The lab was a shadow, the Void gone.

She was Eleven—and this summer was hers, shining in glossy color.

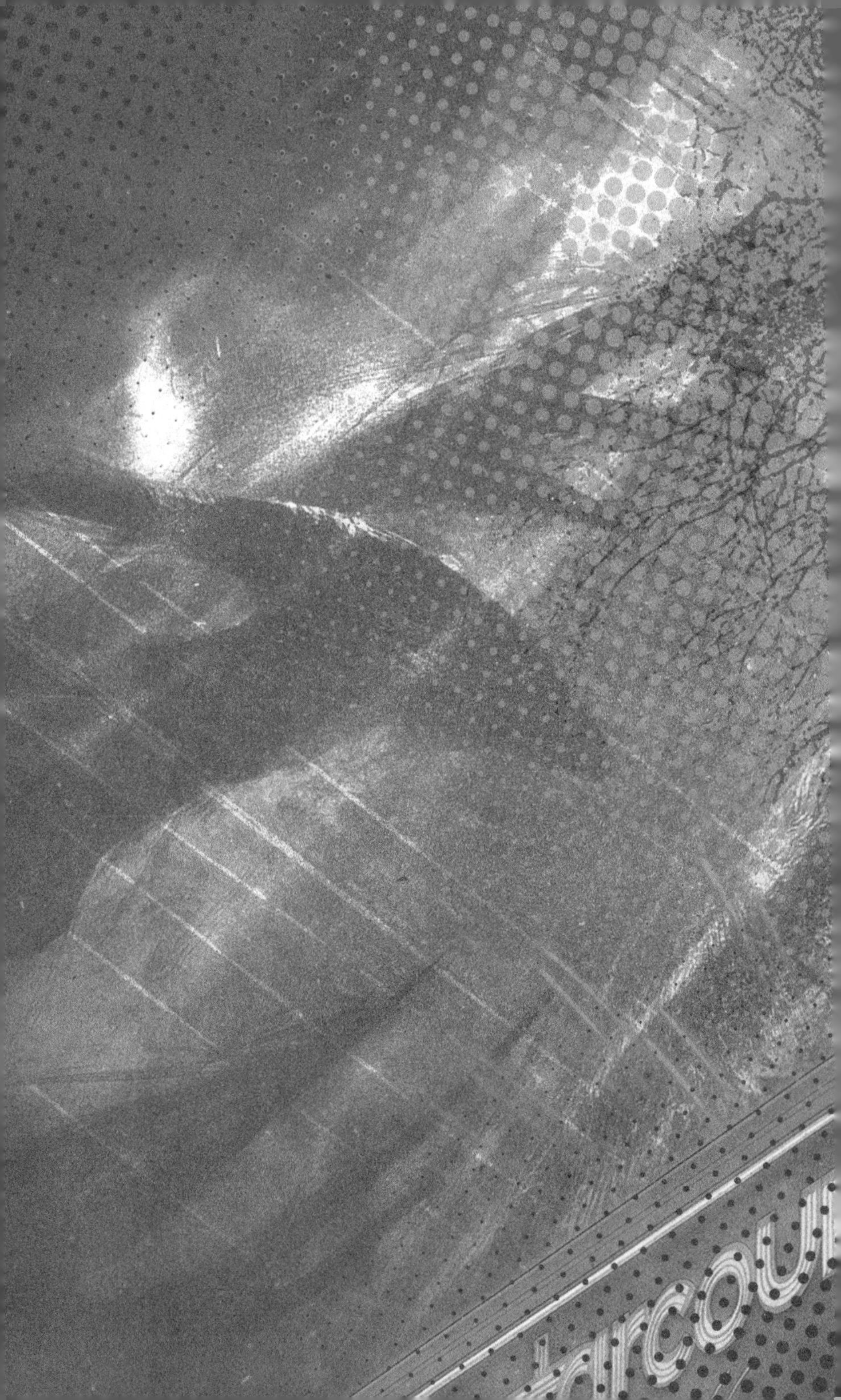

CHAPTER TWENTY-NINE

The glass doors of Flash Studio swung shut behind them, and they emerged into Starcourt Mall's bustling corridors, still buzzing from their glam photo shoot. Bags from their shopping spree dangled from their arms, while El clutched her signed Polaroid, the edges worn from her grip, the ink of her friends' signatures smudging her fingers. Her blowout curls, still stiff with hair spray, bounced with each step. The group strutted like rock stars, glitter from their photo shoot sparkling on their cheeks, the high of their glam session pulsing through them.

"We're basically MTV material now," Max giggled,

grinning at Lucas. "Ready for *our* close-up, Mr. Sinclair?"

Lucas puffed his chest. "Forget MTV. I'm *Soul Train* royalty." He moonwalked, dodging Max's playful swat, their chemistry sparking. "Admit it, you dig my suave moves."

"In your dreams," Max shot back, but her grin gave her true feelings away. She blushed when their eyes met. Their fingers found each other, their hands interlacing.

Mike's arm brushed El's, his smile shy but warm. "You looked so beautiful in there," he said, his voice soft, stirring memories of their couple shots—his arms around her, the camera's flash freezing their shy grins.

El's cheeks warmed, her neon-pink Spencer's earrings catching the light. She felt like a whole new person after the last forty-eight hours with her friends, sneaking out to Slumber Fest, winning the scavenger hunt and going on the shopping spree, scoring the photo.

Will glanced from one couple to the other, then sighed dejectedly to himself. "Sheesh, I can't wait until Dustin gets back from camp so I'm not the fifth wheel."

The couples broke apart and surrounded him, making him feel included. Will cracked a small smile. They wound their way toward the escalators, then took a lazy descent. El's eyes swept over the packed atrium.

Suddenly—

The mall dimmed. The overhead lights flickered wildly, plunging the mall into a strobe of jagged shadows.

The escalator whirred to a halt, the elevator stopped mid-descent, all the people stopped in place, and Madonna's

"Like a Virgin" warped over the speakers, slowing to a guttural, demonic drone.

El froze, a chill spiking up her spine, her powers humming unbidden, a restless storm beneath her skin. Her breath hitched, the air thick with a dread she knew too well.

Will stiffened, rubbing the back of his neck, his face draining of color.

He grabbed El's arm, his grip tight, eyes wide with panic. "You feel it, too?" he hissed in her ear, their shared trauma vibrating between them. Their eyes locked, and then another vision hit.

El's sight blurred red, thunder rumbling in her skull, not from the mall but from . . . *down there.*

A crimson rift tore open in her mind's eye, and she saw it—a portal wrenching apart, tentacles clawing through it.

"El, what's up?" Max's voice cut through, sharp with concern.

Lucas and Mike turned, their laughter fading, faces creasing with worry. El blinked, and the vision dissolved like smoke—the lights blinking on and stabilizing, the escalators slowly starting back up, the people meandering by—but the chill clung to her bones.

A hot droplet of blood swelled in one nostril. Her heart pounded, the horrific vision still fresh.

Before she could speak, Mike's lips brushed her cheek, soft and grounding, his hand cupping her shoulder.

"You okay?" he asked, his voice steady, pulling her back to the present.

El wiped her nose, smearing the blood, hiding the dread simmering in her gut.

"Fine," she lied, her voice small, her eyes darting to Will. His gaze was haunted, but he forced a tight smile, a silent pact to keep their fear unspoken—for now. She nodded, clutching Mike's hand, her powers quieting, though the mall's shadows seemed to writhe.

"That's all behind us, remember?" Mike went on, recognizing her haunted look. "We stopped it—together. We're safe now."

"Of course." El forced a smile to quiet his worries. "It's over. For good."

"*Freaky* power surge," Lucas said, shrugging, oblivious to the undercurrent. "This place's wiring's gotta be worse than my grandma's toaster." He nudged Max, grinning. "Bet it's haunted by, like, actual ghosts."

"Haunted?" Max snorted, flipping her ponytail. "Yeah, where are those Ghostbusters when you need them?"

"Who you gonna call?" Lucas parroted. "But seriously, maybe we need to try that phone number."

The group laughed, the tension easing, but El's senses probed the air, catching a whisper of *wrongness*—something stirring beneath the mall, unseen, alive—but she suppressed it. Bad memories held power, almost like a magic spell. Even buried in the past, they could still affect you with their dark magic and pull you under. She had to stay strong—and move forward.

With her friends.

They pushed through the glass doors, stepping into the blinding sun. They strode through the mall parking lot, Max turning lazy circles on her skateboard, and plowed into Hawkins. Their town hummed with summer—kids cannonballed into the public pool across the street, their splashes mixing with car radios blaring "Summer of '69" as they drove by. The air smelled of chlorine and hot asphalt.

El glanced back again—the mall's facade loomed in the far distance, the glass doors reflecting the sky, hiding secrets. A chill crawled up her neck. She could feel it—bad things lurked back there.

This time, Will grabbed her arm gently, coaxing her to turn away. The shadows had to be left—behind them. Only they had the power to turn away.

"D&D night tonight? Mike's basement?" he said, forcing cheer. "No bullies crashing our party this time!"

Mike smirked, nudging Lucas. "Pretty sure I can smoke you both."

"Keep talkin' like that," Lucas shot back. "I'll nuke your paladin with a fireball." He made an explosion noise.

Max rolled her eyes. "Can't live with them—can't live without them. Ugh, kill me now."

El giggled as the guys teased each other. "Same."

"Dude, *Gremlins* was insane," Mike went on, his eyes lighting up. "Those things would trash Hawkins worse than Dustin's nacho-cheese farts."

Lucas cackled, mimicking a Gremlin's screech, flailing his arms until Max shoved him, laughing.

"Gross!" Max said, wrinkling her nose. "*Ghostbusters* is the superior film. Slimer's way cooler than Gizmo."

Will nodded, high-fiving her. "Totally agree! Slimer's got style."

"Style?" Mike scoffed, grinning. "Gizmo's cute. Slimer's just . . . slime."

They bickered, ambling down the sidewalk, their voices weaving into the town's pulse. El smiled, the normalcy a shield, though the chill lingered, whispering of what lay beneath Starcourt.

Max spun her board, ollieing over a curb, her grin fierce.

"This summer's ours!" she said, catching El's eye. "Right, El?"

El nodded, her blowout catching the breeze, her heart full despite the dread.

"Ours," she echoed, glancing at Mike, then at Max and Lucas, and finally at Will, their presence a promise. Dustin would be back from camp soon, bound to regale them with his adventures.

They roamed, the mall shrinking behind them, Hawkins sprawling in its summer glory—kids racing BMX bikes, their chains clattering; teens slurping Slurpees on curbs, their lips stained blue. Max led the charge, her board weaving lazy arcs, Lucas jogging to keep up, teasing her about her pro skater dreams. Will sketched as he walked, capturing Max on her board, while Mike and El trailed, their hands clasped, her earrings glinting in the late afternoon sun.

But behind them, beneath Starcourt, unseen, rats scurried

through the underbelly, their claws clicking on concrete, eyes glinting in the dark. Russian voices whispered through vents, clipped and urgent, their words lost in the hum of machinery. Something stirred below, a pulse of malice waking in the shadows, its tendrils reaching for the surface.

El's powers thrummed, sensing the dark horizon. Max glanced at El, her grin softening. El smiled back warmly at her friend. For now, all was well.

They headed off, oblivious to the mall's underbelly stirring, their voices fading into Hawkins's summer hum.

The sun blazed hot and strong, but even in the afternoon glow, dark shadows loomed in the corners, whispering of dangers yet to come.

But no matter what happened—one thing was clear. They would face it . . .

Together.